NIGHT SCHOOL FOR SCANDAL

ANGELA MEADOWS

Published by Xcite Books Ltd – 2012

ISBN 9781908262257

The story contained within this book is a work of fiction. Names and characters are the product of the author's imagination and any resemblance to actual persons, living or dead, is entirely coincidental.

Printed and bound in the U.K.

Cover design by Sarah Ann Davies

To Lou

Acknowledgements

I would like to thank Antonia and all the team at Xcite for encouraging me to complete the story of Joyce and her friends and for knocking the manuscript into shape. I would also like to acknowledge the inspiration I got from reading my copy of *The Joy of Sex* by Dr Alec Comfort all those years ago in the 1970s.

Chapter One
Let's Start a School

Eileen drew the Ford Escort to a stop outside the Old School. The building looked dark and mysterious without any street lights in the village to illuminate it.

'Would you like to come in for coffee?' Joyce said as she opened the passenger door, twisted around and placed her stiletto heels carefully on to the narrow pavement.

'Don't mind if I do. Not much else to do this evening,' Eileen replied. She got out and locked the car door. Joyce was already through the wide gates and approaching the front door of the school house. Inside it was warm and cosy so Eileen flung off her fur jacket and settled on the comfy Dralon sofa.

'Will Maxwell House do?' Joyce called from the kitchen, 'milk and sugar?'

'That's fine, milk, no sugar.' Eileen stretched out her long stockinged legs and looked around the room. There were pictures hanging on the peach-coloured walls. One was a wedding photograph in which she recognised Joyce and her recently deceased husband.

Joyce entered bearing a tray which she placed on the coffee table in front of the sofa.

'I've brought a few biscuits too,' Joyce said, placing a coffee cup and small plate in front of Eileen.

'Oh, thank you, Joyce. How exciting!'

Joyce looked surprised at Eileen's sarcasm.

'Is something troubling you, Eileen?' she asked.

'I'm sorry, Joyce, I didn't mean to snap, but is this it?'

'Is this *what?*'

'The rest of our lives.'

'What do you mean?'

'Well here we are, in our forties, you widowed and me divorced. It's the 1970s and everyone's having fun – well nearly everyone – and what have we got to look forward to – an evening of flower arranging followed by a coffee and a biscuit.'

Joyce sat beside Eileen and nibbled on a chocolate-covered digestive. She brushed off a few crumbs caught on her acrylic-covered bosom.

'I know what you mean, Eileen. Things can be a little boring.'

'A little boring! Life has become a sorry succession of shopping trips, coffee mornings, afternoon tea, evening classes and WI.'

'I suppose you could find a man.'

'A man! I've just got rid of one who went off with his twenty-year-old floozy. I don't want to get involved with another man, thank you very much. No, what I need is sex.'

'Eileen!'

'I'm sorry to be coarse, Joyce, but I mean it. I don't want to be saddled with a man day and night but I would like to be made love to again. To feel that thrill that ripples through you, down there; to feel my breasts being caressed; to feel his cock throbbing in my hand.' Eileen noticed that Joyce looked a little flushed. 'Don't you feel it, Joyce?' she added quietly.

Joyce nodded.

'You're right, Eileen. Since Bill was killed in the accident I have missed, um, it. Not that we got up to much recently. I think we were past lust.'

'That's what I need – a bit of lust. Not soppy love which saddles you with a relationship until you fall out and get divorced all over again. Just quick and cheerful lust.'

'I don't know how we could go about getting it.'

'We?'

'Yes, I may not be as bold as you, Eileen, but I feel the same. I don't want to spend the next thirty years becoming a wrinkled, bitter old crone. I want some life too.'

'We could go to a discotheque.'

'And mix with all those young people?'

'You've still got a good figure, Joyce, and those legs of yours ...' both looked at Joyce's crossed legs, the shimmering nylon-covered calves and the red high heels.

'So have you, but we'd look as out of place as two Maltesers in a box of Black Magic.'

'Well, where else can you meet men out for a good time?'

'A pub?'

Eileen snorted.

'Well, I don't know what your village pub is like, but the blokes in my local would barely muster a hard-on between them.'

Joyce nodded and giggled, 'Ooh, Eileen, you are naughty.'

Eileen sipped at her coffee, thinking for a moment.

'You know, Joyce,' she said eventually, 'We have all these evening classes – flower arranging, cake decoration, dress-making. It's a pity they don't have one for sexual intercourse. You know, the college provides the experts and the materials, you pay your fee and get what you want from the course.'

Joyce laughed.

'Now there's an idea. Evening classes for sexually deprived middle-aged ladies. I'd sign up for that one.'

Next morning Joyce was still chuckling over Eileen's outrageous idea. They'd carried on discussing what such a course might include and who they'd have to lead it. As she'd settled down to sleep Joyce had been gripped by desire and her dreams were filled with writhing bodies and huge cocks spurting milky juice. She awoke hot and sticky between her legs, her mind still filled with the images of sexual organs. She made herself a cup of tea, wondering at the effect that the discussion had had. On her way back to her bed she stopped off in what had been Bill's study. From a drawer in the desk she took out a pile of magazines. She carried them and her mug back to her bedroom and dropped them on the bed. She lay on top of the bedspread looking at the garish covers. The publications were Bill's porn collection. Joyce had discovered them when she'd had to start clearing Bill's things after the funeral. She hadn't known that he bought such stuff. Why had he needed it? Was it because he was bored with her, or did he just need some extra stimulation as he was approaching fifty? At first she was going to get rid of them but wasn't sure how. It would be embarrassing if the dustbin men found them when they emptied her bin. So she'd just put them back in the drawer.

Now she leafed through the magazines. She looked at the breasts, buttocks and displayed vaginas. She had to admit the girls were attractive. She glanced at herself in the mirrored wardrobe facing the bed. Eileen was right, although there was a touch of grey in her brown hair, she did still have a figure. A thought passed through her mind, she hesitated, then pulled her nightie over her head. She reclined on the bed facing the mirror, resting on one arm while cupping her breasts with the other hand. They were still firm, not perhaps quite as perky as some of the girls in the pictures but not as droopy as some of those with enormous tits. She slid a hand down to her waist, which was still narrow thanks to all the walking she did around the village. Joyce glanced again at some of the poses in the magazines. She knelt on the bed, thrust her bottom in the air and pushed her arms out in front of her. She twisted her neck to try to see herself in the mirror. She liked what she saw. There was hardly any saggy flesh hanging down and her buttocks were round and taut. She swung round on to her back and pulled her legs up to her chest. Joyce looked through her thighs at the mirror. Her lips were red and full, shiny with the fluid that was seeping from her vagina. She realised that the one difference between her and the girls pictured was the mass of curly brown hair, tinged with grey, that covered her mound. Her left hand moved to cover her sex and her forefinger slipped between her lips finding her little button. She rubbed it and felt the almost forgotten thrill that it produced. The person in the mirror was pleasuring herself, her thighs wide apart, one hand massaging a nipple, the other burrowing into her sex; one, two fingers pushing deep into her vagina. She almost forgot that the person in the mirror was her; it was another's hands but her breasts, her cunt.

The orgasm came suddenly, ripping through her and

bringing a groan from her throat. Joyce flung her arms and legs across the bed as the convulsions continued. Gradually they subsided and she took deep breaths, feeling the sweat cooling on her face and body. She rested for a few minutes then began to casually flick through the magazines. Now it wasn't the pictures that attracted her but the letters and stories – obviously fantasies – and the adverts for sex toys and contacts.

After a light lunch Joyce picked up the telephone and dialled Eileen's number.

'Hello, Eileen, it's Joyce. Are you doing anything this afternoon? Well, what about after your gardening lesson? You're free. Good, well come for tea. I've got an idea.' Joyce put the phone down and returned to the lounge and another of Bill's glamour magazines. She'd spent the morning going through them methodically, comparing articles and readers' accounts and making a note of addresses and telephone numbers. Later she decided that it really was time that she dressed. It wouldn't do for Eileen to arrive with her still in her dressing gown with nothing on beneath it.

She stood naked again in front of her mirror. She looked at the shrub of brown hair between her legs. Presumably men liked the girls in the magazines because they had little or no pubic hair. They must like seeing a woman's hole without the surrounding foliage. Joyce had heard of women having it shaved or waxed off and now she resolved to do the same. She went to the bathroom and found the razor she used on her underarms. She wetted her pubes and carefully began to shave off the hair. The thought of cutting herself scared her so she went about her task very slowly. At last she was sure that she had removed every last pubic hair. She washed the hairs away, dabbed herself dry and applied copious amounts of talc. She returned to the bedroom.

It was a different woman in the mirror now, a wanton, sexy woman whose naked sex demanded to be filled by a long hard cock. Joyce shivered as she was overcome by a tiny orgasm. Dear me, she thought, I'm becoming so turned on I don't even have to touch myself. The bedside clock showed that time was moving on; Eileen would arrive soon. She had to dress but rejected her usual clothes. She found, in her undies drawer, a pair of briefs, suspender belt and a push up bra that Bill had bought years ago and which she had never worn. She put them on and pulled sheer nylon stockings up her legs and, looking in the mirror as she fastened the suspenders, realised that she resembled some of the pictures in the magazines, before the girls were stripped naked. There was a miniskirt in the wardrobe which she hadn't worn for a few years and a ribbed acrylic jumper which she had thought too tight when she bought it but now she revelled in the way that it clung to her breasts and waist. She just had time to do her make-up before the front doorbell rang.

Joyce skipped to the front door and opened it wide.

'Eileen!'

'Joyce. You look, uh, different.' Joyce hurried Eileen through the hallway and took her woollen coat.

'What is it, Joyce? There's something about you that's changed.' Joyce guided Eileen into the lounge recalling at that moment that she had left the pornographic magazines lying scattered on the sofa, coffee table and floor.

'Ooh, what are these?' Eileen squealed, picking up the nearest publication and flicking through the pages, 'Where did you get them?'

'They're Bill's. I found them in his drawer when I was clearing his stuff.'

'Naughty Bill. Didn't you know?'

'Of course not. I've never seen such stuff before.'

'But you have now. You've had a good look, haven't you. That's why you look different. You've been feeling yourself.'

Joyce felt her cheeks turning red.

'Yes,' she said, 'it was what we talked about last night that set me off. The pictures are exciting but I'm not attracted to the girls.'

'No, of course not.'

'It's just their poses made me think about, you know …'

'Having sex.'

'Yes.'

'And did you enjoy it?'

'What?'

'Making yourself come.'

'Yes.'

'So you did.'

'What?'

'Come.'

'Yes. Of course.'

'What do you mean, "of course",' Eileen sighed, 'I try time after time but I rarely bring myself off.'

'Oh?'

'As I said last night; I need a man.'

'Ah well that's what I wanted to speak to you about. I'll just go and get the tea.' Joyce hurried into the kitchen leaving Eileen to flick through the pages. When she returned Eileen was lying on the sofa with her skirt around her waist and a hand inside her white nylon knickers. Joyce placed the tray on the coffee table.

'Just trying,' Eileen sighed, 'can't say I got much of a response.' She tugged her skirt down over her thighs.

'I'm sorry,' Joyce replied wondering how they had become so relaxed about sex.

'You know all these young girls have shaved fannies.'

'So have I.'

'What?'

'Yes, I shaved it all off an hour ago.'

'Really! let's have a look.'

'Eileen!'

'What's wrong? No one else is going to see.'

'Well, all right then.' Joyce tugged at the zip on her skirt, pushed it down over her hips and stepped out of it. She felt very self-conscious standing in her stockings and knickers in front of Eileen, but there was a new feeling of confidence and pride in her which she hadn't felt until today. She pulled her panties down over her bottom and let them drop to her ankles. She felt Eileen's eyes focus on her bare pubis.

'Well! You certainly have got rid of it all. Sit down. Let me see between your legs.'

Joyce sank on to the sheepskin rug in front of the fireplace, kicked the knickers off her ankles and spread her legs, supporting herself on her arms.

'Remarkable,' Eileen said, 'is it sore?'

'A little bit, but I put plenty of talc on.'

'I'm sure if you're not used to shaving it will be. Let me get closer.' Eileen uncurled herself from the sofa and crawled to kneel between Joyce's legs.

'It certainly makes your pussy stand out more,' Eileen said, 'There's more contrast between your red lips and white skin than with the brown pubes. Does it make you more sensitive?'

'I don't …' Joyce's reply was cut short by Eileen's finger touching her clitoris which was peeping between her lips. Joyce shook. Eileen allowed her finger to slide down and in. Joyce gasped. Eileen held her breath as she concentrated on moving her finger. Joyce's elbows gave way and she sank back on to the rug. Her thighs trembled. Eileen slid another finger between the swollen lips. They slipped easily in the slick channel. Joyce groaned and clenched her thighs together, trapping Eileen's hand. Eileen waited till the muscle contraction had passed and gently withdrew her hand.

'Well. That certainly proves something,' Eileen said. She moved back to the sofa and picked up her tea cup.

'What's that?' Joyce asked, sitting up and searching for her knickers.

'You need fucking.'

'And you?'

'Oh, yes. Seeing and feeling your cunt was fun, but I need a cock.'

Joyce stood up pulled her knickers up and put her mini-skirt back on. She sat next to Eileen, knees primly together and sipped her tea.

'Well that's why I asked you to tea, Eileen.'

'Really?'

'Yes. Our chat last night got me thinking and looking through Bill's magazines made me think some more.'

'That's a lot of thinking for one day.'

Joyce giggled.

'Well it wasn't all thinking, I must admit.'

'So what's the big idea?'

'Why don't we open our own school for deprived women?'

'Sexually deprived?'

'Of course.'

'Who?'

'All those women we meet at coffee mornings and evenings classes and WI meetings. It can't be just the two of us who are feeling left out of the sexual revolution. We'll invite women discreetly to join our classes.'

'Classes on what?'

'All sorts of things. You only have to look through those magazines to see all the different ways people get enjoyment out of sex, and there are contacts in the mags to get um, guests, to come to our lessons.'

Eileen looked unsure.

'But where could we do it?'

'Here.' Joyce replied. Eileen looked around the small cosy lounge. 'No, not in here,' Joyce went on, 'come with me.' She stood up, found a pair of slippers alongside the sofa and took Eileen's hand. Joyce guided Eileen along the hallway and out of a door into a dark empty space. Joyce's hand found a light switch and at once the old school hall was lit up.

'In here!' Joyce said triumphantly, 'When Bill and I bought the old school we were going to convert this into a lovely large living area but we only got round to doing up the old school house before he was killed.'

Eileen looked around the space which had once been packed with up to fifty children and their teachers.

'Obviously, it will need some work – curtains, thick carpets or rugs, more intimate lighting, and suitable furniture. But what do you think, Eileen?'

Eileen turned to face Joyce.

'You really mean this, don't you?'

'Yes. Let's have some fun before we end up as wizened old prunes. So, will it do?'

Eileen looked around the hall again.

'I think it's ideal. There's plenty of parking and because

you're right on the edge of the village it's well out of the way of whispering neighbours.'

'So, we'll do it?'

'Yes. I'll help with getting this sorted out while we're planning the course and sending out invitations. It won't take long.'

'What about booking the, um, guests?' Joyce chewed her lip.

'I was the secretary for a theatrical agent, once upon a time. I think I know how to deal with the people we need. Anyway, we'll be paying them for their services so they'll come.'

There were one or two moments in the next month when Joyce regretted embarking on their venture, but only when she was exhausted from a day's scrubbing or painting. Soon the hall had lost its school appearance. Thick red curtains hung from the windows, the ceiling was painted black and the walls covered by mirrors and prints of classical gods and goddesses frolicking in the nude. On the polished wooden floor were large rugs with thick piles and sheepskins together with a plentiful supply of floor cushions and bean bags. In the centre of the room was a king-sized brass bedstead with a thick feather mattress covered in orange sheets and bedspreads. There was also a chaise longue and three sofas arranged in a semicircle. The old pendant lights had been replaced with a variety of standard lamps that cast light on to the bed and chaise longue and left other parts of the hall in seductive darkness. Joyce and Eileen had not omitted other necessities such as a film projector and screen, a powerful stereo record player and a bar stocked with a variety of drinks.

Joyce and Eileen stood in the hall admiring their handiwork.

'There's something else we'll need,' Eileen said.

'What's that?' Joyce asked.

'I'll show you.' Eileen left, while Joyce wondered. A minute or so later Eileen returned holding a large Wedgwood style biscuit barrel.

'Biscuits?' Joyce said.

Eileen removed the lid. 'Condoms.'

Joyce laughed and dug into the jar pulling out a handful of packets.

‘I’ll put it on the bar, shall I?’ Eileen replaced the lid.

‘Yes,’ Joyce said, ‘So that’s it, we’re ready. All we need now is some, what shall we call them? Clients, pupils?’

‘Students.’

‘That’s it – students of sex.’

‘Shall we try out the bed?’ Eileen walked to the middle of the room, kicked off her shoes and sat on the bed. Joyce went to a bank of switches. Most of the lamps went out leaving the periphery of the hall in darkness. The bed sat in a circle of light provided by two overhead spotlights. Joyce joined Eileen in the light.

‘It’s a bit bright, don’t you think,’ Joyce said.

‘Yes, but it needs to be bright here so that everyone can see what is going on.’

‘What is going on?’ Joyce asked as Eileen tugged at her skirt.

‘I’m getting in the mood,’ Eileen replied, ‘Is your fanny still bare or have you let it grow back?’

‘It got very itchy so I’ve had it waxed off.’

‘Waxed? What did the girl in the salon say when you said you wanted it all off?’

‘Not a lot. Everyone is having bikini waxes now and apparently quite a few girls have most of their hair removed.’

‘Let me see.’

Joyce helped Eileen remove her skirt and then pulled her blouse over her head. She wriggled out of her new tiny knickers and lay back amongst the soft pillows and blankets.

Eileen caressed her smooth mound.

‘It feels really soft,’ Eileen said.

‘That’s nice,’ Joyce murmured, ‘Don’t you want to undress?’

‘Well, yes, I think I do.’ Eileen paused and pulled off her own top and skirt. Underneath she wore a matching set of lacy black bra, suspender belt and knickers and sheer black stockings. She removed her knickers and knelt between Joyce’s outstretched legs.

‘There, what do you think? Do you think a man would like to get his hands on my body?’

Joyce looked at Eileen's slim waist and flat stomach. Her pubic hair was as black as the hair on her head.

'Oh, I think so,' she said.

Eileen lay down beside Joyce and their hands moved gently across each other's stomachs until their fingers found each other's cracks, the one bounded by thick black hair and the other naked. They moaned in unison as they moved together, fingers slipping in and out of wet vaginas until Joyce came with the now familiar groan.

'Are you sure you want a man?' Eileen asked raising herself up on an elbow and looking into Joyce's flushed face.

'I think so. You've given me a lot of pleasure but I'm looking forward to being able to do things with a man.'

'Yeah, me too. There's nothing quite like having a thick hard cock pushing between your legs is there. Well, we will have to see how our course works out. What are we going to call our class anyway?'

Joyce lay still, shielding her eyes from the bright spotlights.

'I suppose it has to be clear what it is but sound respectable.'

'Hmm, yes.'

'How about, the Ladies' School for Sex.'

'A bit too direct,' Eileen pondered, 'What about the Ladies' College for Intercourse.'

'Not quite, especially as it may not all be about intercourse, as such.'

'That's right. I know, the Ladies' College for Erotic Arts,' Eileen said triumphantly.

'I like that. A bit mysterious and all embracing.' They hugged each other giggling gleefully.

'You know,' Eileen whispered in Joyce's ear, 'we're really going to have to be bold and put aside all Protestant ideas of chastity and decency. You're going to be doing things you've never thought of doing before and probably doing them with other people around watching. Is that what you want?'

'Yes. It sounds exciting. Do you?'

'Oh, yes.'

'Good. Now,' Joyce announced, 'do you want to see if I can get you to come?'

Eileen looked into Joyce's eyes.

'Do you really want to?'

'Yes, I'm quite determined that it doesn't have to be a man that can get you to orgasm.'

'Well, it's up to you. It may take some time.' Eileen lay on her back and opened her legs.

'Don't worry, I've got the energy,' Joyce said straddling her. She lowered her head until it was between Eileen's thighs. She stretched out her tongue until it touched the lips of Eileen's sex. Eileen moaned.

Chapter Two
The Students

Joyce relaxed on a sofa in the old school hall now decorated as a plush, warm venue for sexy exploits.

'Well, it's ready. What do we do now?'

Eileen turned from the full length mirror where she had been examining herself.

'We need some students and a programme. Did you get those cards printed?'

'Yes, they arrived this morning. I've got them here.' Joyce rummaged in her capacious handbag and pulled out a polythene bag filled with business cards.

'Ooh, let me see.' Eileen ran to Joyce and took the card proffered to her. It was black and red with ornate writing saying, "The Ladies' College for Erotic Arts" with a telephone number – Joyce's. 'Yes, they look just right,' Eileen said.

'So, what do we do with them?'

'Keep a supply with you at all times and hand them to anyone who you think may be a possible. Let me have a handful.'

Joyce divided the cards in half, gave a stack to Eileen and replaced the others in her bag.

'And what about the programme? What are we going to do?'

'Ah, I've had a few ideas about that. Those old porn mags of your Bill's gave me some ideas. Let's do a list and start making some plans.'

'Ooh, that sounds exciting.' Joyce shivered with the thought of actually arranging for some naughty sex.

* * *

Drying herself after a shower, Susan caught sight of herself in the mirror. Her breasts were still firm and pert and her stomach flat. She could feel proud of her body but she felt tired and jaded. The trials of looking after a two-year-old on her own made her feel more than her twenty-five years. The old anger gave her an acid taste in her mouth. Was it really over two years since that rat, Dave, had walked out on her?

She dropped the towel to the floor and had a good look at herself. Would another man fancy her? Why not? She was young and had a good figure. She wrapped her arms around herself imagining being cuddled, a hand caressing the wispy blonde curls on her mound, a finger slipping into the crack between her legs.

She shook herself. What was she thinking? It had been well over two years since someone had fucked her, and that was Dave the rat. No other man would surely want her now with a two-year-old in tow. But she missed the tender touch of fingers and tongue on her body, the thrust of a hard prick into her wet cunt. Gosh, how they used to get up to it in the days before she became pregnant, before Dave ratted on her and left.

Surprisingly, after all she had been through, there were still fond memories of their first dates at college discos. She was training as a beautician and Dave was on a course for apprentice electricians. He'd been shy at first and she had had to urge him on to the dance floor. It had all changed after their first fumbling encounter on the bed in his digs. He couldn't get enough of her then. His penis always seemed to be pushing against his jeans and would spring out the moment she pulled the zip down and pulled aside his Y-fronts. More than one pair of nylon tights had been ruined by his eagerness to practically tear off her clothes, and bury his manhood in her. He didn't have much imagination. Perhaps it was the electrician in him – insert plug into socket was his motto. So long as she was flat on her back with her smooth legs apart he was happy. It could be on the bed, the floor, the dining table, the sofa, even once on a beach in South Wales. She hadn't minded; she enjoyed the feeling of being filled, the rhythmic thrusts, the spurt when he came and now and again the mind-numbing, muscle-cramping, leg-clenching, nipple-tingling pleasure of her own orgasm.

They got married when they were both twenty-one and had steady jobs. Setting up home together had been fun. They didn't have much cash and the rented flat was small, but all they needed was a bed. That was where they spent most of the time when they weren't at work. It was when they decided to try for a baby that things started to change. She had been on the pill for more than four years by then and read some reports in papers that being on it for a long time could cause health problems and the idea of a baby was fun. Dave had seemed to accept the idea that a baby was the next step in their relationship but once she became pregnant his mood seemed to change. He didn't fancy intercourse with a foetus in her womb and because he couldn't think of any other way of having sex, they touched and kissed less. Then he started going out for evenings, meeting up with mates in the pub she thought. A month before the baby was due he left; didn't say anything, just came home early one day while she was still at the salon, packed a bag and went, leaving just a note to say he wouldn't be back.

Susan didn't want to think about that last month before Hannah was born. She had been upset, angry, depressed. The worst thing was discovering that Dave had set up home with another girl her age across the other side of town. Her parents and friends had helped her through the birth, settling into a council flat and getting the divorce, but all the time she had felt alone and unloved. Now two years later, with her lovely, petulant, charming, determined, daughter, she had little time to think about herself. At least she was now able to do a few sessions a week at the salon while her mother looked after Hannah. She was beginning to relate to other people again, and, like now, beginning to notice her own body again.

She enjoyed her work helping women to feel good about themselves. There was a lot of satisfaction in painting nails and tearing off the wax strips to leave soft, smooth skin. Lately she had begun to wonder why the women did it, the waxing that is. Was it to be more attractive to men – husbands, boyfriends, gosh, perhaps even lovers? Some wanted more than just legs and arms done. More and more girls were getting their crotches trimmed so that they could wear the skimpiest bikinis without showing any hair. There was even that older woman, what was her name, Joyce, who wanted it all off. Susan recalled the pale, smooth appearance of Joyce's mound and crack when she had finished the task. Was she getting satisfied by someone who fancied a hairless pussy? But Joyce was old, well a lot older than her. Why couldn't she get some action?

Hannah cried out, and Susan hurried to see to her needs. It was time to get dressed, deliver Hannah to mother and get to the salon for another morning of waxing and nail varnishing.

'You seem surprised to see me,' Joyce said sitting at the table in front of Susan.

'Oh, I'm sorry, Mrs, uh, Blandford. I hadn't noticed who my first appointment was and, well, I was thinking of you this morning.'

'What made you think of me, dear?'

Susan blushed. Why had she said that? Now she had to think of an explanation.

'Um. I suppose it was about your last appointment.'

Now it was Joyce's turn to blush.

'You don't get many for that treatment do you?'

'Quite a lot of young women, but not older ones,' Susan bit her tongue. She'd put her foot in her mouth good and proper, but Joyce seemed to be considering it a joke. She leaned closer to Susan and whispered, 'You know, it makes me feel sexy being all smooth down there.'

Susan gasped. Surely Joyce was recently widowed.

'You've, um, got a man?' Susan whispered. Joyce shrugged.

'Not just yet, but I have my hopes. Look you're on your own, aren't you?'

'Yes. I've got Hannah of course …'

'But you haven't, uh, had "it" for a while, have you?'

'No.'

'Well, why don't you join us?' Joyce fiddled with her handbag and pulled out a card which she passed secretively to Susan. 'We're meeting next Wednesday evening; half past seven; my place, the Old School. Surely you can get a babysitter for your daughter.'

'Yes, my mother does ...' Susan looked at the card. The Ladies' College for Erotic Arts, she read. It sounded mysterious, and exciting.

Joyce sat up straight and placed her hands flat on the table.

'I suppose we had better get on with it, hadn't we, dear,' she said, winking.

'Good morning, Edith. You're looking thoughtful.'

Edith put her coffee cup back on its saucer and looked up to see who was speaking to her. It was Eileen, another occasional participant in the WI coffee mornings.

'Oh, hello, Eileen, how are you?'

'I'm fine, but what about you. Didn't I hear that your husband was in the Laurels now?'

'Yes, Stanley's become so poorly with this Alzheimer's that I couldn't look after him any more. He needs the special treatment they can provide in the nursing home.'

'You must be finding life different. You've been looking after him for a while, haven't you?'

Edith nodded and thought about the long years of looking after her disabled husband.

'Since he came home from the war. The Alzheimer's is just one more thing on top of his weak heart and useless legs.'

'Well, you've kept yourself fit and healthy.'

Eileen's compliment lifted Edith's spirits and she straightened her back to give herself her full height. She looked down at Eileen.

'One of us had to be. Pushing him in his wheelchair and lifting him in and out of bed has given me muscles I never had as a young thing. In fact I don't know what I'll do now he's not there at home all the time.'

'Yes, being on your own can be difficult.'

'And there's the other thing.'

'What other thing?'

'Sex.'

'Sex?'

Edith smiled to herself. These younger women didn't think

that old'uns like her thought of sex. Well it was fun to show that they were wrong.

'Yes, despite Stanley's difficulties we found our ways of getting some satisfaction, well, we did until he started going doolally. I miss it now. It's not quite the same on your own is it?'

Just for a moment she recalled the delicious feeling of rubbing her sex against Stanley's face while he lay on the bed; feeling his tongue flick inside her fanny, his nose rubbing against her little button; rocking her bottom to and fro until she came in a thigh trembling spasm that trapped poor Stanley's head in her groin.

'No, I know what you mean.' Eileen was fumbling in her handbag. She pulled out a red and black card and placed in Edith's hand. 'Why don't you come and join us, next Wednesday evening, seven thirty. I'll pick you up in my car.'

Edith read the card – The Ladies' College for Erotic Arts. Hmm, could be more interesting than sitting in front of Coronation Street with her cocoa.

Betty was panting by the time she reached her front gate. It was a long walk from the shops carrying her shopping bags.

'Good morning, Betty.'

For the first time Betty noticed Eileen, who lived up the road, walking towards her.

'Oh, hello, Eileen,' she puffed.

'You've got your hands full there. You could do with a car to carry all that back from the shops.'

'Fat chance of that. Tom's away.'

'Oh. He's a salesman isn't he? He must be away quite often.'

'Yes, he covers the whole of the south. He's off most weeks.'

'That must be difficult for you both.'

'For me, yes,' Betty said bitterly, 'but not for him.'

'Oh?'

'He's got his floozies. One in every city I think.'

'You mean Tom has lovers?'

Betty wondered why Eileen was shocked. After all hadn't her husband run off with a younger woman?

'That's what I mean.'

'But he comes back to you.' Eileen sounded almost wistful.

'Yes, more's the pity. I suppose it means I get my housekeeping out of him.'

'Don't you feel envious?'

'Envious?'

'Of these other women; getting his, ah, service.'

'They're welcome. I can't say that Tom ever gave me much in the way of pleasure. Mind you I don't suppose any man would want to now. Look at me.'

Betty showed off the bulges she had in all the wrong places. She was usually embarrassed by her fat but Eileen had hit a nerve

'You're not so bad, Betty. There are plenty of men who like something to get hold of. Wouldn't you like to have a bit of attention?'

Betty thought about the last time she had had some "attention" paid to her. Actually it hadn't been Tom but his boss, Frank, at a company do a couple of years ago. He had pulled her playfully into the stationery cupboard and before she knew what was happening he was kissing her with his tongue down her throat and a hand pulling her knickers down. He slipped two fingers into her cunt and had her gasping and shaking in no time. Then he'd tipped her forward over a pile of boxes of manila envelopes and thrust into her from behind. It was all over almost before the disc jockey had played one record by the Jackson 5 but the memory had lasted a lot longer.

'Yes, I suppose I would,' Betty said dreamily. Eileen was thrusting a card into her hand.

'Why don't you join us, next Wednesday evening, half seven. I'll give you a lift.' Eileen stepped past her and walked on along the street. Betty looked at the curly writing on the card – The Ladies' College for Erotic Arts. What's all that about, she wondered?

It was almost dark when Susan walked up to the door of the Old

School. The cold spring evening made her glad she had put her coat on but she was beginning to feel a bit silly in her denim miniskirt and tight skinny rib top. What was this Ladies College all about?

Joyce opened the door very quickly after she had pressed the bell push. She was wearing a halter neck maxi dress that left her arms and shoulders bare.

'Hello, Susan. Come on in, it's a bit cold out there, isn't it.'

Joyce led her down the narrow hallway and through another door into a large open space. The ceiling was invisible and there were mysterious shadows between the pools of light made by the lamps and spotlights, but her eyes were drawn to the huge bed in the centre of the room covered with soft cushions and a fur bedspread. There was no one else in the room.

'Shall I take your coat, dear?' Joyce asked. Susan noticed that it was a lot warmer in the hall and was happy to remove her coat. 'Take a seat. I'm sure the others will be here soon.'

Susan walked to one of the sofas that partly ringed the bed and sank into it. It seemed to embrace her, encouraging her to curl her nylon-smooth legs under her. Her skirt rode up exposing even more thigh. A distant ringing signalled some more arrivals and soon Joyce was showing in three other ladies. Joyce introduced Susan to them and added.

'This is Eileen. She and I have organised this little do.'

'And this is Edith and Betty.' Eileen pointed to a tall, elderly woman and a rather short and plump woman who like Eileen and Joyce appeared middle-aged. Susan began to feel a bit of an outsider.

'Now, who would like a drink?' Joyce asked, 'We have wine or perhaps you would prefer a sherry or a martini.'

Soon they were all seated in a semi-circle on the sofas with drinks in their hands. Susan listened to their chatter. Eileen stood up, coughed and the talking stopped.

'Now, ladies, Joyce and I are glad you could come to the first session of the Ladies College for Erotic Arts.' Betty giggled. 'Our purpose is to have fun, sexy fun.'

'I don't see any men,' Edith said, 'You're not a pair of lesbians, are you?'

‘No, we’re not,’ Eileen went on, ‘not that we’re against a little mutual stimulation, but we’re all here because we want a bit of cock.’ Joyce made a little gasping noise. ‘Yes, I’m going to be coarse and to the point. We all want to feel a man’s body rubbing against us, his hands and tongue exciting us and his penis sliding into our pussies.’

Susan felt herself nodding. She could almost feel it happening as Eileen described. Her crotch was already getting moist and her cheeks flushed.

‘I can see that the thought of sex excites some of us,’ Eileen went on, ‘but what we intend doing here in the College is more than simple in-out fucking,’ Joyce giggled again, ‘we are going to explore all the ways we can get pleasure and satisfaction with and without a man to provide the tool. Every course needs a textbook and ours will be this,’ Eileen picked up a book from the coffee table beside one of the sofas, ‘you may have heard of it; it’s called *The Joy of Sex* and we’ve got a copy of the paperback version for each of us.’

Joyce picked up a small pile of the books and handed them to each of the ladies.

‘Now don’t worry about the cost. There may be some expenses for the course, but for now Joyce has very generously stumped up the cash to ensure that we have a good time. Now we’d like you to read through the book to get some ideas.’

Susan flicked through the pages of the copy she was given. There were pictures of a man and a woman having sex in all sorts of ways. She blushed at the drawing of a woman stroking an erect penis but there was a little tingle between her legs. She closed the covers. Eileen was still talking.

‘We have to lose our inhibitions and join the sexual revolution. That means losing any embarrassment about our bodies or what fucking involves.’

‘Hear, hear,’ Joyce called.

‘I’m all for Women’s Lib,’ Edith added.

‘Ooh, it will take a lot to stop being embarrassed by my flab,’ Betty said.

Susan kept quiet and wondered what inhibitions she had to lose.

'Now to get us in the mood,' Eileen continued, 'Joyce is going to show us a film. It's not of her last summer holiday, I can tell you.'

'Come and sit in front of the screen,' Joyce said getting up from her seat, 'I'll get the projector started.' Susan and the others followed Joyce to the end of the room where a cine projector was set up on a stand. There were chairs, cushions and bean bags on the floor in front of a large screen. Edith immediately went to one of the upright chairs and sat down.

'I don't think lounging on the floor will do my back much good,' she said.

'Oh, I don't know, I think it's fun,' Betty said flopping on to a bean bag. Her nylon dress rode up exposing the stocking tops on her fleshy thighs. Susan curled her legs under her on a large, soft, floor cushion, again wishing she hadn't worn such a short skirt. The lights in the room went out and Susan got the thrill she always had when the lights went down in the cinema.

'Now I think I know how to do this,' Joyce said, 'it was Bill's hobby, well one of them. He had a cine camera and was always filming when we went on holidays, but this isn't one of his films. Eileen found it advertised in a magazine. I hope you are sitting comfortably.' She pressed a button and a whirring and clicking began.

The screen lit up with patterns and shapes and then settled down into a slightly grainy, fuzzy picture. There was no sound and as far as Susan could make out there wasn't much in the way of story but a young woman soon had her clothes removed and was rolling around on a bed showing off her bare breasts and bottom. The camera zoomed in on the hairless crack between her legs. The man who had helped remove her clothes reappeared naked. There were glimpses of his erect penis before he knelt between the woman's legs, lifted her calves up and apart and buried his manhood in her. The woman writhed and shook as he pumped her. He seemed to keep going for much longer than Susan could recall Dave the rat doing but eventually he shuddered. The man withdrew and the camera zoomed in for a final shot of white come oozing from the woman's crack. The screen went white and the film flapped as it revolved on the spool.

Susan found she was still staring ahead at the blank screen, mesmerised by what she had seen. The projector light went out just as the lights in the room came on. Susan shook herself and looked around.

'Ooh, didn't he have a big one,' Betty giggled.

'I can't see that the woman got much out of it,' Edith commented, 'he just banged it in and got his end away.'

'Exactly,' Eileen said, 'these films are made for men. They can wank themselves off in a few minutes while watching the woman get laid. We need something more. I don't know about you ladies but it takes a bit more to make me come. So during this course we will be learning how to make the most of what's available.'

'I don't see any young men here,' Edith said.

'No, not this evening, but we will. What I want you to do now is choose a mirror,' Eileen pointed out the six wide full length mirrors between the windows around the hall, 'then remove your clothes and examine every part of your body, and I mean every part.'

'Why?' Susan asked.

'So we become familiar with ourselves and can start to learn about how we react when we can see and touch ourselves.'

'I'm not taking all my clothes off,' Edith complained, 'Some of my bits can't bear exposure at my age.'

'Well, take off what you're comfortable with.'

The ladies got up from their seats and dispersed. Susan headed for a mirror close to the corner. When she stood in front of it she found that a spotlight had been positioned just right to illuminate her. She glanced at her image then to her left where Eileen was already wriggling her tight red pencil skirt over her hips revealing a back and red suspender belt and knickers. In the mirror she could see the backs of Edith and Betty. Betty was struggling to pull her dress over her head while Edith had removed her cardigan and yellow blouse to reveal a cream basque.

Susan looked back at herself. How strange could it be to strip off with a group of older women around her? Was this the best way to get a bit of a life? Well it was probably safer than venturing out on her own to a pub, and the ladies seemed very friendly and pleasant. She lowered the zip on her skirt, undid the top button and pushed the stiff denim down over her hips. The skirt slid down her smooth legs. She stepped out of the skirt and pulled the tight top up, above her breasts and on over her head. She dropped the top onto the carpet and faced herself. She'd put an old, sexy, half-cup bra on but it was a bit tight now after having had Hannah and she didn't like what she could see. She reached behind her back and unclipped it. The bra sprang off releasing her nipples and full breasts. They jiggled a bit but she was proud that they still remained firm. Then slowly she rolled her tights and knickers down from her waist, over her buttocks and slowly revealed her blonde pubes. Susan balanced ungainly on one leg while pulling her tights from the other and then, there she was – naked.

Susan glanced again at Eileen. She too was naked and sitting straight backed and cross-legged on the floor like a yogi. Her eyes were closed and her fingers played with her fanny. Eileen appeared to be somewhere else. Susan looked again in the mirror. Betty too was naked and sitting on the floor but in a less tidy position and looking something like a sack of potatoes. Edith was still on her feet and her appearance made Susan gasp. She was still dressed in flesh coloured stockings joined by suspenders to the cream basque which gave her a figure which belied her age. Her buttocks did not sag and, reflected in the mirror, Susan could see the wisps of hair around her sex. Susan thought Edith looked incredibly sexy.

'Look at yourselves in your mirror,' Eileen said apparently coming back to the world, 'and touch your body; feel your fingers on your skin. Get used to the feeling and discover where you like to be touched most.'

Susan did as she was told. She knew her nipples were sensitive. Gently she brushed them with her hands. They were hard in moments and sending tingles from her toes to the top of her head. There was a heat between her legs and she could feel her lips swelling. Is it really so easy, she thought. She sank to her knees splaying her thighs and reached with a hand into her sex. Her forefinger slipped easily into her crack and her thumb found her nub. She rubbed it and in moments she was drifting on a cloud, whereabouts unknown. The tingling within her became an electric shock, muscles locked and she cried. For seconds she was held in the grip of her orgasm and then there was release. She collapsed forward, the muscles in her vagina clenching and unclenching.

'Well, my dear, I wish I could come as easily as you,' Joyce's gentle voice spoke in her ear and her warm hand caressed her back, 'are you sure you need a man?'

Susan rolled over and looked up to see the four older women looking down on her with looks varying from wonder to delight on their faces.

'Oh, I think so. I'm surprised it happened with all of you around me.'

'You may not agree, but I think you could be quite an exhibitionist, young lady,' Edith noted.

'I think that's been a most successful start,' Eileen said, 'Let's have another drink and chat about it.'

Chapter Three
Party Time

The doorbell rang. Joyce pulled on a nylon housecoat and hurried to open the Old School front door. A man in a dark grey suit stood on the doormat, a large suitcase by his side. Joyce noted that he was probably in his early thirties and had thick, dark hair down to his neck. She was pleased to see that he was slim and looked as though he kept himself fit.

'Ah, you must be Mr Winter. Do come in,' she said.

'Thank you, Mrs …?' he said obviously searching his memory.

'Oh, call me Joyce. Come on through.' She led him down the hallway and into the main room. She looked at him to see his reaction as he entered the hall. She wasn't disappointed. His eyebrows rose when he saw the big bed, the soft sofas, the plush rugs, the seductive lighting and the other four women in various states of undress.

'Here he is. This is Mr Winter,' Joyce called then turned back to the visitor. 'Bring your case in. You can put it on the floor, or on the bed if you wish.'

Mr Winter walked into the centre of the room and placed the case down beside the bed. He turned to face the five women who had formed a half circle around him.

'This is Susan,' Joyce said starting at the end of the line, 'then there is Betty, Edith and Eileen.' Joyce watched his goggle-eyed look take in Susan's slim figure in white bra and knickers, Edith's older but majestic form in black basque and stockings, plump Betty in her fluffy dressing gown, and Eileen, seductive in her fake-fur-edged negligee that just came down to her thighs.

'I … I'm sorry I'm a bit late. I'm not used to these country roads. We don't usually do, um, house calls,' Mr Winter said nervously.

'Well, we thought it would be a bit like a Tupperware party,' Eileen said, 'You show us what you have to sell and we decide if we want to buy.'

'My mother has been having Tupperware parties for years,' Susan said. 'Her house is filled with plastic containers.'

'I think they're very useful,' Betty said.

'We're not here to discuss Tupperware,' Eileen said, 'perhaps Mr Winter would like to get started.'

'Oh, just a moment, Eileen, Perhaps he would like a drink,' Joyce said, 'Would you like something to drink, Mr Winter, we have red or white wine, sherry, or perhaps you'd prefer a cup of tea or coffee?'

The young man looked at each of the ladies in turn.

'Oh, red wine, please.'

Joyce hurried to the drinks cabinet to pour the wine and returned to the group. She passed the glass to Mr Winter who took a gulp and then looked slightly more relaxed.

'Thank you. Perhaps if you'd like to sit down and, uh, make yourselves comfortable, I'll make a start.'

Edith and Betty sat on a sofa while the others arranged themselves on the floor. Joyce noticed that Mr Winter's eyes seemed fixed on Susan's thighs.

'Right, um, well,' he began, 'As I said, we don't usually sell our goods this way, it's usually all by mail order, so I'm not really used to, uh, talking about them, but, well, Joyce persuaded me to come and visit you so we'll give it a go.' He opened the case and took out a white object. Joyce thought it looked like a rather straight, smooth banana. He held it up with pointed end upwards.

'This is our most popular dildo,' he said, 'solid plastic, hygienic, modern design.'

'Looks like one of them rockets they send up into space,' Edith said.

'Um, what is it for?' Betty asked.

'You stick it up your vagina,' Eileen replied. Betty looked shocked.

'It is a penis substitute,' Mr Winter explained. 'We have them in various sizes and colours, this is the most popular.' He reached into the case and drew out a variety of similar objects, in black and shiny silver. 'We also have straps that they fit in.'

'Straps?' Joyce asked.

Mr Winter put down the dildos and pulled a black leather object from the case. He demonstrated how the white dildo fitted through a hole in a wide strip and held up the contraption to show how the straps and buckles fastened it around the waist and crotch.

'Once the woman has tightened the straps the dildo will be held firmly,' Mr Winter continued.

'The woman?' Betty said.

'Of course, you silly,' Eileen said. 'Can't you see it's to allow a woman to fuck another woman.'

'Oh,' Betty said red-faced.

'We are not a group of lesbians,' Joyce said, 'but we are looking for ways to get pleasure and improve the satisfaction of intercourse with a gentleman.'

'Of course,' Mr Winter said, somewhat bewildered. 'You may use a dildo on yourself or it can be used by a man while he is, um, recovering between, uh, episodes.'

'It may work,' Eileen said, 'may I feel one, the black one I think.'

Mr Winter handed her the object. Eileen felt its weight and smooth surface and practised her grip on it. She lifted her negligee to reveal that she was naked underneath. She put the point of the dildo between her legs, rotated it around and then gave it a gentle push. She gasped and opened her legs a little.

Joyce saw Mr Winter's eyes widen as he watched Eileen slide the dildo into her hole. His cheeks reddened and sweat appeared on his forehead.

Eileen pulled the dildo out and let her housecoat drop.

'Yes, not a bad feeling. Better than nothing,' she said.

'But not the same as a man's thing?' Edith asked.

'No, it's a bit hard, and of course you have to move it

yourself to get any real feeling.'

'Ah, um, many people, er, women, prefer a vibrator,' Mr Winter said. He pulled another silver and black cylinder from the case, 'this is a popular design. It has a motor that makes it vibrate.' He twisted the blunt end and it began to whine and throb in his hand, 'It runs on batteries,' he added.

'It's rather noisy,' Susan said, 'It might wake up Hannah if I used it at home.' The other ladies nodded knowingly.

'It doesn't have to be inserted,' Mr Winter continued, twisting the end to shut it down. 'It has attachments for stimulating the nipples and clitoris or for massaging muscles.' He fitted a cup shaped piece to the end of the vibrator

'Oh, let me have a go,' Betty said. She took the instrument from Mr Winter's hand, twisted its end, then undid her dressing gown and pulled out a large, saggy breast. She touched the buzzing vibrator to herself. The cup just fitted over her pale red nipple

'Ooh, that tickles,' she said, her eyes closed, 'It's actually quite nice,' she added in a dreamy voice. She transferred the vibrator to her other nipple and was soon swaying.

'Do you have another one?' Susan asked.

'Yes,' Mr Winter said, delving into his case, 'we have other models that have more resemblance to the, ah, male member.' He drew out a pink rod which had veins and folds and a tip which did indeed have the shape of the glans of a penis. He handed it to Susan.

'Oh, it's soft on the outside and not slippery.'

'It has a rubber skin which is easily washable with soapy water.'

'How do I turn it on?'

'There's a switch on the base.'

Susan pressed the button and the vibrator began to move in her hand making a more subdued and muffled noise compared to the other.

'That's a lot quieter,' Susan noted, 'I could use that at home.'

'It is our top model. A bit more expensive than the other one.'

'Perhaps I can give it a try out.'

'Please do.'

Susan got up from the floor and went to another of the sofas. She snuggled up amongst the cushions and wriggled her knickers down her legs. Joyce found herself watching avidly as Susan spread her thighs and parted her pussy lips. She held the tip of the softly whirring vibrator against the opening of her vagina and gently pressed. There was an audible intake of breath followed by a long, soft moan. Joyce watched the rod disappear inch by inch inside Susan. Her face and neck became flushed and her breathing increased in rate. Her thighs began to shake and her moans became louder.

'Oh, oh, oh,' Susan cried. Suddenly she arched her back and flung her arms out. Joyce could see the vibrator buried up to its base in her cunt with juices oozing out from around it. The others cheered and clapped.

Susan groaned and relaxed.

'Shall I help you, my dear?' Joyce asked.

'Oh, yes, please.'

Joyce placed a hand between Susan's thighs finding the switch on the end of the rubber cock. Then gripping the end of the vibrator she tugged gently and it slid out, emerging with a glutinous plop.

'There, was that good?' Joyce asked.

'Phew, I'll say. Better than using my hand anyway.' Susan pushed her hair from her brow and wiped sweat from her eyes, 'Not quite the same as a real bloke, but a pretty good substitute. I think I'll have to have one.' She twisted around to sit facing Mr Winter again. He seemed to have been struck senseless.

'Shall we move on?' Joyce said resuming her seat.

Mr Winter shook himself. 'Yes, yes, of course.' He looked into his case.

'Do you have any other devices?' Edith asked.

'Oh yes,' Mr Winter replied, pulling out what looked like a string of Christmas baubles. There were three small white plastic globes connected by string. 'You might find these, um, interesting.'

'What are they?' Edith asked with a mystified look on her

face.

'They are called Chinese balls. One is solid and the others contain a ball bearing that rolls around inside.' He demonstrated by holding the string and letting the balls hang down. When he swung them from side to side the three balls moved independently and erratically, like Mexican jumping beans.

'What do you do with them?' Edith asked again.

'Well, um, a lady inserts them in her, er, vagina, and as she moves around they, um, stimulate her.'

'I see,' Edith said, 'They sound intriguing. May I try?' Edith stood and took the balls from Mr Winter's hand. The others watched as she walked out of the hall. Joyce noted that Mr Winter seemed to be impressed by her long shiny black legs in the high heeled shoes and the tight black satin basque that contrasted with her silver hair. Despite her age she had a slim figure which the boning held in a very seductive shape.

'We also have various items of clothing,' Mr Winter continued, handing out G-strings, crotchless knickers, quarter-cup bras, suspender belts and nipple tassels, which the ladies examined and commented on while passing them to each other.

'Do you have them in larger sizes?' Betty asked, 'I think this would cut me in half if I tried it on.' She held up a tiny triangle of black lace with the corners joined by short lengths of string. The others laughed. Edith reappeared walking slowly and swaying from side to side.

'How do the Chinese balls feel?' Eileen asked

'An interesting sensation,' Edith replied, lowering herself into the sofa carefully, 'the young gentleman is quite correct. Each movement provides a stimulus. I quite like it.'

'Are you going to keep them in?' Joyce said.

'Oh, yes, for a while. It could be quite exciting to go about one's daily chores with the balls up one. It will make a trip to the butcher's more of an adventure.'

'Now, Mr Winter,' Eileen said in determined fashion, 'you have shown us lots of things for women. What about for men? Do you have things that can help a man during intercourse?'

'Well yes, I do, do you have husbands who might like to try some items?'

‘No there aren’t any husbands for us to worry about,’ Eileen said firmly.

‘There aren’t any men here,’ Mr Winter pointed out.

‘Oh yes, there is,’ Joyce giggled.

‘There’s you,’ Betty exclaimed.

‘Come on show us what you’ve got,’ Eileen said.

Mr Winter’s face turned red from his collar to his fringe. He rummaged in his case.

‘Well, um, I do have a variety of novelty condoms,’ he said handing out a number of packets, ‘these come in various colours and, uh, flavours, and there’s ribbed ones and nobbly ones.’

‘Why would you want a nobbly condom?’ Susan asked.

‘They give extra, um, friction, which is supposed to give greater feeling for the man, and uh, the woman.’

‘Oh, let’s see one,’ Eileen ripped open the cellophane covering and pulled out the rubber. She gave it an experimental stretch and the others peered at the little hard knobs that covered it.

‘You’ll have to put it on so we can see how it works,’ Edith said.

‘Put it on?’ Mr Winter gulped.

‘I’ll help you,’ Joyce said, kneeling in front of him and reaching for the belt on his trousers.

‘Let me take your jacket. You must be warm in here,’ Eileen said, standing and moving behind the young man. She pulled his jacket off his shoulders, immobilising him while Joyce undid his belt and buttons. His slip-on shoes and socks slipped off easily, then Joyce tugged on his trousers and they fell to his ankles. Already there was movement in his groin and a mound appeared, pushing against the white cotton of his Y-fronts. Eileen completed pulling the jacket down his arms.

‘Rather boring pants,’ Joyce observed, yanking them down.

Mr Winter’s penis sprang out and bobbed up and down. The ladies stared at the erect rod. It grew some more as they gazed and the foreskin peeled back. The hole in the pink, shiny glans was like an eye which appeared to be looking at each of them.

‘Ooh, that’s a big un,’ Betty said.

'I haven't seen one that size since before the war,' Edith reminisced.

'It's no use, I can't resist. I have to hold it.' Joyce said. She encircled the member in her right hand. She squeezed. The protruding four inches swelled even more, the knob becoming purple and the skin taut. She reached between his legs with her left hand to cup the sac.

Mr Winter groaned.

'I think we need to remove your tie and shirt, so you can breathe,' Eileen said, quickly and efficiently loosening the tie and unbuttoning his shirt. Mr Winter stood naked in front of them, his cock held firmly in Joyce's hand.

'Now let's see what this condom looks like when it's in place.' Eileen stretched the open end of the rubber over the shining knob. With a little twisting and tugging she eased the pink knobbly material over the glans and along the broad shaft, all of which did nothing to lessen Mr Winter's erection. Joyce removed her hand and they knelt back to look at their handiwork. Mr Winter rocked forwards and backwards.

'I think I preferred it without the condom,' Susan said.

'Yes, it is quite a fine specimen,' Joyce agreed.

'But it is supposed to improve satisfaction,' Eileen said.

'I think the young man needs to lie down,' Edith said noting that his swaying was increasing.

Eileen stood up and helped Mr Winter to lie on the bed. He lay flat on his back on the fur-covered mattress, his cock as upright as the cliché flagpole. 'Now let's see if it works,' Eileen said. She straddled him and flung off her fur-trimmed negligee. Joyce heard him gasp as he took in Eileen's trim figure and firm bust. She raised herself up, positioned his rubber-coated cock between her swollen lips and then slowly lowered herself onto it.

Joyce watched the penis disappear from view, inch by inch.

Eileen gasped, 'Oh, it is big. It feels as if it's tearing me apart.'

As his cock rose into Eileen's pussy, Mr Winter was stirred into action. He grasped Eileen's buttocks and thrust upwards.

Eileen cried out as his cock was rammed in up to the root

and his balls slapped against her buttocks. Her thighs trembled and she collapsed on to him, her nipples brushing his chest and his balls squeezed into her crack. He began to thrust up against her weight and she responded by riding him. He was gasping now and shouting out repeatedly, 'yes, yes, *yes*.'

Eileen lifted herself up so his cock almost slipped out, glistening in the lamplight. He grabbed her buttocks in both hands and pulled her down as he arched his back and thrust up. His cock slid into her dripping cunt and he cried out one last triumphant, '*yes!*' Eileen bent her head back and trembled all over her pink, sweating body then sank forward over him.

They lay still for a moment.

'Well, Eileen, did it do the trick?' Edith enquired.

'Oh, yes,' Eileen panted, rolling off Mr Winter and stretching out on the bed.

'Now, Mr Winter, you must have something that will help a man keep going.' Joyce said.

'What? Oh, yes,' Mr Winter sighed and heaved himself into a sitting position, his legs dangling over the side of the bed, his still half erect penis hanging between them. 'If you look in the case you'll see a box labelled "Arab Strap".'

Joyce knelt and rummaged through the assorted objects remaining in the case, wondering what the purpose of some of them were. She found a small cardboard box clearly marked "Arab Strap". She opened the box and took out a small collection of leather straps connected to a stainless steel ring. She held it up. It looked a little like the harness a child might put on a toy pony, but the ring was wrong.

'The ring goes over the cock,' Mr Winter said.

'Ah, I see,' Joyce replied. The loosened condom slid off his semi-stiff but wilting prick and she deposited it on the floor. Then she gripped the sticky shaft in her right hand and slipped the ring over the glans. It slid down easily and rested against his curly brown pubic hair.

'Now fasten the straps around the base, under my balls,' Mr Winter instructed. Releasing the penis, Joyce took hold of the two ends of the strap and brought it round the root of his penis. She fed the end the buckle and pulled it tight. Mr Winter gasped, but the effect was miraculous. Almost at once his cock leapt up and expanded to its full dimensions the ring now digging into the shaft and immobile.

'That feels good,' Mr Winter said in a trembling voice. Joyce made the strap secure. There were still two straps hanging down.

'Where do these go?' Joyce asked.

'They fasten around my balls and provide extra pressure,' Mr Winter explained between little moans as his penis throbbed. Again Joyce took hold of each end of the strap and wound it around the scrotum. She tightened the buckle as Mr Winter let out another gasp of what sounded like pleasure.

His testicles resembled a shiny red apple dangling from a sturdy branch. Joyce could not resist reaching out to pluck it off. It was hard and warm and, thankfully, securely attached.

'Now if you please, another condom quick. I need some relief.' Mr Winter appealed, rising to his feet.

Joyce picked up a packet at random and tore it apart. She stretched the rubber over his throbbing cock. It was an interesting shade of mauve. Then she threw off her housecoat and clambered on to the bed alongside Eileen. Mr Winter knelt at her feet his erect penis contrasting with the black leather of the straps. He lifted her feet up and apart. Joyce bent her knees and realised that her fanny was open and visible not just to Mr Winter but to the other ladies too. She didn't care; she just wanted to be filled by this thick, long cock. Mr Winter did not take his time. He leaned forward until the tip was between Joyce's lips, paused as she gasped in anticipation, then thrust. Joyce felt the swollen glans slide all the way up her moist channel and then the hard cold steel ring against her lips. Mr Winter gave an extra shove and she felt the metal buckle pressing against her clitoris. Every movement sent sensations running from her groin to each extremity of her body.

Mr Winter rocked backwards and forwards. At the end of each inward thrust Joyce groaned. Her eyes were closed and all her thoughts and feeling were concentrated in her cunt, experiencing every slide and push. She could feel her orgasm beginning somewhere far off and rushing towards her like an express train. It ran her down just as Mr Winter came. She felt his semen spurting just as her muscles locked, gripping his cock firmly in her vagina.

He let out a long groaning sigh and collapsed with his chest pressing against her breasts. They lay together for moments, their sweat mingling and their breathing coming together in short pants.

Joyce could feel that although Mr Winter had come his penis was still erect inside her. He slowly withdrew and she saw the slick hard rod emerge from her hole still as hard and long as when it went in. The dangling testicles wobbled.

'Is it my turn?' Betty said, standing and divesting herself of her dressing gown. She stood naked.

'Kneel please,' Mr Winter said clambering off the bed. Betty knelt on the carpet presenting her ample and fleshy rear to the salesman. He lowered himself to his knees and parted her buttocks with his hands. His cock found its target and he leaned forward.

Betty let out a startled 'ooh' and responded to his thrust by arching her back and pushing back against him. Joyce was amused to see the slim, bony, young man bouncing against the well-padded rear of the woman. They kept at it for some minutes, and Joyce felt like congratulating Mr Winter on his stamina. Betty moaned and groaned and her bulges took on a glowing, pink tinge and a patina of sweat. At last, when Joyce wondered if Betty could take much more, Mr Winter let out a shout and froze. Betty subsided into a heap and Mr Winter's cock slid out. It was still erect in its web of leather straps.

'Please. Help me get it off,' Mr Winter appealed. Joyce leapt off the bed and knelt in front of him undoing the buckles and pulling the wet leather from around his balls and cock. With the constraint released his penis quickly shrank and his scrotum became wrinkled. Mr Winter puffed out his cheeks.

'Phew, that was some session.'

'I think you all deserve a drink after that exhibition,' Edith said getting up to fill glasses at the drinks cabinet.

Betty picked herself up and put her dressing gown back on.

'I think if we do much more of this, the weight will drop off me,' she said. The others laughed and clinked glasses.

'I think we have begun to achieve our objectives,' Eileen said as they each picked up a glass, clinked them and toasted the Ladies College for Erotic Arts.

Joyce showed Mr Winter to the front door. His suitcase was considerably lighter than when he arrived and there was a thick wad of five and ten pound notes in his pocket. As on his arrival he looked the epitome of the travelling salesman.

'Well, thank you for coming, Mr Winter,' Joyce said holding the door open.

'Thank you, Joyce. You know, this evening has been so, um, successful; parties like this may become a common way of distributing our products. Good night.'

Chapter Four
The Studs

'Hey! Look what I've got.'

Johnny let go of the weight bar held against his chest. It crashed onto the mat. He glared at Mick.

'What did you put me off for? I had that one.'

'Sorry, mate,' Mick said, holding out a sheet of paper, 'I wanted you to see this.'

Johnny glanced at the sheet without taking it from Mick, then picked up a towel from the floor and wiped the sweat from his arms and neck.

'What does it say – models required? Poncing around in fancy clothes, is it?'

Mick took a closer look at the piece of paper. 'No. It says "life models required".'

'What does that mean then?' Johnny towelled his thick thighs.

'It's what they have at art classes, isn't it. Living models for artists to paint.'

'Posing?'

Mick grinned.

'Yeah. You up for it?'

'Who's asking?' Johnny dropped the towel and stood in front of a long mirror admiring the muscles of his arms and shoulders as they contracted and relaxed beneath the glistening skin.

'It says it's the Ladies' College for Erotic Arts,' Mick read.

'Some women keen on painting the naughty bits,' Johnny said, gripping one hand in the other and tensing his arms.

'Yeah, I reckon they could do with some choice meat like you and me,' Mick said finding himself admiring Johnny's performance, again. 'I need the cash – don't you?'

'How much they offering?'

'Competitive rates for comprehensive service,' Mick read again.

'What the fuck does that mean – comprehensive service?'

'Fuck knows. Look they give a phone number. I could ring and find out more.'

'You do that. I'm going to pump up a bit more.'

'I'll get on to them when I've had a work out.' Mick pulled off his tracksuit top revealing an array of muscles almost as impressive as Johnny's; well, he hoped as much.

Johnny dismounted from his rusting bicycle and pushed open the iron gate to the Old School.

'It had better be worth pedalling this far out of town,' he said pushing the bike up the short path.

'The woman said that they would make sure we were properly paid for the job,' Mick said following.

'Not quite the same as x pounds per hour, is it?'

'She was very nice on the phone. She said her name was Joyce. Asked all about us, what we were studying, that sort of thing. Sounded like my mum.'

Johnny rested his bike against the wall and pressed the doorbell. Mick put his bike against Johnny's and carefully wound a chain around the rear wheels. He snapped the padlock shut as the door opened.

'Hello boys. Mick and Johnny is it?' Mick looked past Johnny and saw a woman who was indeed about the age of his mother, a little on the short side with grey-flecked brown hair. She was wearing one of those horrible, knee-length, nylon housecoats.

'I'm Johnny. He's Mick.'

Joyce's eyes looked up and down each of them.

'Oh, lovely. I'm Joyce. Do come in boys.'

They entered a narrow hallway and Joyce closed the door behind them.

‘Go on through, boys – down the hall.’

Johnny led the way, pushing open a door at the end of the hall and stopping suddenly. Mick collided with him.

‘What did you stop for?’

‘Take a look at this.’ Johnny stepped forward, allowing Mick to pass through the door and look at the room.

It was a vast bedroom but apart from a huge bed there were sofas and spotlights.

‘I don’t see any painting gear,’ Johnny said.

‘Perhaps they haven’t got it out yet,’ Mick replied, then his eyes saw the other four women coming to greet them. There was a young one, an old one, a fat one, and another that looked about his mother’s age but taller than Joyce. Not one of them looked like an artist in paint-spattered overalls but all looked as though they were dressed for a special night out. The young one wore a denim miniskirt with knee-high black boots and a tight ribbed top. The old one had on a calf-length black leather skirt slit up the side and a black silk shirt. Even the fat one looked attractive, wearing a paisley patterned purple tunic top over black trousers.

‘Hi, I’m Eileen. Come and join us, boys.’ That was the fourth one, the other middle-aged woman, wearing a brightly coloured jump suit.

Mick followed Johnny into the room, finding it difficult to take his eyes off the multi coloured furs on the bed.

‘Come and join us on a sofa,’ the fat one said, sitting down and patting the cushion beside her. Mick sat and found himself sinking into the soft upholstery. ‘There, that’s nice, isn’t it?’ the fat woman went on. ‘I’m Betty.’

Mick noticed that Johnny had stayed standing, planting his feet apart and folding his arms. Joyce bustled up.

‘Now, boys, I expect you’d like a beer, wouldn’t you.’

‘I don’t pollute my body with alcohol. Water will be fine,’ Johnny said.

‘Oh, good. I mean, very sensible,’ Joyce flustered.

‘I’ll have a glass of water too, please,’ Mick said.

‘Two glasses of water, coming up,’ Joyce said, retiring. The other three women sat on the semi-circle of sofas and Mick noticed their eyes travelling up and down Johnny's body.

'So, you do Keep Fit, do you?' Eileen asked.

'Pumping iron, we call it,' Johnny said in the slow drawl he liked to put on.

'Oh, you mean like that foreign man, Arnold Swatsunbugger, or something. I saw his picture in the paper,' the woman in the miniskirt said.

'Arnold Schwarzenegger's the guy, lady. Reckon he'll be famous one day.'

'Not sure I like all those muscles bulging out of places where most men haven't got muscles,' the oldest woman said.

'Only one bit of muscle, we're interested in, eh, Edith,' Eileen said and Mick wondered if she meant what he thought she meant.

'I think you'll find it's not muscle,' Edith replied, 'No, I like to see a fit man, a strong man, but those twitching muscles, ugh.'

'You've seen a lot of this "pumping iron" then?' Betty asked.

'Only, now and again, on ITV,' Edith said, sticking her nose in the air.

'You have to put on those poses in competitions to show how well ripped the muscles are,' Mick explained.

Joyce handed a glass of water each to Mick and Johnny.

'So are we going to see these muscles of yours then?' she asked.

'If that's what you're paying for, lady,' Johnny said. 'Where do we prepare?'

'Well, right here if you like, or you can go behind there.' Joyce pointed to a black zigzag screen in a corner of the room almost invisible in the shadows.

'Right. Come on, Mick.' Johnny poured the glass of water down his throat and strode to the corner. Mick took a swig, put the glass down and trotted after him.

In the semi-darkness behind the screen Johnny started to pull his sweatshirt over his head.

'What do you think they want?' Mick whispered, pulling the zip of his top down and finding himself enraptured as usual when Johnny's smooth muscular chest appeared.

'Well, it's not daubing paint on a canvas, that's for certain.' Johnny pulled off his training shoes and white socks. Mick took his tracksuit top off and removed his shoes. Johnny pulled at the string at the waistband of his tracksuit bottoms and tugged them down over his hips and thighs. Mick felt his eyes bulging.

'Hey, what are you wearing? Is that a posing pouch?'

Johnny's genitals were encased in a shiny orange fabric and dangled between his thighs. Mick could see that his taut, smooth buttocks were naked.

'Yeah, got them mail-order from one of the mags. Just the job for posing in front of a bunch of women, don't you think?'

'Yeah, great.'

Mick self-consciously pulled his own trousers down revealing his old black swimming trunks. Why did Johnny's body hold so much fascination for him? He was mesmerised by the curved outline of Johnny's large cock and balls inside the elasticated orange cloth.

Johnny experimented with a few arm and leg tensions checking his muscle definition.

'This'll stun 'em.' He strode out of their hide into the light and view of the women. Mick stumbled along behind. There were murmurs of approval.

Johnny stood under a spotlight in front of the sofas and put on a pose taking care not to contract his muscles to their greatest extent. Mick stood by his side, out of the circle of light.

'Very good, boys,' Eileen said clapping her hands.

'You said you wanted "life models",' Johnny said proudly. 'What for?'

'We'll get to that in a minute,' Eileen answered. 'First, we'd like to see all of what you've got to offer.'

'All?' Johnny seemed to have lost his glib talk.

'She means we want to see what you've got in that orange sack you're wearing,' Edith said.

This wasn't how Mick had expected it to be. He had thought that they would be discreetly nude, posing on a chair, or pedestal surrounded by artists behind easels. Standing here in front of the women lounging on sofas seemed somehow more exposed.

'Yer, gerrem off,' Betty said laughing.

'OK,' Johnny said, a defiant tone in his voice, 'Come on, Mick. Show the ladies what you've got.' With one brief tug the skimpy garment was pulled down and his penis and testicles spilled out. The orange knickers slipped down to his ankles and he stepped out of them planting his feet apart.

Mick couldn't stop himself staring at Johnny's tool hanging down his thigh and the wrinkled sac. He'd seen it before of course, when they were showering after a workout, but something was different. Usually Johnny's penis sprang from a nest of blond curls. Now there were just a few wisps of hair on his pubes. He's trimmed his pubic hair so that it didn't protrude from the posing pouch; Mick smiled. That was just like Johnny to get everything just right.

'Come on, Mick. You too,' Joyce called. Mick was jogged out of his day dream and hurriedly pulled his old saggy bathers down his legs. His penis popped out half erect. He felt his cheeks turn red.

'Ah, now that's better,' Betty said. 'We thought you were both uninterested.'

Johnny turned and glared angrily at Mick's swollen cock.

'What are you after, ladies? You said you wanted life models but don't go telling me you're painters cos I don't see any brushes.'

'That can be arranged,' Betty giggled.

'Now, boys,' Joyce said calmly. 'Perhaps we should explain. Yes, we said we wanted life models, not for painting, but to experiment with, to mould into a form we like. We are exploring the erotic arts and we need some live models to work with.' She turned to each of the other women, 'we think they'll do, don't we, girls.'

'Well, they're good, young flesh,' Edith said

'They've got all the right bits.' Betty giggled again.

'And I am sure they will soon get in the mood, when we get started,' Eileen added. 'Don't you think so, Susan?'

Mick noticed that the quiet young woman was licking her shiny red lips and her cheeks were red.'

'Oh, yes,' she said.

'Well, let's give them something to get excited about then, girls.'

Mick stared in amazement as each of the women began to undress in front of them. Susan was the most eager. She tore off her top and pulled her mini-skirt down in moments. Mick's half erect penis leapt to attention as his eyes took in her bare thighs, tiny black panties and her breasts resting on a black bra that did nothing to contain them. In another moment or two the knickers and bra were gone to and she stood up dressed only in the black, high heeled, knee boots. Her crimson nipples were hard and seemed to point up at him. His gaze descended to the blonde curls at her groin. He felt his cock straining to stretch towards her and his balls ached. He wanted to take her in his arms to wrap himself around her, embed himself in her. He took a half step towards her and she moved towards him.

'Now, girls, remember it's two between five and it's not all about fucking.' Joyce spoke sternly. 'Remember what you have read. It's a gourmet meal; don't rush to the main course.'

Joyce's voice grabbed Mick's attention for a moment, although he didn't take in her words. He noticed that Betty and Eileen were also naked and approaching Johnny; his purple headed, circumcised cock sticking out above the horizontal. Mick gasped; it must be nearly a foot long and his balls dangled beneath it.

A hand grasped Mick's cock. He looked down expecting to see Susan's hand gripping him but it was Joyce. All thoughts of her resembling his mother were erased from his mind. She actually looked very attractive; OK, older than Susan, but her tits were still firm and she still had a waist. Her hips were a little broader than the younger woman but the smooth hairless pubis with the swollen red lips was what drew his eyes.

'Good, I've got your attention,' Joyce said, 'Now Mick you've got to remember that as well as a cock you have a mouth and two hands. You have to use all of them to satisfy Susan and me.'

Mick saw Johnny being dragged to the bed by Betty and Eileen with Edith, stripped to a black basque and stockings close behind. Then he was being pulled down to the thick fluffy rug. Susan was beneath him and her breasts were within reach. He reached out with a forefinger and touched a nipple. It quivered and Susan gave a little gasp. He lowered his mouth to the other, feeling the hard bud between his lips. He sucked and felt the body squirm beneath him. Fingers gripped his cock and a hand cupped his balls. As his lips rubbed against the nipple the fingers caressed the length of his penis and slid over his knob. He had to stop sucking as a groan rose from his own throat.

'Perhaps that's a little too much, too soon,' Joyce whispered removing her fingers from his manhood. She moved to lie alongside Susan with Mick kneeling between them. She took his spare hand and placed it between her legs. His fingers found her moist crack and slipped inside. Now it was her turn to moan, as one, two, three fingers groped inside her. Mick realised that while his prick ached to shoot his load he wanted this feeling to last. He lowered his head to Susan's breast again and let his hand slide from her other breast over her belly to her wet cunt. His cock rubbed against her side as his mouth and two hands worked.

Mick found that if he concentrated on the two women it just about took his mind off his straining prick and tight testicles. He worked the fingers of his two hands in unison, making patterns in the vaginas of the two wriggling, groaning women. He kept his mouth busy moving from one nipple to another to another; feeling the different textures and consistency of the two pairs of breasts. Both women were moving as one, like a pair of puppets on his hands. They moaned and begged and shivered and shook. Susan was first to come with a long drawn out cry, but Joyce was not long after, sobbing with joy. Mick felt both vaginas clench around his hands with pulses of pressure as the muscles contracted repeatedly.

'That's it. I need it,' Susan said, no longer the quiet one. She moved away causing his hand to slide out of her. She sat up and pulled him down. He rolled on to his back his cock reaching for the ceiling. Susan stood astride him and slowly bent her legs. Her fanny touched the tip of his cock and he gasped. Down,

down she came and his cock slid effortlessly into her cunt. He was watching her, watching the look of ecstasy on her face as he filled her. Then his view was obscured by thighs and buttocks. A dripping hairless cunt was pressed against his face. Without a thought his mouth opened and he reached with his tongue. He felt folds of skin and then he found the smooth, slick surface of her vagina. He lapped and sucked, drinking Joyce's juices. His chin rubbed her little nub and his nose slid along the crack to her arse while Susan's cunt continued to slide up and down on his cock. To Mick his tongue and his cock were one; he was all cock, buried in pussy, two pussies, and, yes, here it came, a tsunami of spunk welling up from his core. He arched his back and pushed up as hard as he could, spurting his spunk deep into Susan's deep cleft. He sucked and drank Joyce's effusion as his orgasm locked his whole body. Susan subsided, her buttocks squeezing his balls and his head was gripped by Joyce's thighs. He was smothered by her buttocks.

'I think you'd better move; you might suffocate him,' Susan's muffled voice reached Mick.

'Oh, yes,' Joyce giggled, 'mustn't do that, must we.' She moved and Mick gasped cool air. He opened his eyes and saw Susan sitting astride him, and beyond, on the bed, he could see Eileen riding Johnny while Betty and Edith did things with his hands. They too reached a climax and fell into a heap of panting flesh.

'Now, ladies, let us not forget the dessert,' Joyce said, 'let us have a little mouth music as Dr Comfort calls it. Time to move on, I think.'

There was no conversation but all the women moved. Mick felt a moment of regret when Susan got up and left his soft, wet penis lying amongst his matted hair, but then Edith stood over him. Grey hair and lined face attested to her age, but her figure in the basque and stockings was anything but unattractive.

'Now, young man,' she said, 'let's see what your powers of recovery are like.' She pushed his feet apart, knelt between his knees and lowered her head to his groin. Her tongue traced the length of his dormant prick, then circled his balls, first one then the other. Already he felt a stirring.

'Good. Good.' Edith muttered between strokes with her tongue, 'I haven't had such a response since before the war.'

His cock stiffened and rose. Edith's tongue touched his knob. Mick gasped and shivered. How could she know just the right place and pressure to get that reaction? Was it the skill of a mature woman? Her lips touched the tip in a kiss then parted and a hot ring slid over his knob. She gripped the top of his shaft with her lips and her tongue played all over his glans enclosed within her mouth. He was fully recovered now, his cock hard, erect, ready to burst again. He gasped as Edith's lips slid further down his shaft, his knob touched the hot flesh at the back of her throat, and went further. Mick couldn't believe it. Edith was swallowing his cock. It was tight but oh, so hot and smooth. Difficult though it was, Mick raised his head so that he could see her mouth devouring his tool. Down, down went her lips, until her nose was pressed against his pubis. Mick was transfixed; his whole throbbing cock in her mouth and gullet. Edith lifted her head revealing his glistening shaft. She allowed his knob to just leave her lips. She gasped and filled her lungs, then lowered her head once more. Again he felt the delirious pleasure of her mouth sliding down his cock, not so far this time because she started lifting and lowering her head. His cock was like a piston sliding in and out of the cylinder that was her mouth and throat. He couldn't take much of this, much as he wanted it to last for ever. His cry when his orgasm came was of joy and regret. Joy for the burst of pure ecstasy and regret that it would not last. His semen fountained into Edith's mouth and she sucked and swallowed every last drop. Mick subsided in a shuddering wreck and Edith gently released his shrunken member. She rocked back on to her heels.

'Where on earth did you learn to do that?' Eileen asked.

'Oh, I had to be imaginative after Stan was injured. We could never have intercourse in the normal way, but with a bit of work he could get an erection and I learnt to enjoy making him come in my mouth. This young man took a lot less time and effort I can tell you.'

'But how do you take his whole length?' Betty asked.

'I don't know. Practice I suppose. Mind you I was a little

worried there; Stan was never as big as this magnificent boy.'

'Well, my turn now,' Eileen said, 'I need the practice. It's not something I allowed Eric very often. Perhaps that was why he ran off with his young bit of stuff.'

Mick was on the point of dozing off when he felt another set of lips grip his cock. No, not again, surely, he thought, but his insatiable penis thought otherwise. It was almost as if he was separated now from his genitals. His cock soon responded to Eileen's attention and Mick felt like a spectator watching and feeling the stirrings in his groin.

'I've had enough of watching,' Betty said, 'I need something.'

She planted her feet beside Mick's head, heels against his shoulders and crouched down over Mick's head. Her fleshy buttocks touched his chest and her hair tickled his nose and lips. Betty sank lower and now her lips touched his. He flicked his tongue between the folds of skin and flesh. She rocked back and fore, rubbing her protruding clit against his nose. Mick found he could concentrate on licking out her cunt while far away Eileen's lips and tongue were working up and down his shaft and sucking on his balls. Time became meaningless while Mick lapped at Betty's cunt and Eileen worked his cock once again into a throbbing rod of potency. Mick felt that he was floating in some sublime paradise as he chewed on Betty's clitoris sucking air through the folds in her flab while his penis trembled to every touch of Eileen's tongue. At last the familiar feeling grew in his groin and erupted from his shaft. His lips closed and pulled on the morsel of flesh, and Betty too came with an earth shaking tremor.

Betty flopped forward letting cool air reach Mick's head. Eileen lapped at his balls and shrinking tool relishing the final drops of his spunk. Mick sighed and listened to his heart recovering from its activity. He closed his eyes, just wanting to sleep.

There was clapping.

'Well done.'

'Good one.'

Mick opened his eyes and saw, Joyce, Susan and Johnny

sitting on the edge of the bed looking down at him.

'That was really good,' Eileen said licking her lips.

'Ooh yes, I got a nice one then,' Betty giggled.

'I'll put the kettle on,' Joyce said, jumping off the bed.

'Oh, yes, look at the time. I'd better be getting off,' Susan said.

There was activity all around Mick. He sat up to find that Johnny was already pulling on his pouch.

'Fun's over,' he said, 'time to get dressed by the look of it.'

Mick followed Johnny behind the screens and they pulled their clothes on. When they emerged all the women had dressed except Joyce who arrived with a tray of mugs, still naked. They sat around for a few minutes drinking instant coffee, engaging in a little half-hearted and stilted conversation and then they were being ushered to the front door.

'Thank you, boys,' Joyce said, pulling on her housecoat. 'Same time next week?'

Johnny shrugged, and Mick nodded.

'Oh and here's what we promised you.' Joyce reached into a pocket and drew out two five pound notes. She handed one each to Johnny and Mick. Johnny grunted his thanks.

'Thank you, Joyce. It's been, ah, a pleasure,' Mick said. He unlocked the bikes and they mounted and waved to Joyce as they cycled off.

The cycle ride back to their shared house was refreshing. It still wasn't late when they got home, locked up the bikes and went in.

'Fancy a drink,' Johnny said pushing open the door to his room.

'Um, well, yeah.' Mick wondered what Johnny meant. He followed him in. Johnny opened his wardrobe and picked up a bottle of whisky. He looked around for a glass and a mug and poured two generous measures. He passed the glass to Mick.

'I thought you said alcohol polluted the body,' Mick said staring at the golden liquid.

'It does, but sometimes it helps put things in perspective, such as this evening.'

Mick took sip. He wasn't used to spirits and the liquid burned his throat. He coughed.

'It was something else, wasn't it? Those women were insatiable.'

'Yeah, I thought they were a bunch of old biddies but they sure knew how to bring a guy off, and were willing to pay for it.' Johnny sprawled on his double bed.

'Susan wasn't old, but that old dear, Edith – well the way she took my cock …' Mick felt his penis hardening at the thought of what had happened a short while earlier. Johnny grinned.

'Yeah, her and the others; couldn't get enough of it, could they?'

Mick had a vision of Johnny's huge erection.

'Not surprising once they saw your whopper.'

Johnny smiled and rubbed his groin.

'Yeah, well, you've got to make an effort to please the ladies.'

'What, like wearing that pouch and trimming your pubes.'

'You noticed!' Johnny looked leeringly at Mick. 'You like looking at cocks, do you.'

'No, well, yes, well you know, for comparison.' Mick was embarrassed. 'In the mags the guys seem to have small, uh, packages.'

'That's because they've pumped up their thighs and chests.'

'Yeah, but yours looked pretty huge even before you got an erection. How do you do it?'

'I'm not sure. I suppose I was always pretty big, but when I was a kid and decided to get into bodybuilding I decided to treat my cock like a muscle group.'

'What do you mean?'

'You know how we pump each set of muscles with particular exercises.'

'Yeah.'

'Well I decided to do the same with my cock. Except there was only one way I could think of to exercise it.'

'Wanking?'

'That's it; plenty of it. Practice makes perfect so they say.

I'm up for it five, six times a day.'

'Really?'

'Want to see?' Mick felt Johnny looking at him, gauging his response.

'Uh, yeah, OK.'

Johnny pulled off his sweatshirt and dropped his bottoms. His cock was already straining against the fabric of the pouch. He whipped it off. Once again, Mick was fascinated by the long, thick member and its purple helmet.

'Let's have a look at yours then.'

'Oh, right, yes.' Mick stripped his clothes off without taking his eyes off Johnny's tool. Johnny massaged it slowly with his left hand. When Mick was naked he crawled on to the bed beside Johnny.

'Go on, you know you want to. Hold it, Suck it.' Johnny urged letting go of his tool. It stood up with a slight curve in the shaft. Mick leaned forward. It was something he'd never done before, never really thought of doing; he touched the purple dome with his lips. The various scents of the women evaporated off Johnny's skin and filled his nose – perfumes, sweat, cunt juices. The knob was warm, soft but with a hard core, and the purple skin was pulled tight. He opened his lips and reached out with his tongue, moistened his lips then licked the tip around the small gaping hole. His lips slid over the helmet and his tongue circled it. Mick was elated. He actually had another guy's cock in his mouth, and he loved it. His own penis was straining and demanding attention. He felt a hand grip his balls and squeeze them.

He lowered his head, taking more of Johnny's cock into his mouth. He had to open his mouth as wide as possible. He was sucking air through the narrow gaps. The tip touched the back of his throat. He gagged; he couldn't do what Edith did. He gripped the shaft in his hand and pulled it out of his mouth a little then began to move up and down on it. Johnny's hand moved from his balls to his shaft and started milking him like a cow's teat.

Now he just wanted to make Johnny come. He lubricated the glans and shaft with his saliva and bobbed his head faster and faster. It felt like nothing he had experienced before, a stiff rod banging in and out of his mouth. It went on and on. He was fit so didn't tire; he just wanted to keep going. Suddenly, Johnny tensed; his grip tightened on Mick's cock and a torrent of salty, eggy, fluid shot into Mick's mouth. He gulped, struggled to avoid choking, recovered, sucked and licked, holding the softening cock in his mouth.

Johnny's body relaxed and then he was rubbing his hand vigorously up and down Mick's dick. Mick tensed, and closed his mouth on Johnny's shrinking shaft as his own semen gushed from his cock.

Johnny released his grip and Mick let the penis slip from his mouth. He collapsed with his head beside Johnny's feet.

'Yeah, not bad. Didn't know you were a cock-sucking queer.'

Mick was confused. This evening had revealed so many desires that he'd almost been unaware of.

'I didn't know either.'

'Well, suits me. I don't care whether my cock's inside a cunt or a mouth, and your mouth is as good as any. So until we meet up with the ladies again, you'll do.'

The taste of Johnny's spunk was still on Mick's tongue. He thought about sucking Johnny's cock again and sinking his own tool into the women's fannies or mouths. Apparently they were all available; a pretty good deal. The future looked like being fun.

Chapter Five
The Camera

Joyce poured tea into the china cups and passed one to each of the women.

'Now, girls, I have a task for you,' she said wrapping her housecoat around her and sitting down on a sofa.

'A task?' Edith asked.

'Yes. I want to plan next week's activity, since we seem to have come to the end of this evening's exercise.' Joyce waved a hand at the two boys asleep on the bed, each with an arm draped tenderly over the other's naked body.

'Ooo, what have you got for us?' Betty said eagerly.

Joyce got up and crossed the room to a cupboard, opened it up and took out a brown cardboard package. She brought it back to the semicircle of sofas and sat back down with the box on her knees.

'What have you got?' Susan asked, leaning forward.

Joyce opened the box and took out a flat, white, rectangular object.

'What is it?' Betty asked, peering at it.

'It's a camera,' Eileen said, proud of her knowledge.

'Strange-looking camera,' Edith said.

'Oh, I know,' Susan said, leaning even closer and brushing her bare breasts against Joyce's arm, 'it's one of them instant cameras, isn't it?'

'That's right,' Joyce said. 'It's called a Polaroid Land SX something or other.'

'What does that mean?' Betty asked looking mystified.

'I don't know what the name means,' Joyce said, 'but once

you've taken a picture the camera produces a photograph – straight away.'

'You mean you don't have to take the film to Boots?' Betty said.

'That's right. The camera does everything for you.'

'I see,' Edith said, slowly as if she was thinking carefully, 'so that means we can take photographs of us having sex and not worry about what the nosy people at the chemists will think.'

'Yes. It's completely private but we can take photos of some interesting poses.'

'Well, come on, show us,' Eileen urged.

'Well …' Joyce was reluctant, 'the films are very expensive. I don't want to waste a shot.'

'You won't. Come on; take one of me,' Eileen said.

'Well, all right, just the one.' Joyce pressed a button and the rectangular box sprang into an oddly unsymmetrical machine but with a lens that revealed its purpose. Joyce stood up carefully holding the camera in front of her. 'How are you going to pose, Eileen?'

'How about this?' Eileen lifted her feet on to the sofa, pulled her knees up and apart giving Joyce a full view of her bush.

'I expect that will do,' Joyce said squinting into the viewfinder.

'What about flash?' Susan said.

'That's what I am doing,' Eileen said. The others giggled.

'No, I mean light.'

'Oh, yes,' Joyce said returning to look in the box. She plugged a flashbulb pack into the camera and returned to bend close to her subject. There was silence as everyone held their breath, then there was a flash of light followed by a mechanical whirring sound.

'What happens now?' Edith asked.

'We have to wait for a minute, while the picture develops,' Joyce said.

A few moments later the fully developed photo was in her hand and the ladies all peered at the picture of Eileen's vulva.

'Well, I can't say that Eileen's fanny interests me much, but

I suppose the boys may find it exciting,' Edith said with a sniff.

'Yes, well that's the task I'm setting you. I want you to each plan a pose that we can photograph that is exciting to look at.'

'Like what?' Susan asked.

'Anything. Look through your *Joy of Sex* and see what you can think of. It could be of you on your own, two of you together or with the boys or whatever.'

'What are you going to do with the pictures?' Edith asked.

'That's up to you. If you want to keep them you can.'

'I think it'll be fun,' Betty said giggling, 'although I don't know who'd want to look at pictures of my flab.'

'Oh, I don't know, Betty,' Eileen said, 'Some of the old masters painted lots of pictures of women shaped like you; and anyway, you've lost quite a bit of weight since we started meeting.'

'It's all this exercise I'm getting.' Betty chortled again.

'Right, so you know what you've got to do.' Joyce clapped her hands, 'I think we'd better wake the boys up and pack them off.'

Joyce rolled a piece of Blu-tack between her finger and thumb before pressing it against the back of the photograph. Then she pushed the photo against the wall alongside the others and bent to look at it. She stood up straight, stepped back and reviewed her handiwork, just a couple of dozen small photographs arranged in neat rows; but what photos! She smiled as she thought back over the evening and took another close look at each of the prints.

First up had been Betty. She was keen to get started as soon as all the girls were in the hall and the boys had arrived on their bicycles.

'I want it to be seen that a bloke can find his way through all this flab and give me one,' Betty said.

'What position do you want to use?' Eileen enquired, being methodical and organised.

'I want it from behind?' Betty said, quite forthright. She undid her dressing gown and, standing, let it fall from her shoulders. She showed off her body in all its voluptuousness.

Joyce thought that despite being considerably overweight Betty exuded eagerness for sex and both boys, fitness fanatics though they were, could sense it. Johnny's cock was already signalling his enthusiasm to get on with the job.

Betty knelt on the thick rug in the open space between the sofas and the bed. She thrust her large fleshy bottom up and tucked her head in her arms resting on the floor. Her breasts splayed out on either side of her and her stomach sagged towards the carpet. Johnny approached her from behind and pushed her feet and legs apart. Then he stood between them and reached down wrapping an arm around each thick thigh. He grunted and lifted Betty's arse off the floor, his thigh and arm muscles bulging with the effort. He lined up his cock with her red-lipped pussy and thrust in from his hips.

'Ooh!' Betty cried as she found herself impaled while hanging upside down.

'Oh, wait a moment. I haven't got the camera ready,' Joyce called, rushing to get into a position to capture an image of Betty and Johnny in action. She peered through the viewfinder.

With sweat glistening on Johnny's straining muscles he thrust in out and out of Betty's crack. Momentarily the shaft would emerge from the folds of her buttocks and then disappear again.

Joyce waited and then pressed the switch. There was a flash of light just as Johnny was fully withdrawn. Joyce collected the photograph and waited for it to develop while Johnny continued to pump into Betty, who groaned and sighed in succession. Joyce managed a second shot just as Johnny froze, his hips vibrating with the tension of an orgasm and Betty let out a long low moan of pleasure.

Gently, Johnny lowered Betty to the floor and then relaxed. Sweat ran from his chest down his abdomen and mixed with the semen and juices dripping from his slack penis. He sank to the floor and sat cross-legged, breathing deeply.

The ladies clapped and shouted their congratulations. Slowly and carefully Betty pushed into a sitting position.

'Phew! I didn't expect that,' she said, 'No one's picked me up for a long time.'

'That lad is strong,' Edith agreed.

'Did you get any photos?' Betty asked.

'Oh yes,' Joyce said.

'Are they any good?'

'Judge for yourself.' Joyce passed the two damp prints to Betty. 'Be careful not to touch them while they're still wet.'

Betty looked from one photo to the other, grinning broadly. 'There's no doubt what's happening, is there?'

The others got up to look over Betty's shoulder at the pictures.

'Nope, you can see you're being fucked,' Edith said, shocking the others with her no-nonsense language.

'They've come out well,' Eileen said, 'You're becoming quite a photographer, Joyce.'

'Well, the camera does it all really,' Joyce said modestly, 'Now, I'll go next so someone else can have a turn with the camera.'

'I'll give it a go,' Eileen said, reaching for the camera, 'What are you going to do?'

'Wait and see, but you will need to get up high over the bed so that you can look down.'

Eileen looked mystified, 'How am I going to do that?'

'I got the step-ladders out of the garage. They're over there.' Joyce pointed to the corner of the room. Johnny went to fetch the ladders and erected them at the end of the bed. Eileen took the camera and clambered unsteadily up the rungs. Standing on the top she peered through the viewfinder.

'Well, come on then. What are you going to do?'

Joyce flung off her housecoat revealing her mature but firm naked body.

'I'm ready for you, Mick. Remember what I said to you earlier,' she called out.

Mick needed no second bidding. Throwing off the towel he had chastely held around his waist, he moved towards the bed, his erect cock bobbing up and down. He lay down with his head towards Eileen, his penis a vertical flagpole. Joyce climbed on to the bed and squatted over Mick, facing him. Slowly she lowered herself until her shaven pussy kissed the swollen purple head. Mick trembled. Joyce dropped another couple of inches, driving the shaft into her tunnel.

'Shall I take a photo?' Eileen called.

'If … you … like,' Joyce said between gasps.

'Hold it right there?' There was a flash and a whirr. Joyce let out a cry and sank down engulfing Mick's cock. Joyce knelt with her thighs stretched wide either side of Mick's body with his manhood buried inside her. It felt as though it was piercing her whole body. Her mouth was open taking small, quick breaths.

'Is that it?' Eileen asked.

'No …' Joyce replied, 'Wait a moment while, huh, I get into the pose.' She lifted herself up and a few inches of Mick's cock reappeared. He took her hands in his. Slowly and carefully she stretched out her right leg, steadying herself on Mick's rigid arms, and moved it around until it was beside Mick's left shoulder. Then she did the same with her left leg. Now she was sitting on Mick's cock and balls. He grunted quietly. Joyce leaned back holding Mick's hands firmly and gently lowered herself, letting go of his hands at the last moment. Man and woman lay flat on the bed, her legs over his, with his cock still most obviously inserted in her vagina.

'Now,' Joyce said. 'Take a few before he slips out.' She wriggled a little and brought a groan in response from Mick.

'I see. The X position. Very athletic,' Eileen said, 'Those yoga lessons obviously did some good, Joyce.'

Joyce watched as Eileen leaned over them, aiming the camera. There was another flash. She closed her eyes and concentrated on contracting her pelvic muscles. Mick was moving somehow and she could feel the small thrusts that his penis made in her cunt. It felt as if she was in paradise; a constant stimulation, a never-ending pleasure. There were a few more flashes and then at last she felt the rising tide of an orgasm. As she came, with muscles throughout her body rippling, she felt Mick's penis throb and spurt. He let out a guttural cry.

The electric currents subsided and Joyce felt the penis shrink and withdraw. She forced herself to open her eyes and sit up.

'Well, did you get the shots?'

Eileen had dismounted from the ladders and came to her with the prints in each hand.

'Yes. I think they capture the pose.'

'I think they do,' Joyce said surprised to find the photographs of her naked body in mid-climax strangely exciting.

'My turn next, I think,' Eileen said. 'I'm being greedy. I need both boys for my pose. You can stay on the bed, Mick.' She handed the camera back to Joyce and shucked off her robe. Joyce reluctantly gave up her place on the bed.

Eileen climbed on to the bed and crawled between Mick's legs. She leaned forward and brushed her erect nipples against his chest in a zigzag motion descending down his abdomen. When she repeated the movement, Mick let out a small gasp. The next time, Eileen lowered her head to his chest and dragged her tongue across his skin from side to side making sure that she licked each of his nipples and then his navel. She rubbed her nose in his luxuriant pubic hair and before reaching his penis. Still wet with his come and Joyce's juices it was already thickening, lengthening and changing from a sad, drooping willy to a proud, erect cock.

'Yes, that's more like it,' Eileen murmured as Joyce set off the first flash. Eileen pressed her lips to his knob as it emerged from its cover and sucked it into her mouth. Mick moaned and his body stiffened.

Johnny climbed on to the bed, his penis ready for business. He knelt behind Eileen and grasped her hips, took aim and thrust. His aim was true as his long cock buried itself in Eileen's cunt. Her body jerked forward and more of Mick's shaft disappeared into her mouth. She coughed and raised her head releasing the knob from its moist enclosure.

'Yes, Johnny,' Eileen gasped. 'Do it!'

Johnny needed no encouragement. He swayed back and forth on his knees, his long prick disappearing into and emerging from Eileen's tunnel. Eileen's head fell again on Mick's cock and moved in time with Johnny's thrusts.

'Move your arms, Johnny,' Joyce called, manoeuvring the

camera into position. Johnny put his hands behind his back and continued fucking, touching Eileen only with his thrusting cock. The camera flashed.

'Yes, yes,' Mick urged, arching his back and raising his penis in time with Eileen's bobbing head. The camera flashed again.

Johnny let out a roar like a lion, grabbed Eileen's hips and thrust in so fast and deep that his balls slapped against her mound. His buttocks tensed and he threw his head back and shouted. Mick lifted his body off the bed forcing his penis into Eileen's throat and cried out. There was another flash.

Both boys relaxed and subsided, their cocks spilling out of their respective holes, wilted and spent. Eileen collapsed onto Mick's chest, panting.

'I don't think that pose is in *Joy of Sex*,' Edith said.

'Well, not both at once,' Betty agreed.

'I've wondered what it would be like to have a prick at each end,' Eileen said between breaths.

'And what did it feel like?' Joyce asked.

'Tremendous. It felt as though they were going to meet in the middle and I was a bead on a string, sliding up and down. One moment my mind was on the cock I was sucking the next it was on the cock filling my fanny.'

'So, do you want to see the photos?'

'Yes please, Joyce.' Eileen swung off the bed, leaving Mick and Johnny lying in two comatose heaps. She took the prints from Joyce's hands and looked at the images.

'Aren't we wanton?' Eileen commented.

'We are, but I feel the need for a cup of tea before we have Susan and Edith's turn; and I think the boys need a short rest.'

Joyce placed her cup on its saucer.

'Now, who's next? Susan or Edith?'

'I'll do it,' Susan said quietly.

'And what have you chosen, Susan?' Joyce asked. The young woman reached for the plastic carrier bag that she had put beside the sofa. She pulled out a length of soft black rope.

'I'd like to be tied up.'

‘Ooh, a bit of bondage,’ Betty cooed.

‘Why do you want to be bound, dear?’ Edith asked.

‘I’m not sure. Since I’ve been on my own I’ve had to make all the decisions myself so perhaps I’d just like all responsibility taken out of my hands.’ She tugged on the bow holding her negligee together and let it slip from her shoulders.

‘So, who is going to do it?’ Joyce said.

‘Johnny knows what to do,’ Susan said glancing at the muscular young man sitting naked on the side of the bed. He smiled at her.

‘It’s my pleasure, darling,’ he said. He stood up and approached her, taking the bag in one hand and her hand in the other. He pulled her to her feet and drew her towards the bed. She sat on the mattress and shuffled into the centre. Johnny delved into Susan’s bag and pulled out a black leather strap.

‘What’s that?’ Betty asked.

‘A gag,’ Eileen said, ‘It’s got a ball that fits in the mouth and the strap does up behind her head.’

‘I hope she can breathe properly,’ Betty said.

‘Can’t you see? The ball has got a hole through it so she can breathe all right, but won’t be able to speak. Exciting isn’t it.’

Johnny knelt behind Susan and placed the gag around her head. She opened her mouth and the ball slipped between her teeth. Johnny threaded the strap through the buckle and pulled it tight. He checked that it was fastened securely.

‘That’ll keep you quiet,’ he grunted. He drew a length of the cord from the bag and, holding Susan’s arms above her head, wound it around her wrists before tying it off with an expert knot. He pushed her down gently so her head rested on a pillow. Then he used another length of rope to fasten her bound arms to the brass rail that ran along the top of the headboard. Johnny moved to the foot of the bed and grasped Susan’s right ankle. He wound another length of rope around it then tied the end of the rope to the post of the footboard. Her left ankle was similarly bound in rope and then he pulled on it, forcing her legs wide apart, before tying the rope to the other post.

‘That’ll stop her wriggling,’ Johnny said.

‘I should think so,’ Joyce said, circling the bed with the

camera in her hands. 'It was a good idea to get black rope, Susan. It is very dramatic against your lovely white skin.' She climbed the stepladder and took a couple of shots of the young woman spread-eagled on the bed.

'What happens now?' Betty asked.

'I think that is up to Johnny,' Eileen replied. 'He has his victim as he wants her and can do whatever he likes with her.'

Johnny was kneeling beside the bound and gagged young woman. He caressed her breasts with his hands then lowered his head to lick and suck first her left nipple then her right. Joyce could see Susan's muscles tensing as she attempted to wriggle but Johnny had tied her very effectively and she remained fixed in position. Johnny spread his kisses over her stomach while still rubbing his fingers lightly over her breasts. She gurgled faintly and Joyce could hear a faint whistle as air was drawn through the ball gag.

Johnny climbed astride Susan and shuffled his knees back until Susan's nose rubbed against his arsehole and his balls dangled against her chin. He lowered his head between her legs. Joyce crept close focussing the camera as his tongue flicked up and down her crack. Susan's lips swelled and a droplet of fluid oozed from within. Her pelvis moved imperceptibly but the bindings on her ankles kept her motionless.

Johnny parted her lips with his fingers and extended his tongue into her vagina. The camera flashed and a moan emerged from the gagged mouth between his buttocks. He pressed his face into her, reaching deep with his tongue and rubbing his chin against her clitoris.

If she had been free she would have been writhing and crying out. Joyce watched Susan's muscles straining against her bonds as Johnny took her closer, but not quite to orgasm. Then, when he judged the moment was right, he swiftly moved and knelt between her legs his immense cock searching for cunt, and finding it, driving in. Somehow, Susan arched her back tightening the ropes around her wrists and ankles to get an inch of movement. Holding himself up on his arms, with his hand placed either side Susan's armpits, Johnny thrust his hips forwards and backwards. Each pump drove his cock nine inches into her lubricated hole and then withdrew for another thrust.

Joyce took photo after photo as Johnny kept at it, minute after minute. Susan's arm and leg muscles were in a constant state of agitation and the air whined as it passed in and out of the ball in her mouth. With a final groan Johnny drove his cock deep into Susan's cunt and, bending his arms, sank onto her.

'That was quite something, don't you think?' Joyce said looking at the prints she had taken.

'Yes, but I think we should release Susan, before she goes into cramp,' Eileen said pushing Johnny off the girl.

'Oh, yes,' Joyce said putting the camera and photos down and climbing on the bed to release the buckle holding the gag in place.

Each of the ladies helped undo the ropes and soon Susan was sitting up rubbing her wrists and ankles while Johnny lay breathing deeply.

'Well, what do you think?' Joyce said after showing Susan the pictures.

'It was fantastic. I couldn't move but I seemed to sense every touch far more than usual, and when he was inside me I felt like I was just a fucking machine which kept on producing orgasms.'

'Would you do it again, love?' Betty asked.

Susan thought for a moment.

'Yes, I would, with someone I trust like Johnny. I'd like to explore other positions and ways of being bound.'

'I think we have a bondage specialist in the making,' Eileen commented.

Joyce turned to Edith.

'Now it's your turn. What have you got for us?'

'Oh, I think you will find my pose a bit different. It may shock you too. Mick is my willing helper.'

Joyce saw the boy slouched on a sofa, unselfconsciously naked, become tense and give a thin smile. Edith undid her robe, removed it and stood revealed in her familiar black stockings and basque. She still insisted that no one would want to see her ageing wrinkles and veins, although her flat stomach and firm buttocks were a testament to a fit body, despite her years.

From her capacious handbag Edith took out an object that mystified Joyce for a few moments. Black leather straps dangled from a white V-shaped object. The arms of the V were about seven inches long and over an inch in diameter. The apex of the V was a larger ball. Joyce examined the object and saw that the arms of the V were moulded like two penises sprouting from the same ball sac.

'It's a double dildo!' Joyce exclaimed when she realised what she was seeing.

'That's right, dear,' Edith said taking a pot from her bag. She opened the top and took out a finger full of grease that she smeared on one penis. 'A dried up crone like me needs a bit of lubricant,' she explained.

Edith squatted and parted her labia with one hand while positioning the greased penis with her other. Then slowly she inserted the dildo into her vagina. The other ladies looked on avidly. Soon the whole shaft was inside her and she blew air from her cheeks. She stood up with the spare penis thrust out from her mound and buckled the belt around her waist. With one strap attached to the dildo passing between her buttocks and another fastened tightly at the front, the belt held the contraption firmly in place. Joyce moved in and took a couple of photos from different angles.

'Now, Mick. Time to get in position,' Edith said. Joyce was at a loss as to what Edith intended but as Edith covered the exposed white cock in lubricant, Mick moved and knelt in front of her. He lowered his head and arms, parted his knees and raised his behind. Joyce, standing just behind Edith, relished the view of Mick's testicles and semi-erect penis dangling between his thighs and she admired his firm, smooth buttocks. Then she noticed the red rose of his anus and realised what Edith intended.

'Really, Edith. I don't recall this pose in the *Joy of Sex*,' she said.

'Well, the author is an old fuddy-duddy and only thinks women should be buggered. Since queers enjoy the activity I don't see why all men shouldn't have a taste of it.'

Edith dropped to her knees behind Mick and shuffled closer until the firm plastic dick was between his buttocks. She placed a hand on each cheek and spread them wider apart. Mick's hole was pulled taut. Another shuffle forward and the cock touched the red ring.

'Now, relax, my boy,' Edith ordered and pushed her hips forward. The well-greased tip of the dildo slid inside Mick's arse, stretching the ring. He groaned but didn't flinch. Joyce ducked down to see what was happening and saw his penis twitch and harden. Edith pushed again and the shaft began to disappear inside Mick's anus. His penis quivered again and grew as big, if not bigger, than Joyce had ever seen it. The foreskin peeled back and the purple knob glistened and rubbed against the carpet. Joyce started taking photos as often as the instant camera allowed.

'Oh, oh, yes,' Mick moaned incoherently. Edith rocked gently backwards and forwards. Joyce saw a flush rise from her neck to cover her face, her eyes were unfocussed and she muttered inaudibly.

Mick's whole body trembled as the dildo slipped in and out of his arse. He began to move his own hips against Edith's rhythm driving the cock deeper and harder. He lifted up his head, arched his back and cried out. Semen spurted from his cock forming a pool on the floor.

Then Edith let out a long drawn out sigh and sank back to sit on her calves. The dildo slid from Mick's anus and he too let out sigh.

'Hey, Mick. I didn't know you liked a bit of arse action,' Johnny chortled, 'let me know when you want a real cock up your behind.'

Mick chuckled, 'I'm not sure I could take your monster.'

'Well, we'll just have to try it out, won't we? You never know what you can do until you try.'

Joyce helped Edith to her feet and unbuckled the belt. Edith pulled the cock from her fanny and then collapsed onto a sofa.

'Well, that was quite something. I wasn't expecting to climax,' she said breathing heavily.

‘I think it was a very powerful climax to our games,’ Eileen said.

Joyce looked again at the photo of Edith thrusting the snow-white cock into Mick’s arse. How much things had changed in the first weeks of the College, Joyce thought. She recalled Eileen’s brazen need for a cock and the slightly wary group of ladies at their first meeting. She felt that at first they had been content to accept any titillation or experience but as these photographs showed, now they were bolder and willing to direct the confident young men in ways that they wanted and not just what turned on the boys. I wonder what the next few months will bring, she thought.

Chapter Six
Alfresco

'It's a lovely day. Why don't we go out for a picnic?' Eileen said.

Joyce looked out of the kitchen window at the bright May sunshine and thought that it would be a change to go out for the day.

'What a good idea. It is very warm. I'll see what I've got in the fridge.'

It didn't take long to hard-boil some eggs, butter some bread and to pack cheese, tomatoes, crisps and a cooled bottle of Mateus Rosé in a shopping bag with a couple of glasses and plates.

'Let's take your car,' Eileen said.

'Oh, all right, I don't mind.' Joyce didn't use the big Rover very much; it was Bill's car more than hers, at least before he had died.

They loaded up the boot with the picnic, a blanket and, at Eileen's insistence, Joyce's Polaroid camera. They set off out of the village. Eileen directed Joyce down ever smaller country lanes until they were well into the country and away from the main routes. Joyce manoeuvred the big car up a track across a piece of common land to the edge of a wood.

'This will do nicely,' Eileen said. They had stopped in a grassy dell surrounded on one side by trees and by shrubs on the rest.

'It's very secluded,' Joyce agreed, pulling up the handbrake and switching off the engine. There was no sound of other traffic, just birdsong and the chirping of insects.

They unfolded the blanket onto the grass and unpacked their simple lunch. Together they sat on the grass. Joyce was already feeling warm in her blouse and slacks. She realised that Eileen had dressed much more suitably for the weather in a short cotton skirt and vest.

'This is more like it,' Eileen said, sipping her wine, 'but I feel like getting some air to my skin.' Before Joyce had a chance to reply Eileen was pulling off her vest and unfastening her skirt. She was surprised when Eileen didn't stop there but unclipped her bra and pushed her knickers over her thighs. She stood up and stretched her naked body.

'Eileen!' Joyce exclaimed.

'What's the matter? There's no one to see us. Get your camera out and take some pictures.'

'You planned this didn't you?' Joyce said, realising Eileen's intention, 'Coming out for a picnic was just an excuse so that you could get your clothes off outdoors.'

'Yes, well it's something I've dreamed of doing and now, well, we're realising our dreams what with the College and everything.'

'That's true.'

'And it is such a beautiful, hot day – the first of the summer.' She spread her arms and spun around on one leg. Joyce thought she looked wonderful with her black hair flowing and her breasts jiggling. Eileen stood by the side of the car.

'Come on, photograph me.' She posed by resting her right arm on the roof of the Rover and holding her left hand behind her head.

'Oh, all right.' Joyce picked up the camera, opened it up and peered through the viewfinder. She pressed the button and the instant print emerged from the cartridge.

Eileen moved towards the front of the car and reclined on the wing with one hand behind her resting on the bonnet. Her other hand cupped her breast and caressed her nipple. Joyce stepped forward to get a closer picture and noticed that Eileen's nipples were hard and erect.

Eileen's hand drifted from her breast down over her stomach to her crotch. She curled a finger in her black pubic hair. The finger slipped into her crack. Joyce watched her rubbing herself, her eyes closing and her mouth dropping open slightly.

'Hi ya, ladies. Can I help you?'

Joyce almost dropped the camera at the sound of the voice. It had a Birmingham accent with a hint of the Caribbean. She turned to see a dark-skinned man approaching along the track from the woods. He was tall, and looked to be in his twenties or thirties. A fuzz of afro-style hair framed his smiling face and he wore jeans, a rather grubby T-shirt, battered brown boots and he carried a sailor's style kit bag over his shoulder.

'Well hello,' Eileen said. Joyce turned her head to see Eileen's eyes fixed on the young man but with her fingers still in her pussy. She made no attempt to hide herself.

'Eileen!' Joyce looked from Eileen to the young man. He was just a few steps away now and had a broad grin on his face. He dropped his bag beside their picnic and put his hands on the buckle of his jeans.

'What's the matter, Joyce?' Eileen said, 'Don't you think the young man is keen to see us.'

'Yes, but …' Joyce saw the man unfasten his buckle and unbutton his fly. His cock was pressing hard against the cloth waiting to be released. 'Who are you? What are you doing?' Joyce asked.

The man took his eyes off Eileen for a moment to look at Joyce.

'The name's Winston. Winston Gibbs, missus. It looks like I'm going to bring a little colour to your photos.' He put his thumbs in the front of his jeans and pants and pulled them down. A long, black cock leapt out. Eileen gasped and fixed her eyes on it. Joyce's eyes too, were drawn to the long, taut tool gleaming in the bright sunlight. Winston paused to pull off his boots and socks and to drop his jeans and pants to his ankles. He stepped out of them and dragged the vest over his head.

Joyce felt admiration and desire fill her as she gazed on Winston's body. His dark chocolate skin was flawless and smooth. There was not a hint of spare flesh on his muscular frame. His eyes however, were fixed on Eileen and hers on his long, thick penis that was pointing towards her. She reached for it and encircled it in her hand. Her white hand looked small against the thick, black shaft. She tugged him towards her. He reached out to touch her breast.

'Come on Joyce, get clicking,' Eileen called, 'What was that Paul McCartney song? Ebony and Ivory.'

Joyce had forgotten the camera in her hands in her concentration on Winston's body. Eileen was right – the contrast of her white skin with Winston's was indeed a striking sight. She fired off a shot but while the print developed, Winston moved.

He pushed Eileen back so that she lay over the bonnet of the Rover, parted her legs dangling over the wing and placed himself between them. He positioned his cock against her fanny and pushed. Eileen shouted.

'Oh, yes. You're huge. No, don't stop. Give it to me.'

Winston didn't need a second invitation. He thrust his hips forward and his buttocks tensed. Joyce moved to the front of the car and watched. Winston stood upright with his hands gripping Eileen's hips, his cock sliding in and out of her cunt, juices matting her pubic hair. Eileen's shoulders hammered against the bonnet as she moved in time with his thrusts. She carried on shouting, urging him to fuck her, as hard as he liked. Winston obliged while Joyce clicked the camera.

It couldn't last long of course. The young man was obviously eager and very quickly he froze with his cock rammed to the hilt in Eileen's vagina. Eileen let out a long drawn out groan.

Winston stepped back pulling his penis out of its burrow. It flopped between his legs dripping semen, reduced but still substantial. Eileen pulled herself off the car stiffly and staggered to the picnic blanket. She lay down and reached for her wine glass. She took a swig then offered it to Winston who sat by her side and took the glass. Joyce joined them.

'So, Mr Winston Gibbs. I'm Joyce and this is Eileen. Where are you from?'

'Well, Missus, I was brought up in Smethwick in Birmingham. My ma and pa brought me with them when I was two years old when they moved from Antigua.'

‘What are you doing here?’ Joyce asked

‘I’m travelling, looking for work. I thought I’d take a short cut to the town, but got a bit lost and ended up wandering through the woods. I was pretty relieved when I saw your car. Not as pleased as when I saw you ladies, mind.’

Joyce noticed his cock twitch and grow.

‘How about you, lady?’ Winston said, ‘Would you like some of it.’

Joyce looked at the erect cock straining up to her from where Winston lay on the ground.

‘Go on, Joyce,’ Eileen encouraged, ‘you know you want it.’

Joyce felt her cheeks redden but she started to slide her elasticated slacks over her hips. She stood up and pushed them down her legs. Winston got up and standing in front of her, his penis pressed into her stomach, he grabbed her knickers in both hands and tugged them down to her knees. He thrust a hand between her thighs, his fingers seeking out her fanny, slipping between her lips, exploring her crack.

‘Hey, man, you’re wet,’ he said. He withdrew his hand spun her around and lifted her up. Joyce found herself laid down, face first over the bonnet of the car. Her slacks and knickers were pulled from her feet and then her thighs were pushed apart. She felt the questing knob of his cock between her buttocks. It found its target and he rammed it in. A grunt was forced out of her throat. She couldn’t move, trapped against the hot metal of the car her feet dangling uselessly. There was just the monstrous cock filling her channel and grinding forwards and backwards. He’s using me, she thought, for his own satisfaction; I’m just a simple fuck, and I love it. Fucking again so soon after his first orgasm, he took longer and Joyce was convulsing with pleasure when she finally felt his spunk shooting up inside her. She sighed with pleasure.

‘I’ve got some good shots of you there,’ Eileen said. Joyce turned her head sideways and saw Eileen holding the camera and a handful of prints. She hadn’t heard the shutter at all.

‘But I think, our fun’s over – the weather’s changed,’ Eileen went on. Joyce felt Winston slip out of her and move away. Cool air caressed her sweaty backside. She pushed herself on to her feet and looked up. The sun had disappeared behind a huge black cloud. Drops of cold rain fell on her.

'Quick, shove everything in to the boot,' she said, bursting into action. Joyce gathered up the picnic things in the blanket and dumped them in the boot, while Eileen picked up the discarded clothes and Winston's bag and chucked them in as well. The rain was falling heavily now.

'Get in the car. You too, Winston.' Joyce got into the driving seat and fastened the seatbelt across her blouse. Sticky spunk oozed from her slit and ran down between her buttocks and the leather seat. It felt strange. She realised that Eileen and Winston had both got into the wide, flat, back seat. Joyce started the engine and turned the windscreen wipers on. They struggled to clear the torrential downpour from the glass. Carefully she manoeuvred the car around to take the return route along the rutted track which was already filling with water. The wheels slipped on the mud, but Joyce kept control by concentrating hard.

It was a few minutes before they reached a metalled road and Joyce could relax to look in her mirror. Eileen was sitting with her head against the padded leather wheel arch with her knees drawn up beside her ears. Winston was kneeling on the seat, his black bottom rising and falling as his cock slid in and out of Eileen's cunt. In between moans of pleasure Eileen was urging him on and he grunted in reply.

'Don't make a mess on the leather,' Joyce called out, more in hope than expectation. There was no reply.

Joyce pulled out on to the road. The windows were beginning to steam up so she turned on the fan and heater. Throughout the journey back home each glance in the mirror showed Winston's arse continuing to bob up and down. Eileen's entreaties became weaker and less intelligible.

At last, as Joyce drove the car into the driveway beside The Old School, Eileen let out a loud sigh and Winston's buttocks stopped moving. The car came to a stop beside the door to the kitchen. Joyce looked for her keys in the glove box. It was still raining hard.

'We'd better leave everything in the boot for now,' Joyce

said, 'we can dash inside. That is unless you want to stay in the car; although a nosy neighbour may notice what you are up to.' She pushed her door open and made a dash for the door, fumbling the key into the lock and opening it. Still naked, Eileen and Winston ran into the kitchen behind her.

'Well, here we are,' Joyce said. 'How about a cup of tea?' She began filling the kettle.

'Oh, yes, I could do with a drink,' Eileen said pushing back her sweat-matted hair.

'You couldn't rustle up a sandwich or something too?' Winston asked.

'Oh, yes, I'm sure I can.' Joyce opened the larder, 'Will luncheon meat do?'

'That'll do fine, Missus.'

'Right, well, Eileen, take Winston into the lounge while I get tea and sandwiches made.' Eileen took Winston's hand and guided him from the kitchen.

It took just a few minutes for Joyce to prepare a pot of tea and a plate of sandwiches. She carried the tray into the lounge. Winston was slouched in an armchair. Eileen knelt on the carpet between his legs her mouth around his cock. Joyce placed the tray on an occasional table beside the chair and gave Winston the plate of sandwiches. He tucked into the food with gusto, while Eileen's tongue continued to lick up and down the shaft of his partially erect penis.

Joyce sat on the sofa cradling a cup of tea.

'So, Mr Gibbs, tell us a bit more about yourself. You're from the West Indies, you said.'

'Yeah, though I don't remember anything of Antigua. As far as I'm concerned I'm a Brummie. My pa got work at the Austin factory and after school I started there too, well British Leyland it is now.'

'So why aren't you working there?'

Eileen had lifted up his cock and was licking the come off his balls. She was oblivious to the conversation.

'Well it was dead boring working on the line.'

'And?'

'They sacked me.'

'What for?'

'It was victimisation. My mates agreed. They were going to come out to support me.'

'But?'

'Well they found something else to strike about.'

'Why did they sack you?'

Eileen had gone back to sucking on the knob of the penis, her head bobbing and down as her lips stretched around the shaft.

'They were jealous. It was racial discrimination.'

'There was a woman involved, wasn't there?'

'Yeah, well, I did have a bit of a go with the secretary of one of the directors.'

'And they found out.'

'They caught us in the board room.'

'You were having sex with a secretary in the company board room?'

Winston grinned. 'On the big table actually. I think the guy who caught us wished it was him.'

Joyce finished her tea and put the cup down.

'Hmm. You couldn't find another job in Birmingham?'

'No. Any job I went for got buggered by my old bosses. So I decided to get out and try elsewhere.'

'What do you do?'

'Anything really. I've got lots of skills, my pa taught me house decorating and repairs, gardening, you name it. Ain't got no qualifications, tho', but I could put this place to rights.'

Joyce looked around. The Old School needed a lot of work which she couldn't manage.

'Where are you living?'

'Nowhere. I've been wandering, sleeping rough most nights.'

Eileen had paused for breath, holding Winston's thick shaft in her hand, the knob an inch from her mouth.

'Are you going to give Winston a job, Joyce?'

'I'm thinking about it.'

'Go on, do it. It'll only cost you bed and board and a bit of pocket money.'

'There is the spare room he could have. Are you interested, Mr Gibbs?'

'I certainly am, Missus.'

'Come and have a look at the room.'

Joyce put her cup and saucer down and stood up. Eileen released her grip on Winston's prick allowing him to stand.

Joyce guided Winston and Eileen up the stairs and into a bedroom at the back of the house. She and Bill had put their spare double bed in the room along with a wardrobe, dressing table and chair and still there was space left over.

'This'll do me fine,' Winston said. He went to the bed and tested the mattress, 'Yeah, nice and firm. Let's test it out.' He grabbed Joyce's arm, drew her towards him and gave her a gentle shove so that she fell onto the bed. He followed her, kneeling between her legs. He lifted her ankles on to his shoulders and positioned his cock to enter her pussy. Joyce watched the long black rod disappear into her and felt it filling her channel. With her legs raised she could make little contribution to the movement, but Winston vigorously rammed his tool in and out. Sweat glistened on his chest, his skin gleaming like a mahogany piano. With a deep thrust and a loud groan he ejaculated. Joyce gasped and felt a moment of regret as the cock slid from her. He withdrew and allowed her legs to flop onto the bed.

'Yeah, I think it'll do.' Winston said stretching out on his back, arms folded behind his head. He turned towards Eileen, 'You can carry on with what you were doing now.'

Eileen didn't hesitate but was on the bed, sitting astride his legs and licking the spunk off his cock, without a comment.

Later in the afternoon, Joyce was in the kitchen washing up the picnic things and the tea cups. She had put on her housecoat and slippers to do the chores. Eileen walked in still naked.

'Winston would like a drink,' she said.

'Can't he do anything for himself?' Joyce said.

'What do you mean?'

'Well, since he arrived he's had you cart his bag up to the room and sort through his dirty laundry and he's had me providing sandwiches and drinks and doing his washing. He's spent all the time on the bed.'

A dreamy look came over Eileen.

'Eileen, are you listening to me or are you just thinking about his prick?'

'Sorry, Joyce. What were you saying?'

'Look I'm sure Winston is a lovely bloke and will do odd jobs around the house, but he likes having women at his fingertips, doing what he wants.'

'Yes.'

'Well I think he needs to be taught a lesson before things get out of hand and he has both of us acting like his slaves.'

'I see what you mean.'

'Look, the girls will be here soon. He doesn't know about the College. Keep him occupied upstairs until I say it's time to come down. I'm sure you won't have any trouble doing that, will you.'

'No, OK.' Eileen filled a glass with water and returned upstairs. Shortly after, Joyce heard faint cries of excitement coming from the upstairs room.

Joyce pushed her head around the door. Winston was still lying on the bed with Eileen kneeling over him brushing her tits across his chest while he fondled her pussy.

'Come on down,' Joyce whispered.

'What's up, missus?' Winston asked.

'Come downstairs. There's something we'd like to show you. We're sure you'll like it,' Joyce said. Eileen agreed and climbed off the bed.

'Well, OK. It had better be worth it,' Winston hauled himself upright and followed Eileen and Joyce out of the bedroom and down the stairs.

Joyce opened the door to the hall and beckoned Eileen and Winston through. She took a look around and was pleased to see that the girls had got in position, as requested. Susan was riding Johnny on the bed, kneeling over him, back straight, her fanny rhythmically engulfing his foot-long erection. Johnny moaned and urged her on. Meanwhile Edith sat on a sofa with her legs splayed and Mick kneeling on the floor between them, his head buried in her muff.

'Hey, what are those honkies up to?'

'They're pleasuring the girls, Winston. Welcome to the Ladies' College for Erotic Arts.'

'What is this?' Winston continued to stare at the women getting their pleasures from the boys.

'We are an education establishment devoted to ensuring that us women get as much pleasure out of sexual activities as men.'

'What have you done to those guys?'

'Oh, we've just shown them that there are many different ways of getting satisfaction – theirs and ours.'

Betty came towards them, her breasts wobbling under her fluffy dressing gown.

'Oh, you've found a new one. He's pretty. I'm sure he'd like to fondle my tits.' She shucked the dressing gown off her shoulder, took Winston's hand and dragged him to the sofa. She sat him down, knelt astride him and pressed her ample bosom against his face. His cock hardened rapidly. Betty raised her fleshy arse and lowered herself onto his rod.

'Ooh, that is nice,' she said, continuing to rub herself against him.

Despite his afternoon of exertions with Eileen, Winston proved his insatiability by quickly coming in Betty. She heaved herself off and then Susan, fresh from fucking Johnny stood in front of him, grabbed his head and pressed her semen-dripping cunt against his face.

'Lick me dry, lover-boy,' she said, rubbing her fanny up and down his face.

Over the next couple of hours Winston experienced his cock, mouth, and hands being used by the five women to excite themselves. Joyce was impressed by the number of times he was brought to an orgasm although his effusions became less. Not once was he allowed to choose the position and he was encouraged to suck and lick each of the women in return for attention to his cock.

Finally, with his energy failing Winston was beckoned by Eileen to fuck her as she lay on her back on the bed. Somehow his cock still stiffened and he slid it into her eager quim. Eileen wrapped her legs around his thighs. Edith clambered on to the bed behind him with her strap-on-dildo thrusting out from between her legs. She positioned the knob against his arse. Meanwhile, Johnny also joined them on the bed and crouched at Eileen's head. His long penis thrust towards Winston's head.

As Edith eased into his rear hole he gasped and opened his mouth. Johnny took the opportunity to thrust his knob into Winston's mouth.

Joyce watched Winston's face carefully. First of all there was shock then a flash of anger then as Eileen wriggled beneath him, an expression of sublime pleasure. He sucked on Johnny's cock hungrily while redoubling his efforts inside Eileen and forcing the dildo deeper into his arse.

It all came to an end rapidly with both men ejaculating. Johnny, Winston and Edith flung themselves apart panting hard leaving Eileen gasping on the bed.

It took a few minutes for them all to recover.

'What was all that about, man?' Winston asked.

'We want to show you that we're all equal here,' Joyce explained. 'We can express our desires and everyone else will join in if they wish. Everyone contributes and no one sits around giving orders.'

'I see.' Winston was thoughtful.

'Do you still want that job?' Joyce asked, 'No one will be your slave, but if you work hard you can get all the sandwiches and sex that you want.'

Winston was silent for a moment.

'Yeah, Missus, I get what you mean. Yeah, I'll take the job.'

Chapter Seven
Triptych

The finger circled Joyce's nipple sending ripples of pleasure through her. There was hot air on her other breast and then warm, wet lips wrapped around the nipple. The tension of the gentle sucking added to the sensations from her other nipple and she shivered with pleasure. She opened her eyes to see the chocolate brown sky over her that was Winston's chest. Behind her head came slurping noises as Betty sucked on his cock.

Joyce was pleased that Winston had proved easy to change. He had soon learned that giving pleasure was as enjoyable as taking it. He could still be demanding as he had the energy and stamina of three men but now he stopped to think what the women might want before handing out his orders.

Winston's tongue left her nipple and traced out a wet sinuous course down her stomach and over her hairless mound before slipping between her lips. His abdomen moved over her head and there was a small smack of lips as Betty released his knob. His stiff rod knocked gently against her forehead, cheek and chin. She bent her neck and reached for it drawing the wet glans into her mouth. She sucked liked a calf at its mother's teat.

The tongue slipped deeper into her crack and his chin rubbed against her clit. She spread her legs wider and thrust her hips upwards so he could press his face harder against her fanny. He began to rock, his face rubbing up and down her pussy and his long, thick cock easing in and out of her eager mouth.

It was certainly not the first time he'd ejaculated this evening but it wasn't long before he shot another load of spunk down her throat. She swallowed gratefully as her own orgasm took her and she clasped her thighs around his head.

It was many moments before the shuddering spasms faded and she released him panting. He fell to her side on the carpet pulling his reduced but still meaty penis from her mouth. She drew breath and turned her head to look around.

On the bed Susan was riding Johnny enthusiastically and urging him to match her vigorous movements. Edith was kneeling with her head pressed into the cushions on the sofa with Mick fucking her energetically from behind. Eileen sat beside Edith avidly watching what was happening with a hand rubbing between her legs. Betty she could not see but presumed she was still lying behind her.

What a wonderful scene, Joyce thought; wouldn't it be nice to record this picture of relaxed pleasure.

Later, Joyce plumped the cushions after the girls and Johnny and Mick had gone and Winston had retired to his bedroom. Only Eileen was left, putting the vibrators and other sex toys away in their cupboard.

'I think it would be nice to have a picture of us all together having sex,' Joyce said.

Eileen looked up from caressing a huge penis-shaped dildo.

'What do you mean?'

'Well, I think we make a very interesting ensemble when we're all, um, at it.'

'You've taken lots of Polaroid photos.' Eileen pointed to the array of prints stuck to the wall.

'Yes, but they are rather small. I was thinking of something bigger, to fill the space on that wall.' Joyce pointed to the blank, black wall above the drinks cabinet. The walls were very high in the old school hall.

'Hmm, yes, I see what you mean. A large photograph perhaps.'

'I was thinking of a painting.'

'Oh. You want an artist to come and paint us while we fuck.'

'Well, I don't know how it would work but something like that.'

‘I do know a few people who know artists. I’ll ask around and see if there is anyone suitable who’d like to do it.’

‘Be discreet. We don’t want everyone knowing what we get up to here.’

‘Don’t worry, the Ladies’ College for Erotic Arts will remain a little known secret.’

It was just a few weeks later when a ring on the front door interrupted proceedings. Betty paused from sucking on Winston’s cock. Johnny stopped pumping his penis into Eileen’s cunt while Susan and Mick took breath during a sixty-nine. Edith put her favourite double dildo down on the seat beside her and Joyce got up and pulled her housecoat around her. She went to answer the door. A few moments later she returned leading a greying bearded man.

‘This is Algernon Pugh, the artist,’ Joyce announced. He paused as he entered the large hall and his eyes widened as he took in the naked men and women scattered amongst the bed and sofas.

‘Good evening, ladies and gentlemen,’ he said in a posh accent.

‘Come and join us,’ Edith said, tapping the sofa beside her. Algernon walked across the carpet, carefully circling where Mick and Susan sprawled on the floor. He glanced at Johnny and Eileen on the bed and sat down beside Edith placing his large leather holdall on the floor at his feet. Joyce went to fetch a tray of drinks and offered them around, starting with Algernon.

‘I understand you would like me to paint a portrait of you ladies,’ he said sipping the wine.

‘And the boys,’ Joyce said.

‘You would be nude?’ Algernon went on.

‘Oh yes,’ Eileen said, sitting on the edge of the bed.

‘Well, not all of us,’ Edith disagreed. As usual she was wearing a tight-laced black basque that held up her breasts and hid the bits she insisted were too saggy to be put on general view.

‘And you wish to be posed in a tableau?’

‘Making love,’ Joyce said.

‘Fucking,’ Eileen added more forcefully.

‘I see …’ Algernon stroked his beard and looked at each of them in turn.

‘Would you like us to show you?’ Joyce asked.

‘Um, that may be of use.’

Joyce clapped her hands, ‘Right, girls, back to it, show Mr Pugh what you can do.’

‘Easier said than done,’ Eileen said, ‘Johnny’s lost his erection.’

‘I’m sure it will just take him moments to get it back, but while you’re getting going I’ll show Mr Pugh our gallery.’ She took his hand and guided him to the wall where the photographic prints were displayed. He bent close to peer at each one in turn.

‘Ah, yes, hmm, I see. Oh, very athletic; er, who is that?’ he muttered. He straightened his back and turned to speak to Joyce but his attention was taken by the renewed action taking place on the bed, sofa and floor.

‘I see. You are all very, um, what shall I say, uninhibited.’

‘We’ve joined the sexual revolution. Why shouldn’t we all enjoy ourselves in a safe environment?’

‘Yes, of course. And you would like me to record the proceedings in a work of art.’

‘Yes, a big one, to fill that space.’ Joyce pointed to the wall.

‘I see. That would indeed be a major piece of work.’

‘I’m happy to pay.’

‘I wasn’t thinking of the cost, more of the time. It couldn’t be done in one, ah, sitting.’

‘No, I suppose not.’

‘But I could take a number of photographs to help with, um, details.’ He walked back to the sofa, opened his bag and took out a large and complex camera. He found a big electronic flash gun and fitted it to the camera.

‘So you’ll do it?’ Joyce asked eagerly.

‘Oh yes. I think it will be an interesting task. I will of course have to get in close to explore the, uh, finer points of the poses.’

‘Of course.’

'And I will need to, er, get in the mood, so to speak.'

'Ah, yes, of course, to get inspiration.'

'Exactly.'

'Shall I help you remove your clothes?'

Joyce soon discovered that Algernon Pugh was quite the hairiest man she had ever met. His thick beard seemed to extend down his chest to his abdomen and even his back and buttocks were covered in curly wool. His balls were enclosed in a nest of grey-brown fur. Only his cock and knob were hairless and jutted out palely from the hairy mass.

Joyce didn't relish the prospect of a mouthful of hair so she presented her rear to him and spread her thighs to welcome him in. He knelt and thrust into her with gusto, groaning with effort and pleasure as he rammed his cock in and out of her channel. Joyce enjoyed it but was nowhere near her climax when he spurted inside her and collapsed on her back. He didn't fall in a comatose heap however, but soon heaved himself up and picked up his camera. He moved amongst the couples and triples, leaning close to fire off a shot with a bright flash of the lamp.

Soon he returned to the sofa and sat down to remove a film from the camera and replace it with another.

'How do you get the prints done?' Joyce asked.

'I have an arrangement with an old friend who runs a small photographic business,' Algernon replied, slotting the 35mm film cassette into place.

'Won't he look at the photos?'

'Of course he will, but don't worry, he does a lot of this sort of stuff. Glamour photography is a vital part of his business as the big printers won't touch it. It's amazing how many couples like photographs of themselves at it. I'll get copies for you too.' He returned to firing off shots of the many and varied combinations and positions of the five women and three men.

Finally when everyone, even Winston, was sated and sleepy, Algernon packed away his equipment. 'I'll come back next week with some sketches for you,' he said as Joyce showed him out.

* * *

Algernon kept his word and returned not only eager to join in the activities but also had some suggestions for the painting. The ladies and the men quickly agreed and Algernon helped them get into position. Algernon took lots more photos and made sketches in a big pad of paper. They didn't hear from him again for weeks until Joyce received a phone call saying that the painting was finished and that Algernon would come and fit it to the wall.

They all stood in a semicircle facing the paintings draped in sheets.

'It is a triptych,' Algernon said.

'Oh, what does that mean?' Betty asked.

'It means that there are three sections to the painting; a large central panel and two smaller panels on each side.'

'I see.'

'Are you ready for me to reveal them?' Algernon said to Joyce.

'Everyone has a glass. Yes, I think so. We're ready, aren't we, girls and boys?'

There was a chorus of ayes and Algernon tugged on the sheets. The cloth fell away revealing the three large paintings in thick gold painted frames. There was silence as each of them stared at the canvasses.

'It's not what I was expecting,' Susan said quietly.

'Nor me,' Edith agreed. 'It's modern.'

They each turned their heads from side to side trying to take in what they saw.

'I think I was expecting something like Boticelli's Venus or Michelangelo's David,' Eileen said.

'It's more like a Picasso,' Joyce said.

'I think you all need to step back,' Algernon said. 'You need to take it all in at once, to start with.'

They all moved away and there were a number of "ahs". For a moment Joyce couldn't see what the picture was then it seemed to click into place. It leapt into view and suddenly it all made sense.

'I get it,' she said, 'it's very clever.'

Filling the main panel were the figures of Eileen and the three men. Eileen was kneeling astride Johnny, riding his cock. Mick was kneeling over Johnny's head and Eileen's head was leaning forward sucking on his knob. Winston, meanwhile, was kneeling behind Eileen with his tool inserted in her arse.

The life size image of Eileen being penetrated by three penises was just one aspect of the painting. The scene was fractured like a broken mirror. Each fragment showed parts of the picture from a different point of view and a different time. On the left, shards showed Mick's penis entering Eileen's mouth, the knob at first visible and then being swallowed up by Eileen's stretched lips. On the right Eileen's buttock and arsehole were seen from various angles some with Winston's cock inserted and one with creamy semen dripping from the hole. At the bottom, were magnifying lens shots of Eileen's fanny, with Johnny's shaft sliding in and his balls swinging. At the top were further images of the tableau from different elevations. As Joyce had noted the composition was cleverly executed so that from a distance the viewer saw the three men in the act of penetrating the woman while up close the details were revealed.

The smaller panels were similar. On the right, Susan and Edith stood facing each other, Susan naked and Edith in her signature basque. Edith's arms rested on Susan's shoulders and her knees were slightly bent so that her pubis was pushed against Susan's. Susan's nipples rubbed against Edith's satin-covered bosom. The fragments revealed what was happening, the women's fannies linked by the double-headed dildo, each riding the other to orgasm.

The left panel was a tessellation of images of Joyce and Betty giving head to each other and shown from every conceivable angle.

Joyce pointed out what she could see and soon each of them expressed oohs and aahs as different parts of the painting were revealed to them.

'What do you think?' Algernon asked.

'I think you have produced a masterpiece,' Eileen said still gazing in awe at the triptych.

‘It is quite remarkable,’ Joyce said, ‘and I don’t think the price comes close to its full worth.’

‘We can, however, show our appreciation,’ Eileen added.

The ladies advanced on Algernon Pugh, feeling for his buttons and groping for the belt of his trousers. He gave himself willingly to their intentions.

Chapter Eight
Showtime

Joyce kicked her left foot high in time with the disco beat of the Bee Gees track. Her bare breasts jiggled. On the next bar with hands on her hips she kicked her right foot, tore at the Velcro and whipped off the G-string. Alongside her, Susan, Eileen, Edith and Betty did the same, all in time. They carried on high stepping for a few bars, giving their audience of Winston, Mick and Johnny flashes of dark, blonde and hairless fannies. The boys clapped and cheered as the music came to an end.

Puffing hard, Joyce bent over. Sweat bubbled on her neck and ran down between her breasts. Eileen was also panting and Edith and Betty had sunk to the floor. Only Susan, the youngest of them seemed not to be short of breath. She went to Winston's open arms and sat on his lap. His fingers slid down her inner thigh and slipped into her wet pussy. She gasped and sagged around him. His mouth found her nipple and sucked.

'Well, I think we're ready,' Eileen said.

'Do you think so?' Joyce asked. 'You don't think one more try?'

'I can't go through it all again,' Betty gasped.

'We're fine,' Edith commented. 'We've just got to think the beat and move in time.'

'Well we'd better be ready,' Eileen said, 'we're on stage tomorrow.'

It was a few weeks earlier when Eileen had burst into the hall, full of excitement. Johnny was fucking Joyce enthusiastically from behind. Joyce looked up at her.

'Hello, Eileen,' she said between Johnny's thrusts, 'you're late.'

'I've been busy and I've got some news.'

'What? Oh, good. Wait he's nearly there. Come on Johnny! Ahhh.' Joyce slumped forward and Johnny's cock slipped out of her channel, dripping spunk on the rug.

Betty and Edith paused from giving Winston a working over and Susan stopped riding up and down on Mick's erect tool.

'I've been on the phone talking to one of the theatrical agents I know,' Eileen began, 'and I've got us a booking.'

'A booking?' the four ladies chorused in unison.

'Yes, an actual booking.'

'What for?'

'Where?'

'When?'

'Who?'

They each had questions and the three men also looked interested.

Eileen went on, 'It's in London, Soho actually, in four weeks time; it's an adult club.'

'You mean a strip joint,' Edith said.

'Well, sort of.'

'You want us to strip off in front of a bunch of lecherous old winos,' Susan said being unusually vociferous.

'They won't be old drunks. It's an expensive club with a select membership, and we won't be simply stripping off; we'll have to put a dance routine together.'

'Dance,' Joyce explained, "I've hardly danced in my whole life. A waltz with Bill was about my limit and he had two left feet.'

'Didn't you do the twist in the sixties?' Betty said. 'I did. Mind you, I wasn't carrying as much weight in those days.'

'The twist passed me by,' Joyce said. 'Bill never wanted to get up and dance, he just wanted to find a corner to snog in.'

'What about you Susan?' Betty asked.

'I did ballet when I was at school. Dave the rat was more into sitting stoned listening to Pink Floyd than getting up and dancing with me. Since I've had Hannah, I haven't had the chance to go to a disco – no time, no man, no money.'

'I danced,' Edith said wistfully, 'I was a flapper. We danced the Charleston. Stanley loved to dance. We went to tea dances when we were courting and did all the old time dances. Even if we were at home we'd dance to the radio when the BBC dance band was playing. Then the war came and we didn't dance any more.'

Joyce watched a small tear run down Edith's cheek. They were silent for a moment as they watched Edith thinking about past times.

Finally Eileen spoke, 'Well, I did the jive, the twist, the locomotion and the rest, until my darling husband left me for a younger model.'

'I think we've got off the subject a bit,' Joyce said. 'You were saying that you've booked us to dance and strip at a London club.'

'That's right.'

'Why?'

'I thought it would be fun for us all to have a day and night out. Now that we are more confident with our bodies why not show them off – and earn a bit of money too.'

'Ah, money,' Joyce sighed.

'How much?' Edith asked eagerly.

'Twenty five pounds. That's nearly five pounds each, even after we've paid for the transport.'

'That's not bad for a bunch of amateurs,' Edith said, nodding her head, 'It'll certainly boost my pension.'

'The money would be very useful,' Susan agreed.

'Talking of transport, Eileen, how were you suggesting we got to London?' Joyce asked.

'I thought we could rent a Transit van and Winston could drive us.'

'Do you think men are really going to want to see us take our clothes off?' Betty looked doubtful, 'Susan is pretty enough, but the rest of us have got a few lumps and bumps.'

'I can assure you that the men won't care about a bit of flab if they can get an eyeful of tits and fannies. My agent friend said that the five of us would go down a storm.'

‘Well’s there’s just one thing for it,’ Edith said.

‘What’s that?’ Joyce asked.

‘We’d better start practising if we’re on stage in four weeks. Sorry, boys, no more fucking for a while.’ Winston, Johnny and Mick looked miserable.

The five ladies got into a huddle.

‘What music should we use?’ Betty asked.

‘What’s that tune, da da, daa, di da da daa?’ Joyce sang.

‘You mean *The Stripper,*’ Eileen said.

‘That’s it.’

‘That’s much too corny,’ Edith said.

‘No real stripper would use that,’ Susan said.

‘No, we need something modern, with it, groovy,’ Eileen mused.

‘Disco,’ Susan suggested.

‘Yeah, that’s it.’

Joyce glanced over at the boys. Finding themselves ignored they’d had to start entertaining themselves. Winston was massaging a magnificent erection while Mick was sucking Johnny’s cock. Joyce thought they could get along by themselves for a while.

‘Do we have a name?’ Betty asked.

‘No, but we need one,’ Eileen said, ‘They’ll want to put it on the notices outside the club. We’d better think one up soon.’

‘How about *Pam’s People?*’ Betty said.

‘Who’s Pam?’ Edith said with a sneer.

‘I don’t know.’

‘*Hot Cocoa*,’ Joyce giggled.

‘It might be what you want to take to bed at night,’ Eileen joked, ‘but I don’t think so.’

‘There’s five of us,’ Susan said, ‘what’s a five pointed star called?’

‘Pentagon?’

‘Pentangle?’

‘That’s a pop group.’

‘It’s a pentacle,’ Edith announced, ‘used in magic.’

‘Well, we’re five old witches,’ Betty said.

‘Speak for yourself,’ Eileen said, ‘but *Pentacle* will do. We can use stars in our dance.'

'Let's get started,' Susan said, eager to begin.

Joyce noticed that Winston was pumping hard on his cock and panting. Mick's head was bobbing up and down, Johnny's shaft sliding in and out of his mouth while Johnny's hand gripped the root of his balls firmly, tugging the sac away from his hard prick so that it glistened purple. They seemed well able to entertain themselves.

The preparations required some extra evenings of rehearsal to which the boys were not invited and Winston was ordered to find somewhere else to go. There were tears and arguments as the steps were practised over and over again. Joyce was amazed at how Edith was able to kick her legs so that her feet were above her head. She must have been quite a dancer in her twenties. Betty proved to be surprisingly lithe, despite her flab and Susan took to the sexy cavorting with ease. Eileen danced and stripped like a professional and Joyce began to wonder what she had done in her youth and why she knew so many people in the theatrical business.

Only Joyce found it difficult. She kept finding herself hopping on a different foot to the others or turning to the left when they turned to the right. While Eileen seemed able to pull off a blouse in one smooth, flowing movement, Joyce found her arms trapped with the collar stuck in her mouth. When Eileen dropped a skirt to her feet she was able to skip out of it in one beat, while Joyce caught hers around her ankles and tripped over.

Eileen was a hard taskmistress and made them go over the moves repeatedly. A week before their date the clothes arrived that Eileen had ordered. There were five sets of sparkly, silver bras, suspender belts, and matching G-strings and ten nipple caps in the shape of a pentacle. The silver theme was repeated in the long, slashed skirt and loose-fitting tassled blouses. Even the flesh-coloured stockings had sparkle. Finally, there were the silver shoes, each with a silver star on the top.

'I can't wear those,' Betty exclaimed. 'Look at those heels. I couldn't walk in them, let alone dance.'

'They're only four inches,' Eileen said matter of factly.

'Four inches of the narrowest stilettos I've ever seen,' Betty replied.

'You can do it,' Eileen urged her. 'It's just a matter of practice.'

Edith examined the bra and suspender belt.

'Do you really want me to wear these?' she said. 'I'm not convinced that men want to see my old scrawny tits.'

'Look, Edith, you look fantastic in your corsets and basques,' Eileen said, 'but we all need to wear the same outfit for this, and your figure is fabulous. The men in the audience won't know or care how old you are. Anyway this isn't about the audience. It's about us having fun and showing that we're proud of ourselves.'

'And the money,' Susan added.

'Oh, yes and getting paid for it is nice too,' Eileen agreed.

'Well, if you say so,' Edith said. 'We're all in this together.'

They dressed in the outfits and went through their dance sequence ending up high kicking in a line with just their signature stars on their nipples. No ankles were broken toppling off the high heels.

The day came for the trip to London, a bright, warm summer's day. They piled into the rented minibus as if they were off on a sightseeing tour of the capital, except they had more luggage than was normally needed for a day trip. They left late in the morning and Winston drove confidently along the motorway. They stopped at a service area for lunch and to stretch their legs. Winston was less sure of himself negotiating the busy London streets; he'd never been to the capital before. Eileen guided him to the West End. They parked and visited Trafalgar Square and the shops of Oxford Street. After tea and cakes in Selfridges they climbed back on board for the short journey to Soho. Eileen was following written instructions from the agent now and they made a few false turns up one-way streets and were jammed in the rush hour traffic for a time before they finally reached a narrow back street.

'Is this it?' Edith asked

'Where?' Betty said, peering out of the window at the tall, smoke-blackened buildings.

'There,' Eileen pointed, 'can you see the poster with our name on it, by the entrance?' Her finger pointed to a closed black door which they had stopped alongside. There was a glass-covered notice board beside it. The poster advertised "Girls, Girls, Girls" with the names of performers beneath. Prominent was a silver star with the title "*Pentacle*" in the centre and the line underneath – "Magic sex from five girls". Joyce was about to ask what the words meant when the door opened and a large man in a dinner suit stepped on to the pavement.

'You can't park there,' he said in a deep gruff voice. Eileen wound down her window.

'We're *Pentacle*. We're performing this evening,' she said brightly. The bouncer didn't smile.

'Park along the street. There's a back entrance for acts. The boss is waiting for you.'

Winston drove a few more yards along the road and managed to park the Transit between a Jaguar and an Aston Martin without touching either. The girls piled out, each with their bags of costume, and followed Eileen to a narrow door with its paint peeling. Winston followed. Eileen rapped on the door. They waited a minute or two until it was opened by a small, thin man wearing a black polo neck and black trousers. He looked past Eileen at the ladies.

'Hi. You must be *Pentacle*. The boss is keen to meet you.' He led them into the building down narrow stairs and corridors, past numerous doors until he stopped at one, pushed it open and stood to the side.

'This is your dressing room. The boss will be along in a few minutes.'

The ladies squeezed into the room. There was barely room for one performer, let alone five. Winston was about to follow them in.

'You can come with me,' the man said. 'We'll find a nice comfortable seat for you to watch the acts.' He pulled the door closed.

'Well, this is a bit cramped,' Betty said, squashed against the one chair placed in front of the make-up desk and mirror.

'I don't suppose they have many acts with five members.' Edith said. 'It's usually single strippers isn't it?'

'We'll manage,' Eileen said, 'let's get dressed.' They shuffled around until each had a little bit of floor space with enough room to wriggle out of their clothes. Without warning the door was flung open revealing a short, fat man in a dinner suit, puffing on a large cigar.

'Welcome, girls. You're *Pentacle,* I gather.'

'That's us. How do you do?' Eileen said, offering her hand.

The man ignored it. 'Delighted, ladies … You're on at ten. We'll see how it goes and if the punters like you, you'll go on again at twelve and two.'

'Oh, we've only got one sequence worked out,' Eileen said.

'Punters don't care. So long as they get an eyeful they don't mind how often they see it.'

'We agreed twenty-five pounds.'

'That's right, per performance.'

'Oh, well, yes, great.'

'Right, I'll leave you to it. Sid will get you refreshments when you need them and give you a shout when you're on.' He backed out and disappeared into the corridor in a cloud of tobacco smoke. The little man, who Joyce guessed was Sid, took his place.

'Have you got your music girls?' he said. Eileen burrowed in her handbag and pulled out a tape cassette. She handed it to him. He gave it a cursory glance and nodded.

'Fine. Champagne, ladies?'

'How much?'

'Don't worry, the first bottle's on the house for guest acts. After that, we'll take it off your earnings.'

'Oh, right. What do you think, girls?' They all nodded and Sid left. He returned a few minutes later with a bottle and five glasses on a tray.

'There you are, ladies. Don't get drunk before your first performance.' He laughed at his joke and left.

Eileen opened the bottle with a satisfying explosion and

managed to avoid spilling too much of the fizzy liquid.

'Well, girls, here's to *Pentacle's* first performance. Let's dance.'

'There's quite a wait before we're on. Do you think we could have a look round?' Edith asked.

'No, better stay here. The manager told me he didn't like performers mixing with the audience before performances.'

'The manager? The fat guy with the cigar?'

'That's right. He was pretty insistent about it. Let's just have our drink, get changed, do our make-up – that's going to take a while with just one mirror – and stay cool.'

They sipped their champagne and chatted before starting to get changed into their stage costumes.

'I need the loo,' Joyce said, slipping out of the door before Eileen could say anything. She wandered along the corridors until she found a door which was marked WC. She spent a penny and set off to return. Somehow, she missed a turning and found herself among the curtains at the side of a small stage. She peered through and saw the auditorium – three or four rows of theatre seats in front of a bar. About a quarter of the seats were occupied by single men. Each had empty seats on both sides of them. They were staring at the stage. Some seemed to be rummaging in their laps. Winston was in the middle of the front row and like the others had his eyes wide open and fixed straight ahead. Joyce shifted her position so she could see through the flats at the stage. She gasped. There was a single divan on the stage on which a young woman was lying illuminated by bright overhead stage lights. The bed rotated slowly. The girl was naked with her legs raised and she held them wide apart. Kneeling between her legs a naked man was pumping his cock into her cunt and making as much fuss over it as he could.

Joyce let go of the curtain and hurried back into the maze of corridors. The chatter and laughter guided her back to their dressing room.

'Where have you been?' Eileen asked as she squeezed into the room. Joyce didn't answer her.

'This isn't a strip club,' she said.

'What do you mean?' Eileen said. Joyce thought she didn't look surprised.

'I got lost coming back from the loo and ended up at the stage. I saw what was happening. It wasn't a stripper performing, but a man and a woman.'

'What do you mean?' Betty said looking confused.

'It's a sex club,' Joyce said. 'There's an audience of men wanking themselves off while a couple have sex on the stage.'

'Are you sure?' Susan asked. 'Perhaps it was one of those gymnastic acts.'

'I know what I saw.' Joyce stared at Eileen, who was trying to avoid eye contact. 'You knew Eileen, didn't you?'

'Well, yes, but so what. We've got our routine.'

'Yes, but will five old dears taking their clothes off – well four old dears and one pretty girl – be enough to satisfy those sex-mad wankers?'

'We'll just have to see, won't we,' Eileen said. 'It's time we all got changed.'

They undressed and put their costumes on in silence. Joyce was angry. She and Eileen had done everything to set up the Ladies' College for Erotic Arts together. Why had Eileen not told the whole story behind their booking?

There was a tap in the door and Sid's voice called out that they were next on.

'Come on, girls,' Eileen urged. 'It's just what we practised – a strip. A dance. We can do it. Let's enjoy it.'

'OK, Eileen,' Joyce said. 'We're here now. If they don't like it, we leave, but we'll give it our best shot won't we, girls?' The other three agreed. Eileen opened the door and led them out. Sid was there to guide them to the stage. There were no curtains in front of the low platform but the lights were down and it was in darkness.

'On you go,' Sid said. 'The lights will go up when your music starts. Give 'em all you've got.' Eileen marched on stage and the others followed forming a V formation with Susan at the front. They were barely in position when the thudding disco beat began and the bright lights came on.

They began to dance. Joyce struggled to find the rhythm at

first and knew that she was behind the others. For the first track they simply danced, kicking up their legs and showing their stocking tops and suspenders, bending low to show their cleavage and turning to show their bottoms in the tight sequinned skirts. Joyce couldn't see the audience because of the bright light in her eyes and neither could she hear any response from them. There could be no one there as far as she knew.

There was hardly a jar as the music moved into the second track and they began to unbutton the blouses, all five of them together. In unison they slipped the thin, sparkly cloth off their arms and showed off their silver bosoms. They wriggled their hips and shimmied the skirts down until in one simultaneous movement they kicked them off. There was a roar from the audience. Joyce smiled – at least someone was watching.

The beat slowed a little at the start of the third track. They swayed from side to side. Joyce reached behind to unclip her bra. In a domino-like effect they each flicked the cups off their boobs and flung the garments to the back of the stage. Ten tits wobbled in rhythm. There was another loud cheer.

Now the tempo increased as, while still dancing, they each unclipped their suspenders and seductively rolled the stockings down their thighs, over their knees and down their calves. They tugged on the toes stretching the shimmering nylon until the stockings flicked off.

Now they were into the final track, loud and fast with a heavy beat. Side by side they kicked their feet high, turned and waved their bare buttocks to the wildly cheering audience. Back facing the front, hands on hips, feet kicked high. Five G-strings flung off, five fannies waved to the audience. They turned, heads down, ankles spread apart, arse and vaginas open to the watching eyes. Down to the floor, spin with bottoms on the stage, feet raised, thighs wide open, moist cunts sparkling in the lights.

The climax of the track passed. They stood, lined up, hands entwined, ready for their final bow. The track finished; the end of the performance. Joyce panted. But the lights did not go out, the music did not stop. A new song began; a slower song, *"You sexy thing"*. Eileen stepped forward, held out a hand and pulled

Winston on to the stage. He gyrated to the music while she pulled his T-shirt over his head then knelt to undo his flies. In moments he was as naked as her and she was kneeling with her tongue flicking along his erection.

Joyce felt silly. There she was standing naked with her three friends doing nothing while Eileen sucked on Winston's glowing purple knob with the audience urging them on. Joyce knew that Winston had the stamina to last for hours while one or the other sucked his penis, but not this evening. Back at the school Eileen would have taken him as he came and swallowed every last drop of his jism but here, on stage, in front of the watchers, she pulled back, releasing the swollen knob just as he spurted. The white cream gushed over her, covering her face and dripping off her nose and chin.

That was when the lights went off and Sid beckoned from the wings.

'Get off now. Quick.' He called in a loud stage whisper. 'Leave your clothes. Someone will bring them to you.'

In something of a daze Joyce followed Susan and the others off the stage and back down the corridor to their room. They shuffled in, all naked with Eileen at the back.

Joyce turned on her friend.

'You had that planned all along, you and Winston, didn't you?'

'No,' Eileen said defiantly, 'not right from the beginning. When we got the booking I thought it was simply a strip. It was a couple of weeks ago when I spoke to the manager that he told me that it wasn't just stripping, that an ejaculation was expected.'

'Why didn't you say?'

'I wasn't sure that you'd all want to have sex in front of an audience.'

'After all the fucking we've done together with the boys.'

'But that's different – in our own place, with people we know.'

The door opened and the manager looked in puffing on his cigar and with a smile on his face.

'Great stuff, girls. Good strip with some good muff views

and a very nice fellation to end it. I could give that black guy a job. Now, how are you going to end your next show? I've got a few guys who'll happily join you on stage. Let's get a bit more involvement from the rest of you ladies.' He backed out and was gone.

'Here's your costumes, girls.' Sid tossed a heap of silver clothing into the room.

Like the others, Joyce was speechless for a few breathless moments.

'The next show …' she said finally.

'I guess they liked us,' Eileen said quietly.

'And we all get a bit of action this time,' Edith said firmly.

'Sounds like it,' Eileen said sheepishly.

'Right, well. I'll need another glass or two of champagne before we sort out this pile of stuff,' Edith said gesturing at the heap of clothes.

There was a louder roar from the audience than the first time when they bared their pussies. Joyce had the impression that the small theatre was fuller than earlier in the evening. As the music slowed Eileen once again drew Winston on to the stage but this time four other men followed. Each one was tall and slim with muscles showing through their T-shirts and tight, tracksuit bottoms. They sashayed on to the stage in time to the music. One approached Joyce, his hands reaching out to cup her boobs. She knew what was required and with one smooth movement reached for the hem of his top and pulled it over his head. She admired the smooth white skin of his chest. Around her she saw olive and chocolate flesh as well as white. She reached down to his hips and tugged the elasticated waist of his tracksuit bottoms over his buttocks. He wasn't wearing pants. His cock leaped out at her. He kicked off the trousers and leaned down to bury his face between her tits.

Joyce felt unsteady. Was it the man's tongue on her breasts or was the floor moving? It was the floor rotating. Somehow the men had arranged for each of the women to spread out in a circle on the revolving stage – the corners of a pentacle, Joyce realised, as her attention was brought back to the hand feeling her thigh and moving inexorably up to her crack. His other hand on her shoulder pressed down and she sank to the floor opening her legs at his insistence. Then he was kneeling over her, his head descending into her crotch and his cock like a dagger before her eyes. She stretched her neck to grab it with her lips and closed her mouth around his knob. Her head spun, partly with the lights revolving over her head, and partly with the effect of the tongue circumnavigating her vulva. She sucked avidly on his glans, relishing the feel of the swollen flesh filling her mouth.

His lips nibbled at her clitoris sending shockwaves up her spine. She wriggled and rubbed her cunt against his mouth urging him to dig deeper with his mouth and tongue. He pressed his face into her and pushed his cock deeper down her throat and then she felt herself approaching the edge and falling over. She shook and gurgled though the cock filled her gullet. He pulled out and spun around. She was still shaking with her orgasm when she felt him thrust deep into her and his testicles slapped against her arse. He pulled out until she felt his knob tickle her clit and then he thrust in deep again. He did it again and again and she marvelled at his strength and stamina until he froze and she felt semen spray over her stomach.

Her breath came in short pants but they were slowing and she turned her head. On her left a man was thrusting into Susan from behind, on her right, Edith, naked as never before, was being thrust into energetically with her ankles around the man's neck.

She noticed that the music had stopped but the noise of the audience had not. There was applause and cheers and shouts urging them on. She looked up at the face of her partner.

'Nice one, lady,' he said as the lights went out.

The five women trooped back to their room and fell into each other's arms in a heap on the floor.

'Well, ladies?' Eileen said. 'Are you still upset with me?'

'Yes,' Edith said, 'we could have done that the first time too.'

Eileen nodded. 'Yes, OK, I'm sorry I should have trusted you. You're all sex mad. So you're up for one more performance?'

'If I can get my breath back,' Betty said, still red-faced and puffing.

Sid arrived with their costumes.

'The boss is really pleased with you. If you do the same at the two o'clock performance you'll earn yourselves a bonus. The audience loved it. We've never had five couples going at it on the revolving stage before.'

After he left, Joyce said, 'Do you know, I hardly noticed the audience.'

'I couldn't see them,' Susan said.

'I couldn't care less who's watching if I'm getting pleasured like that,' Edith added.

'I'd quite like to be able to see the audience watching me,' Eileen said.

'You're just an exhibitionist,' Betty said.

The dancing was a bit less vigorous in their last performance. Joyce found she didn't have the energy for the high kicks but it didn't matter as the audience went wild when they discarded their G-strings and strode to the edge of the stage to show off their cunts and arses. Ten men, including Winston, climbed on to the stage at the end of their performance. Joyce wondered if they were all employed by the theatre or if some members of the audience were joining in the action. She soon found herself riding one man's prick while another stood over him and held his cock out for her to suck. She rode up and down feeling the cock sliding in and out of her channel while gripping the other knob between her lips. She was delighted when both came at once, her face deluged with sticky come with more oozing out around the subsiding cock to trickle between her buttocks.

The stage stopped its circular motion, and the house lights went up. The men left the stage to the ladies who stood up in a line and held each others' hands. They bowed to the cheering audience and padded off the stage. They returned wearily to their room and stood in a huddle, skin against skin.

Winston arrived at the door with another bottle of champagne.

'Compliments of the guys,' he said.

‘Which guys?’ Betty asked.

‘The ones you fucked. Who do you think?’ Winston chuckled and poured the wine.

Sid appeared carrying their stage clothes.

‘That was a knockout,’ he said squeezing out of the way to allow the manager to ease his bulk into the doorway. He waved a handful of five pound notes at them. Eileen took them and counted out the twenty notes.

‘One hundred pounds?’ she queried

‘Yes, ladies, you deserve it after the business we’ve done tonight. Word got around after your first act and we had a full house at the end. Any time you want another trip to the Smoke, give me a bell. You’re welcome on my stage any time. You’re a game bunch of ladies.’

Chapter Nine
Meeting Madam

'Everyone get in,' Joyce said, as she got into the driving seat of the Rover. 'You'd better sit at the front, Betty.'

'Do I get to sit at the front because I'm fat,' Betty said looking affronted.

'Well there will be a squash with three of us in the back seat and you are the biggest of us – I'm not saying fat, mind,' Eileen commented.

'I know I'm fat,' Betty said grinning, 'and I'm sorry the three of you have to squeeze together.'

'I'll sit in the middle so I can give Joyce directions,' Eileen said.

'You haven't told us, yet where we're going. You just said to dress for going out,' Edith said, getting in behind Betty.

'And I think we all look very smart and summery,' Joyce said, peering in her driving mirror.'

'I'll explain when we get moving. Come on, Susan get in,' Eileen said impatiently.

At last everyone was in the car and Joyce and Betty had buckled their seat belts. Winston stood on the door step looking forlorn. He was alone because Johnny and Mick had been told not to attend this meeting of the Ladies' College for Erotic Arts. Joyce wondered what Winston would do on his own without any of them to fuck. He'd probably just watch TV, she thought, wanking himself. She waved, then reversed the car out of the driveway and on to the road. Soon they were heading out of the village.

'Now, Eileen,' Edith said sternly, 'tell us where we're

going.'

Eileen took a deep breath. 'We're going to meet a madam at her brothel.'

Betty twisted in her seat to stare at Eileen. Joyce glanced in her mirror and saw Susan and Edith open mouthed.

'You mean we're going to meet prostitutes,' Edith said outraged, pronouncing every syllable in "prostitutes" carefully.

'That's right,' Eileen said without any further explanation.

'Well! What has that got to do with *The Joy of Sex?*' Edith exclaimed.

'I thought the whole point of the Ladies' College for Erotic Arts was for us women to discover how to get pleasure from sex and to become liberated,' Susan said in her quiet voice.

'You're perfectly correct, Susan,' Eileen said calmly, 'and if you had read your book, Edith, you would know that Dr Comfort has a few words to say about prostitution. He says our western attitude is all wrong and properly trained professionals should be respected as in any activity. He just thinks that if everybody practised his ideas, paying for sex would not be necessary.'

Edith turned away from Eileen to stare out of the window.

'But why do we need to visit a brothel?' Betty asked.

'We, that is Joyce and I, thought it was important that in our study of everything to do with sexual intercourse we should investigate what goes on when women sell themselves for sex. Isn't that right, Joyce?'

Joyce was concentrating hard on controlling the big car but answered. 'Yes. You see, a College is all about education, so we should be learning about things even if we don't approve of them.'

'Well, you could have told us,' Edith muttered.

'Would you have come if we'd told you where we're going?' Eileen asked.

'Hmph,' was Edith's reply.

'Well, we're all here now,' Joyce said, 'and Eileen had better tell me which way to go if we're going to get there.'

They had reached the outskirts of the town and Eileen directed them to a prosperous suburb where large Victorian houses occupied plots of ground behind high walls and hedges.

'Here we are,' Eileen exclaimed, 'Turn up this drive here, Joyce, between the pine trees.' They passed through a pair of tall wrought iron gates which were fortuitously open and drove up a curving, gravel drive between rows of tall, dark coniferous trees. She pulled up outside a colonnaded porch completely out of sight of the road. There were a couple of small cars parked on the gravel and a fine looking Triumph sports car.

'I suppose this is it,' Joyce said, turning off the ignition.

'I bet they're all raddled drug addicts,' Edith muttered.

'Perhaps,' Betty said, 'but someone is making lots of cash to afford this place.'

They got out of the car and stood together in the doorway. Eileen pressed a bell push.

There was the distant sound of a bell ringing but almost immediately the door was opened by a middle-aged woman with glossy black hair wearing a French maid's uniform. She could have been at a stately home except that her skirt was exceptionally short and she wore shoes with very high heels.

'We're here to see Mrs Glover,' Eileen said.

'Ah, yes, please come in,' the maid said in a Midlands accent. She pulled the door wide so that they could step into the tiled hallway, closed it behind them and then led them to one of the front rooms of the house. It was well decorated in modern bright colours with three large sofas arranged in a square around the fireplace and half a dozen dining chairs around the walls beside occasional tables and small bureaux.

'Please take a seat,' the maid said before departing and closing the door. They sat in a cluster on two of the sofas.

'Well, this looks very bright and clean,' Betty said cheerfully.

'All the better to lure in the clients,' Edith muttered.

'Have you looked at the paintings?' Susan asked. They all looked up at the large pictures hanging on the walls.

'They all show naked women,' Joyce noted.

'Yes, but they're all old paintings,' Susan said.

'They're art, not pornography,' Eileen said, 'Old nudes are art, new ones are pornography. Anybody can have a naked woman on their wall if it's an old master.'

Joyce laughed, 'So what is that painting of all of us and the boys, that's hanging on my wall?'

'Oh, definitely pornography. Just because it's a painting doesn't make it art.'

They all laughed at Eileen's strong opinions just as the door opened and two women entered. The first could have been a sister of Betty – in her fifties, somewhat round of face and torso with short, plump legs. She was dressed in a smart two-piece, pale blue suit with sensible court shoes. The other woman was as different from her as Laurel is from Hardy. She was young, definitely no more than about twenty-two and a head taller than the older woman. She wore high heeled sandals that revealed her red painted toenails, a pair of bright yellow hot pants that barely covered her buttocks and a loose white vest that showed off her olive coloured arms and cleavage.

The older woman swept into the room and sat on the vacant sofa.

'Good afternoon, ladies, I'm Frances Glover,' she said. The young woman stood behind her. Joyce looked up at her halo of permed blonde hair and wondered what she was thinking; her face did not show any emotion at all.

'It is very kind of you to see us, Mrs Glover,' Eileen began.

'Oh, Frances, please.'

'Um, yes. We are all members of the Ladies' College for Erotic Arts …'

'And what do your members do in the College?'

'We're interested in all the ways of gaining pleasure of a sexual nature.'

'And you think I may have some ideas for you.'

'Yes, I suppose so.'

'What is it you think I do here?'

'You hire out girls for sex with men for cash,' Edith said gruffly.

'Well, that's not strictly true,' Mrs Glover said. 'It is true that Honey here entertains men willing to pay handsomely for her services, but I do not hire her out as you put it.'

'But you must get something out of her to pay for this lovely house,' Betty said.

'You're right. This property does cost a lot to maintain but I merely rent out rooms to the girls and provide them with some administrative assistance, such as a maid to respond to callers at the door and a telephone answering service.'

'You exploit these poor girls,' Edith grumbled.

'Not a bit of it,' Mrs Glover insisted. 'I think, ladies, you have insufficient knowledge of the service we provide here to make comments.'

'Yes, don't be rude, Edith,' Eileen said. Edith's face turned red but she did not say anything.

'It is quite true that many young women enter prostitution because they are desperate for money,' Mrs Glover said. 'Many fall under the influence of pimps who just wish to exploit them for as long as they're capable of servicing the men.'

'Not much joy of sex there,' Joyce said.

'Quite right and I have nothing but contempt for the men who get their satisfaction by abusing such women,' Mrs Glover said forcefully.

'You can find lots of those women down Gas Street any night or day of the week. Here though, I provide a safe and well-appointed base for women with certain skills who knowingly and freely offer their services to selected men. They charge a considerable sum for what they offer and I can assure you that both parties to the agreement get a great deal of pleasure from the arrangement.'

'So they're not drug addicts then,' Edith said. Joyce saw a flicker of feeling pass across the young girl's face for the first time. She looked affronted and annoyed.

'No drug addict could possibly provide the quality of service that the girls do here. The girls earn lots of money and spend it in various ways. Honey chooses to spend her money on sports cars – such as the one outside. Would you like to say something, Honey?'

The girl stretched herself to her full height.

'I know many people think that selling sex is wrong and exploits women,' she began in a polished accent, 'but I do it because I enjoy sex, I like doing it well and I like having money. I am not going to waste the money I earn on drugs and I don't have sex with men who I dislike.'

'So you can choose your, um, clients?' Susan asked.

'Of course,' Honey replied. 'Like any professional. The clients choose which of us they'd like to negotiate with and we decide whether we want to take up their offer. You should try it, you look attractive enough.'

Susan blushed, but Joyce could see that she was thinking about it. Bringing up a child alone it was difficult for Susan to get enough money to live on.

'Give it a go, young woman,' Mrs Glover said. 'I have a vacant room. There's a new client arriving shortly. I'll suggest he sees you first.'

Susan looked bashful.

'Are all your girls as young as Honey and Susan?' Eileen asked.

'Well, they're not my girls, but the women I do business with vary in age. There is a demand for the attractive, expert, mature woman such as yourself. Do you want to give it a go? Perhaps the two of you together? Many men will happily pay for two at once.'

Eileen looked at Susan and winked, 'What do you think Susan? Shall we?' Susan didn't move for a moment then slowly nodded her head. Mrs Glover clapped her hands with glee.

'Wonderful. Honey, show the ladies up to the Blue Room. When Mr Charles arrives show him in there first and see if they agree to do business.'

Eileen and Susan looked at each other and giggled, then followed Honey out of the room.

'Now what would you three ladies like to do?'

'I'd like to meet more of your women,' Edith said.

'Certainly. Cherry is free at the moment. You can meet her.' Mrs Glover rang a little bell that was on the table beside the sofa and a few moments later the maid entered the room.

'Take this lady up to Cherry in the Lemon Room please, Fenella.' The maid nodded her head and waited at the door for Edith to join her.

'Now, ladies,' Mrs Glover said, turning to Betty and Joyce,

‘how about a cup of tea, then you can tell me all about your College.’

Eileen and Susan found themselves sitting on an enormous bed covered with a pale blue quilt in a large comfortable room that was predominantly blue.

‘What have we done?’ Susan said.

‘I think we’ve agreed to entertain a Mr Charles if he is attractive enough and offers us sufficient cash.’

‘How much is sufficient?’

‘I really don’t know. Shall we see how much he offers and then ask for more?’

‘That’s a good idea, Eileen. Should we get ready?’

‘What do you mean?’

‘Well, take our clothes off.’

‘Oh, no. We mustn’t look too eager and anyway, the gentleman may like to take the wrapping off his purchase himself.’

Eileen stood up to examine the room. There was a very well appointed bathroom attached, a cupboard stocked with drinks, a record player with a stack of records largely by American crooners. In another cupboard Eileen found a supply of pillows and cushions to add to the ones already on the bed. In a bedside drawer there were packets of condoms and a variety of vibrators and dildos, and in another, copies of tasteful pornographic magazines, *Playboy, Penthouse, Forum.*

‘It’s very well equipped, isn’t it?’ Eileen said, ‘I could be quite happy spending my time here.’

There was a tap on the door.

‘Come in,’ Eileen said. The maid opened the door and showed in a tall, slim gentleman. He was dressed in a summer weight business suit and looked to be in his early forties.

‘Good evening,’ he said a little nervously. Eileen bounced up to him and took his hand.

‘Hello, I’m Eileen and this is Susan. We’re here to, um, entertain you.’

‘Very good. Do I have a choice …?’

‘You can have us both together, if you like.’

'That sounds an interesting arrangement. I understand one hundred pounds is the usual fee. What would be the charge for the two of you?'

Eileen glanced as Susan who looked wide-eyed at the sum of money mentioned.

'Oh, I think for the two of us that should be, um, one hundred and, ah, twenty.'

The man shrugged and began to undo his jacket.

'Sounds reasonable. A deal.' He took a wallet from his jacket pocket and counted out a wad of notes.

Eileen looked at Susan again. Susan gave the slightest of nods.

'A deal,' Eileen said, took the cash from Mr Charles's hand and put it in her handbag beside the bed. The maid nodded and stepped out of the room, closing the door. Mr Charles slipped his jacket from his shoulders and began to loosen his tie.

'Let me do that,' Eileen said. 'Would you like a drink, sir?'

'Yes I would; whisky, with a dash of water, no ice.' Susan went to collect the drink while Eileen got on with the business of undressing their client. He was standing in just his very white Y-fronts when Susan offered him the tumbler. He took the glass and raised it to his lips. Eileen knelt and pressed her face against the cloth covering his manhood. She felt a swelling against her mouth and cheek and a growing heat conducting through the thin cloth. There was also a drawing in of breath from above her head.

'I think you should remove Edward's underwear, Susan,' Eileen said standing up and reaching behind her neck to unzip her sundress. Susan took her place on her knees and placed her hand on the hem of the underpants. Very slowly she tugged the garment down. The hem caught, stretched, then flicked off, releasing his manhood. It smacked Susan on the nose. She flinched but recovered quickly and took hold of it in her hand. It grew noticeably and the purple, circumcised knob swelled and glistened.

Eileen was naked. She knelt beside Susan and placed a hand around Mr Charles's testicles.

'You get undressed now,' she whispered, 'I think we've

passed the unwrapping bit.'

She encircled the shaft in her other hand and lowered her head until her lips touched the tip. Her moist tongue slipped out between her lips and touched the hole in the tip of the cock. She felt Mr Charles shiver and a groan came from above her. Eileen smiled; it was having the desired effect. Gently she tugged Mr Charles to the bed where Susan now lay, stripped, legs apart, showing off her wet and swollen cunt.

'I think Susan would like you to lick her,' Eileen said. Mr Charles climbed on to the bed and obediently knelt between Susan's thighs. He lowered his head into her muff and proceeded to lap at her crack. Susan made suitably excited noises which Eileen did not think were at all pretence. Eileen also climbed on to the bed and lay on her back with her head between Mr Charles's knees. She dragged a cushion under her neck, lifting her head so that she could wrap her lips around his cock again. She began to suck.

The maid showed Edith into a room entirely decorated in pale yellow. A young brunette leapt off the bed. She was wearing just a lemon coloured negligee and a dark tuft of hair could clearly be seen at the top of her crotch.

'Who are you?' the girl asked.

'This lady is visiting to learn about what you girls do for a living, Cherry,' the maid explained.

'You're not from the pigs?' Cherry said warily.

'If you mean, am I a policewoman, then quite obviously I am not. They don't employ old dears like me,' Edith said.

'What you here for then?'

'My friends and I are investigating the life of pro … I mean, women who provide sexual services.'

Cherry shrugged.

'Well, I don't mind talking about it, I've got nothing better to do, my first punter this evening has cancelled on me. You can go, Fenella.' The maid left. 'Fancy joining me with a drink, lady?'

'My name is Edith, and yes I would like a drink.' Cherry got up and went to a fridge disguised as a piece of wooden bedroom furniture, 'G&T? It's what I'm having.'

'That will do nicely. Do you live here?'

Cherry began pouring the drinks. Edith sat on the edge of the bed.

'Oh, no. I've got a flat in town. Mrs Glover just rents these rooms by the day, or part day.'

'So she books your clients.'

'No, I book my regulars in, but she looks after any new blokes and points them towards me or whoever else is available.' Cherry offered a full glass to Edith and climbed on to the bed stretching herself out.

'And takes a large cut of your earnings, no doubt.'

'Well, it costs a lot to run this place and keep the pigs off our backs, but I do very nicely, thanks. I couldn't pay for my own flat and all the rest by working in a factory.'

While they talked Edith found herself examining the girl. Her negligee had ridden up her torso and Edith found herself gazing at the Y shaped crease at her crotch and the triangle of black hair.

'Do you enjoy, ah, entertaining your clients?'

'Do you mean do I like being fucked? I call a spade a fucking spade.'

'OK. Do you like being fucked by your clients?'

'I like fucking and some are better at it than others.' While stating her opinion firmly Cherry's hand wandered to her crotch and Edith was enthralled as her finger slipped into her crack. Her eyes stared at Edith gauging her response as she went on. 'Mind you, a finger or a tongue is as good as a cock for giving pleasure.'

Edith rested her hand on Cherry's thigh. 'I am sure I agree with you, my dear.' She slid her hand up the silky skin. Cherry withdrew her finger and Edith's took its place. It slipped easily into the moist channel. The young woman opened her legs and Edith peered admiringly at the swollen pink lips of her fanny. Her finger explored deeper, entering the tunnel. It was joined by a second and a third finger. She probed deeper. All the time Cherry's dark eyes were fixed on her.

'Aren't you feeling warm in all those clothes?' Cherry

asked. Edith was only wearing a thin cotton summer dress over her underwear but nevertheless she was feeling surprisingly heated.

'I am, my dear, but I don't think you want to be faced with my scrawny old body.'

'Actually, I think I do. I think you look beautiful.'

Cherry stirred causing Edith's fingers to slip from her. She knelt and unzipped the back of Edith's dress and eased it off her shoulders. Edith stood and let the dress fall to the floor. She was wearing a thin nylon corset that covered her breasts and abdomen and rather full knickers.

Cherry reached for Edith's hand and pulled her on to the bed.

'Don't you want to take this off?' Cherry said caressing Edith's breasts through the thin material.

'No,' Edith replied.

'Well, you're not keeping these on.' Without warning Cherry pulled Edith's knickers down her thighs revealing her thin pubic hair, silver-grey with a hint of blonde. Edith kicked the knickers off and pushed Cherry down on to her back, easing her legs apart again.

'It was your pleasure we were talking about, young lady,' she said lowering her head to Cherry's crotch. Her lips met the hot, glistening flesh of the young woman's fanny and she pushed her tongue between the lips, drinking in the sweet juices. She searched deep and then swept up to find the girl's long, swollen clit. She sucked it into her mouth and rubbed her teeth gently against it. The girl dropped her arms to her sides and spread her thighs as wide as she could, thrusting her pubic bone against Edith's upper jaw. She sighed and groaned and tossed her head.

'Well, that was a most interesting experience,' Eileen said, as she and Susan rejoined Joyce and Betty in the reception room.

'You satisfied your client, then?' Joyce said.

'Mr Charles was very pleased,' Mrs Glover said returning to the room having shown the gentleman out. 'You two will be very welcome if you wish to rent a room again.'

'Oh, yes the rent,' Eileen said rummaging in her handbag. 'How much do we owe you?'

'That will be twenty pounds for the room hire and ten pounds administrative fee,' Mrs Glover said making a note in a cashbook she kept in a small bureau beside the door. Eileen handed over the notes and gave the rest to Susan.

'Here, you have the rest.'

'Eileen! It's a lot of money.'

'Buy something nice for Hannah.'

'You earned it as much as I did.'

'You need it more than I do. I did it for the pleasure.'

'Was it?' Betty asked, wide-eyed at the sight of all the notes.

'Actually, it was very pleasant indeed. Mr Charles had a very nice cock and some idea how to use it and his tongue.' Eileen looked around, 'Where's Edith?'

'Still with one of the girls, I suppose,' Joyce replied, looking at the ornate French clock on the mantelpiece, 'she's been over an hour with her.'

Just then the door opened and Edith appeared looking flushed and happy.

'Oh, there you are, Edith,' Joyce said. 'We were just wondering how long you would be. Did you and the girl get along well?'

'Yes, we did,' Edith said dreamily. 'Cherry is a very kind young woman.'

'So, she wasn't a raddled, drug-addicted old whore,' Eileen said, smiling.

'Nothing of the sort. I must admit I was wrong to compare the women of this establishment with some of the women you hear about.'

'Very good. We've taken up enough of Mrs Glover's time. We'd better be heading back, and you three can tell me and Betty all about your experiences,' Joyce said rising to her feet.

Another week had slipped by and four of the ladies had had a pleasant evening exploring the joy of sex with Winston, Johnny and Mick. Eileen had not been present and Joyce was surprised and, as the hour became late, a little worried. Susan left to relieve her babysitter and Edith and Betty escorted each other home. Johnny and Mick had cycled off. Winston was washing the glasses and the snack bowls and Joyce was plumping the cushions.

The doorbell rang and rang. Joyce hurried to the door, opened it and found Eileen leaning against the wall of the porch.

'Eileen! What are you doing? You look exhausted.' Joyce examined Eileen's tousled hair, bosom-defining T-shirt, very short leopard skin skirt and high heeled sandals, 'Why are you dressed like that? Where have you been?'

'If you let me in and get me a drink, a long one, I'll answer all your questions.'

Joyce flustered and led Eileen into the front lounge calling to Winston to make Eileen a large G&T. Eileen flopped onto the sofa, her miniskirt riding up her thighs revealing the swollen, protruding red lips of her vulva. Winston delivered the tumbler and Eileen took a long swig followed by a deep breath.

'Now, Eileen, explain. We've been wondering where you were all evening.' Joyce sat in the chair opposite, leaning forward, staring at her friend.

'I've been on the game.'

'On the game?' Joyce didn't understand at first, then comprehension passed across her face. 'Oh, you mean, you've been playing at being a prostitute.'

'Not playing.'

'Really! Where? At Madam Glover's?'

'No. Gas Street.'

'What! With the cheap street-walkers?' Joyce's face showed her horror at Eileen's announcement.

'Yes.'

'Whatever for? Are you all right?'

'I'm fine. A little used, that's all.'

'But why?'

Eileen took another long drink, pulled herself up on the settee and looked at Joyce.

'It was after last week's visit to Mrs Glover. That was a very pleasant experience but it was so obviously the top end, the "nice" side of prostitution – clean, healthy girls, well-off clients, lots of money changing hands. I decided I wanted to see what the other end looked like. So, a few days ago, I dressed up like this,' she tried tugging the skirt down her thigh to no avail, 'and when it was getting dark drove over to town. I parked a few streets away and walked into Gas Street. There were about half a dozen women there, walking up and down slowly, or hanging around a lamp post, obviously waiting for cars to come along. Well, they were pretty suspicious of me at first, thought I might have been a cop trying to catch them soliciting. I gave them a story about being broke and down on my luck and they gave me the benefit of the doubt. I didn't hang around long that evening as they were obviously wary but the next night I did the same. Some of the same women were there and this time they let me talk to them.' Eileen paused to sip from her glass.

'They were all ages. One or two in their teens, a couple older than you or me; and Edith was right, most of them are addicted to something or other and desperate to earn money to get their next hit. They warned me about some of the pimps but they weren't there that early in the night. I told them that I needed to earn some cash. They were a bit possessive of their bit of pavement, so I didn't push it.

The next evening, that was last night, I went again and chatted to some of the girls. They gave me some hints – what the punters want, where to go to do it, how much to ask for, that kind of thing. I just stood by as one by one they were picked up by the men in the cars. Sometimes they'd only be gone fifteen minutes or so before the cars came back and dropped them off.'

'Did they earn much?' Joyce was sitting on the edge of her seat.

'A few quid for a hand job, a bit more for oral. Some of them had rooms nearby which they took the men to and charged a bit more for an hour or so of sex.'

'And did you …?'

'Not until tonight. For some reason there were fewer girls out this evening. A car pulled up. The girl I'd chatted to most, Sharon, pushed me towards it, I think she knew the guy. It was quite a nice car, a Vauxhall Victor I think.'

‘Forget the car, Eileen, what was the man like?’

‘Well, he wasn’t dirty, but he did smell a bit of booze. In his forties I suppose and a bit overweight. He leaned over, opened the passenger door and offered me a fiver for a blow job.’

‘You refused, I take it.’

‘Of course not, that’s what I was there for. I got in. He drove down the street between the old warehouses, pulled into the side of the road and turned the engine off. There was no one else around – it’s a dead end. Then he said, “come on then, I ain’t got time to waste” and pointed to his crotch. That’s when I noticed that his flies were open and his cock was sitting there, exposed. It had been hidden in the folds of his trousers when he’d been leaning forward, driving. It looked really crumpled and forlorn. I reached out to lift it up but he said, “I said a blow job not a hand”. There didn’t seem anything else to do so I lowered my head into his lap, found his cock with my lips and started to suck.’

Joyce’s face was screwed up with distaste, ‘What did it taste like? Was he clean?’

‘Well he hadn’t just come out of the shower but it wasn’t too disgusting. As I sucked he began to get a hard-on but it wasn’t a very impressive cock. Still it meant I didn’t choke when I got to work on it. He put his hands on my head stopping me from lifting it up. It worried me a bit – I thought I might suffocate in his balls. At last I could hear him panting and groaning and then he came.’

‘You swallowed his come?’

‘I had to. He didn’t let me go until after he’d finished and his cock had gone down again. He just pushed me off then and started the car. He turned around and drove back to Gas Street. He gave me a crumpled fiver from his pocket and told to me to get out. That was it.’

‘So then you came here?’

‘Oh no, that was hours ago. It was still light then. Sharon and I had a chat and then another car drove up and again she pushed me towards it. It was a big old Wolseley. The driver looked a bit younger and fitter than the first bloke and he offered me a tenner for a fuck. I got in and we drove a mile or so to the canal. No one around again. He stopped and told me to pull my knickers down. I haven't done it much in car.'

'You did it in my Rover with Winston.'

'So I did. Well that was the first time since I did it in a Morris Minor in the late fifties but even when I was young and flexible it was difficult fitting things together in the cramped space. This car was a bit bigger, I suppose. The seat I was in was pushed back as far as it could go and could recline. He was obviously used to it, because he undid his belt and flies, sort of rolled over the transmission tunnel on top of me and shoved his trousers and pants down. I was trapped, couldn't move a limb but he managed to shove his thing up inside me. He was bigger than the first man and filled me up a bit more. He pushed his feet against the floor and started banging away. His bottom kept on slapping against the dashboard. Anyway I was getting quite worked up when he came. He collapsed on top of me and I thought again that I was going to suffocate; he was such a dead weight. I suggested he get off me and he rolled back into his seat. He wriggled around to get his trousers and pants back on, gave me the tenner and then drove me back to Gas Street.'

'And that was when you left.'

'No. I should have done, though. Sharon had gone and there was just a group of girls I didn't know. Almost at once a white van pulled up. The other women ignored it but the driver beckoned to me. He offered me twenty quid for intercourse. That seemed better still and, after all, I'd hardly spent more than five minutes all together with the first two actually having sex. I got in and he drove to the old gasworks site. It's a patch of rough ground, supposed to be fenced off, but there was a gap that was big enough to drive through. It was almost dark now but I could see that there were a few other cars parked close together. He pulled up and stopped and someone pulled my door open, grabbed my arm and dragged me out. They took me round to the back of the van. There was a mattress on the floor. They pushed me in and told me to take my knickers off. Well I'd forgotten to put them on after the last bloke and left them in his car, so I just hitched up my skirt.'

'Oh, Eileen, did they rape you?'

'I don't know. Was it rape? I'd said yes to having sex with the driver of the van. He was the first. He scrambled in on top of me with his trousers round his ankles. He didn't have pants on but he sure had an erection. He was so eager he practically came before he shoved it in. It was all over in a minute, but as soon as he slipped out of the van his mate, the one who had dragged me out of the passenger seat, took his place. He took his time, got his trousers right off before he got on top of me and squeezed my tits. Mind you it hurt a bit when he entered me. He wasn't one for looking after his woman; he just took aim and banged it in. He kept at it for quite a while, too, and I was beginning to feel a bit knackered when he came.'

'That was it, the two of them?'

'Well, that's what I thought, but I'd forgotten the other cars parked there. They were all in on it.'

'All?'

'I couldn't see much where I was but they moved a couple of the cars so that their headlights lit up the back of the van. I could see silhouettes of men watching what was happening and as one finished with me another started.'

'Oh, Eileen! Are you sure you're not hurt?'

'A bit sore but actually they didn't do anything to harm me. They just wanted a fuck and most of them were so excited that it was about all they could do to get their cocks inside me. A couple of them rolled me over and took me from behind doggy fashion, and one or two only wanted to wank over me.'

'So how many were there?'

'I'm not sure, a dozen perhaps. I think a few of them had two goes.'

'How did you get away?'

'Well, I was getting worried. It had become a succession of fucks, one after the other, and I was getting exhausted. I might even have blacked out for a minute or two. Then a few of them shouted something and they all started running back to their cars. The headlights disappeared and I was sitting on my own in the dark. I scrambled out and hardly had I gone a few yards than the van drove off with its back doors swinging and banging. I think they must have thought the police were on their way. I was left standing on that demolition site all on my own. Well, I got on to the road and walked to where I'd parked my car. Luckily I'd kept my bag hooked around my shoulder so I didn't lose my keys or anything.'

'I'm sure you were lucky, Eileen, really.'

'There's just one thing I'm annoyed about.'

'What's that?'

'They didn't give me the twenty pounds.'

Chapter Ten
Discipline

Eileen parked her car outside The Old School, got out and smoothed down her nylon sundress. She skipped to the door looking forward to an evening of pleasure. She hadn't seen her friend, Joyce, for a week as she'd had various chores to sort out. Now she was eager for the attentions of one of the boys – it didn't matter which.

Joyce answered the door.

'Hello, Eileen, we've been waiting for you, you're a bit late.'

Eileen looked at her watch with surprise. She thought she was on time and her watch confirmed it was only five minutes to eight. What did Joyce mean? She followed Joyce along the narrow corridor and into the large hall. The thick black curtains were drawn shutting out the bright summer evening. The three other women and the three boys were indeed there before her, sitting in a pool of artificial light. Something strange was happening. For a start they were all dressed and none of them was getting in a preliminary bit of fondling or kissing. Susan, Betty and Edith sat on one sofa and Johnny and Mick were together on another. Winston was alone, sitting on the edge of the super-king-size bed.

Eileen followed Joyce into the room and found herself standing facing the three sofas with Joyce by her side and Winston behind her.

'What's going on, Joyce? It feels strange,' she said.

'Ah, well, perhaps it does because we have all decided that you need some discipline.' Joyce said in a schoolmistress tone, which was unusual because she had never been a teacher.

A prickle of fear travelled down Eileen's back. Discipline? That sounded like school. She remembered being called to the headmistress's office to be disciplined for one of her misdemeanours. They were many and varied, usually involving items of uniform or illicit contacts with the boys from the grammar school next door.

'What do you mean by discipline?' she asked tentatively.

'Well, we are a school, or rather a college,' Joyce said, still using her formal tone of voice, 'and all schools need to maintain a level of order amongst their students.'

'Um, yes, but I don't understand. Who has decided that I should be disciplined and what am I supposed to have done?'

'Well, we, your fellow students of the Ladies' College for Erotic Arts have agreed that you should be disciplined,' Joyce said and the other three ladies nodded their heads slowly like the judges at a trial, 'You were absent from last week's meeting and what's more took part in an escapade without inviting any of your fellow students to join you.'

'You mean when I joined the Gas Street prostitutes?'

'That's right,' Edith spoke up sternly, 'you could have been harmed going off on your own like that.'

Eileen had indeed been close to being hurt and the memory was still a little raw.

'OK, yes I suppose it was a little silly to go off and sell myself without telling any of you. I'm sorry.'

'We thought you would say that,' Betty giggled.

'I'm afraid being sorry is not good enough,' Edith said, a severe look on her face.

'I won't do it again,' Eileen insisted. 'I can assure you, one night working on the streets was quite enough.'

'We think you need to be taught a lesson.' Susan's quiet voice chilled Eileen. She couldn't remember the young woman ever sounding so authoritative.

'What do you mean?' Eileen said, her voice trembling.

'As we said at the beginning,' Joyce said, 'we are going to give you some discipline, and as I know you have read your *Joy of Sex* thoroughly you will know what that means.'

Eileen did recall. The words came into her mind now as clearly as if she was reading them off the page. She shivered.

'I am to be beaten?'

'That is correct,' Joyce said sombrely, 'Don't consider that we might get pleasure from seeing you being corrected.'

'But you will,' Eileen said with a cockiness that she did not feel.

'I don't know. It is a learning experience for all of us; a worthy subject for the students of the erotic arts. We shall study your reactions with interest. Perhaps others will require discipline at later date.'

Eileen realised now that her adventure the previous week had just provided an excuse for Joyce and the other girls to plot how they could introduce discipline into their curriculum of pleasure.

'Some people like being beaten,' Betty said cheerfully. 'Perhaps you will, Eileen.'

'And some relish the beating,' Edith said with a curl in her lip.

'Perhaps we will find things out about ourselves,' Susan said.

Eileen was only concerned with one thing.

'How am I to be beaten?' she asked and her lip trembled as she said it.

'There are a number of possibilities and we have prepared for many of them,' Joyce said, revealing to Eileen that she had obviously given some thought to this scenario, 'but we will commence with the simplest – spanking.' She took Eileen's hands, turned her around and led her to Winston. 'Winston has kindly offered to administer the punishment and we have instructed him on what to do. Remove your knickers please, Eileen.'

Winston looked up at her and smiled broadly.

'You mean to beat my bare bottom?' Eileen asked.

'How else?' Joyce replied.

Eileen considered for a moment. She could run out of the room, leave the building, jump in her car and drive away and never see her friends again. She could escape this painful and degrading punishment. But there was something else; a little knot of anticipation in her stomach, the same little thrill that had led her to join the prostitutes of Gas Street and join in all the other daring activities she had done throughout her life. Part of her wanted to know what it would feel like to be beaten and punished. She reached up under her dress and tugged at her panties. They dropped to the floor and she stepped out of them.

'Bend over Winston's knee, please, Eileen,' Joyce instructed. Winston opened his legs. She bent at the knees and waist, lowering her torso across Winston's broad left thigh. He hooked his right leg around her leg closest to him, parting her thighs, and he pressed on her shoulders with his left hand. Her head and arms hung down and her hands brushed against the carpet. His thigh moved under her and she felt her weight shift and she tipped forward so that she was delicately balanced and no longer under control of her position. She was in Winston's hands. She felt his hands on the back of her thighs, lifting up the hem of her dress and tugging it up and back. There was air on her buttocks.

'You may start, Winston,' Joyce said. 'Remember what we said.'

Eileen waited. With Winston's right leg and left arm holding her firmly she could barely wriggle. Her skin tingled in anticipation. How much would it hurt when he brought his right hand down? Surely Winston wouldn't want to hurt her, would he? It would just be a light slap. They were playing a game with her, pretending to punish her, a bit of fun.

There was no warning. One moment she was lying there, almost calm, the next her bottom was on fire. The force of the blow slammed her onto his thigh expelling air from her lungs. It emerged as a roar of pain. Across her left and right buttock her skin flamed. She gasped for breath and sobbed. She wriggled but he still had her held firmly. She pushed her hands against the floor but the force of his left hand on her shoulders held her down. Tears trickled down her face and dripped from her nose.

Joyce was fascinated by the twin globes of white flesh exposed when Winston positioned Eileen on his knee and pulled up her dress. She marvelled at how young Eileen's skin looked, the flesh soft and supple. Winston raised his right hand above his head, looked at her. Joyce gave the smallest of nods. He brought his hand down. The noise surprised her, a loud sharp crack, like a whiplash. For a moment she noted the contrast of his huge black hand splayed out over the white skin, then he withdrew his arm revealing the red hand print, each finger and the thumb clearly defined radiating out from the palm. It seemed to glow like a beacon. Simultaneously came Eileen's cry, an animal roar followed by a tremulous whimper. Behind her she heard Edith, Susan and Betty gasp. Winston raised his arm again.

The cool air did little to soothe Eileen's burning bottom. It felt like a bonfire signalling her humiliation to the watchers. Was that it? Surely one blow so hard was enough; but no, Winston still held her firmly, her thighs parted, her head down, her bottom raised.

A second eruption of fire overlapping with the first but spreading into new territory and another forced exclamation. The tears flowed freely, running down the side of her nose. She cried. Then another, and another, each as heavy and forceful as the last. Her whole buttocks now alight.

Joyce watched the spread of crimson across Eileen's buttocks. Winston was putting as much effort as possible into each blow as he had been instructed to do. Joyce flinched with each slap of hand on skin and cry from Eileen's throat. She could see Eileen's tears but she didn't tell Winston to stop. There was an amazing feeling of power seeing her friend upended and helpless, exposed like a young child and made to endure the pain of the punishment. The thrill that she experienced between her legs surprised her. Were those writers who recommended discipline as a sexual stimulus correct? It certainly seemed so. She turned to look at the other watchers. Mick was vigorously rubbing a massive bulge in his tight, brief shorts and Johnny had a look of intense envy on his face. Who was he jealous of? Eileen for the punishment she was receiving or Winston for the power he was wielding over her. The three women also stared wide eyed. Betty looked horrified, but Edith's expression showed pleasure and Susan was biting her lip anticipating the next fall of Winston's hand.

All of Eileen's consciousness was focussed on her blazing bottom, but there was something else. The fire was inside too. Her vagina was aflame and she knew that her clitoris and labia were engorged. Could anyone see that she was aroused? Was Winston aware of her state?

Another blow blew her mind back to the pain, her whole bottom was an inferno but it raged in her fanny too. The hand fell again, square across her arse, but this time instead of being removed, it lingered. It was hot; hotter than the fire she felt in her cheeks. The hand began to move, the fingers trickling along her crack, lingering around her arsehole, then slipping on between the folds of swollen skin, into the sodden depths. The hand stopped but a finger continued to move, exploring, searching, digging. Two fingers entered her, pushing into her channel. She responded, spreading her legs wider, arching her back to raise her hips. The fingers slid deeper, their passage eased by her effusion. His thumb rotated on her clit. There was a strange noise, a gurgling moan that she realised was her.

Joyce watched as Winston caressed Eileen's quim. Six they had agreed on and six he had delivered. It was enough to turn both of Eileen's buttocks a livid scarlet. Now was the respite and Joyce was amused to see Eileen's response. Despite the pain she must be in from the beating she was arching her back, spreading her thighs, opening her cunt to allow Winston access. The fingers were buried in her vagina and his thumb moved incessantly. Eileen groaned, the sound was so obviously one of ecstasy that Joyce knew that Eileen's beating had aroused her to a new level.

Her stinging bottom and pulsating fanny seemed remote. Eileen had no control over the sensations but she realised that Winston was making an exhibition of her, showing off her punished buttocks and excited crotch. His cock was pressing against her hip, constrained by his trousers. Still his hand worked her, playing her like a musical instrument bringing her to the crescendo of his composition.

'Fuck me, please,' she whispered.

Winston's legs straightened as he stood up. She slipped off

his lap and on to her knees on the carpet, his hand still gripping her cunt and holding her arse up. She felt his hand withdraw to be replaced instantly by his long, thick cock. He rammed it in to her bringing a gasp from her almost as loud as when he had beaten her. Now she had her release. Her orgasm shook her whole body as Winston continued to rock back and forth, thrusting his rod deep into her vagina until he too came and she felt his cream filling her to overflowing.

Joyce was a little astonished when Winston tipped Eileen onto the floor still gripping her pubis. They hadn't planned what to do after the beating. Then he was fucking her with as much energy as he used in spanking her. The redness of Eileen's buttocks infused the rest of her skin as she cried and trembled with her orgasm. It was over in a few moments. Winston withdrew, his penis dripping thick gobbets of semen and Eileen slumped forward, her buttocks still radiating a rosy glow.

'Well, that was successful,' Joyce said, clasping her hands together, 'what do the rest of you think?'

'Winston hit her very hard,' Susan said.

'Her bottom looks sore,' Betty added.

'But she loved it,' Edith pointed out, 'did you see how she asked to be screwed.'

'I've never known Eileen come as quickly,' Joyce agreed, 'she always says how difficult it is for her to have an orgasm.'

'I can hear you, you know,' Eileen said, stretching out on the carpet, holding her dress above her waist so ensuring that nothing touched her burning posterior, 'I hope you are satisfied.'

'Oh, I think so,' Joyce said cheerfully. 'I think we have proved that the pain of a spanking is worth it for the intensity of the pleasure which follows.'

Eileen was very conscious of her sensitive and stinging rear but also of the contented tingle in her vagina.

'You're right, but I think it will be a while before I do anything to deserve more punishment from Winston. My poor bottom will be tender for days.'

'Hmm, yes, it looks like it,' Joyce said. 'Now, Winston, how was it for you?'

Winston looked a little self-conscious.

'I've never lifted a hand to a woman in my life before,' he said apologetically, 'but holding her over my knee and seeing her arse and fanny gave me a right hard-on.'

'So you'll do it again?' Joyce enquired.

'Yeah, if you want me to.'

'Right, well let's have a drink; Susan will you do us the favour? Then we can decide what happens next.'

Eileen sucked on a straw while lying on her front on the floor. The others relaxed on the sofas.

'You have a plan for this evening, I gather, Joyce,' she said, 'I presume it involves more than just my punishment.'

'Well, yes, it does rather,' Joyce said, 'You see having read what *The Joy of Sex* says about discipline – not a lot I might point out – the girls and I decided we needed some more equipment. Winston spanking you over his knee is just one scenario.'

Eileen was mystified, 'What do you mean, more equipment?'

'I had a telephone conversation with Mr Winter. Do you remember him?'

'The gentleman who sells the sex toys.'

'That's it. Well, he made some suggestions and arranged a supplier. Susan can you get the implements to show Eileen.'

Susan put her drink down, got up and went across the room to one of the cupboards in the shadows at the edge of the hall. She returned with a large box made of thick cardboard from which she drew out a variety of items that Eileen only expected to see in museums. Susan laid them on the floor.

'I can guess what their purpose is but what are all these things?' Eileen asked.

Joyce knelt and picked each up in turn. 'Well we have a tawse, a cane, a coiled whip, a cat-o-nine tails, a birch, a paddle and a crop.'

'You bought all these from Mr Winter?'

'All except the riding crop. I had that from when I used to go horse riding, years ago. It's a very good one; Bill bought it for me as a present. I can't imagine that he expected it to be used as we are going to, though.'

'You can't use these when you have someone tossed over your knee,' Eileen pondered. 'Are you expecting your next victim to kneel quietly on the floor or bend over the bed?'

'Well that is a possibility, but you can't rely on someone holding still if they are going to be beaten with a rod or a whip, can you?'

'Well, no, I suppose not.'

'Mr Winter suggested that a punishment stool was a necessary item.'

'Oh. A punishment stool?'

'Gentlemen, can you get it please?' Winston, Johnny and Mick got up and disappeared into the shadows. They reappeared bearing a heavy piece of furniture between them. They placed in on the floor in the middle of the circle.

Eileen examined the structure. It was built out of heavy wood which had been polished and varnished to a glistening, dark brown. There was a platform at one end, about two feet by one foot, with wooden beams protruding from it from which leather straps dangled. From the platform, two sturdy supports rose about nine inches apart and eighteen inches high and curving into what appeared to be a narrow but wide padded seat. The thick legs at the each end also had leather straps attached. Both the platform and the seat were covered in brown vinyl.

'This is a punishment stool?' Eileen asked.

'Yes. I found pictures in an encyclopaedia in the library,' Joyce said, 'Winston built it for us. Didn't he do a good job.'

Eileen noted the well-fitted joints, the smooth, shiny wood and the securely stapled covering.

'So the, uh, victim, kneels over it. I suppose the straps are fastened to stop them escaping.'

'That's right, and the shape ensures that their nether regions are in the correct position to receive their punishment.'

'Well since you've gone to this much trouble, I suppose you expect it to be used,' Eileen said, 'but I hope it's not going to be me. My bottom is sore enough already.'

'No, you're in the clear, my dear. We agreed that six spanks would be your punishment on this occasion.' Joyce nodded.

'You expect there will be others?'

'Don't you. Now you've been disciplined once, don't you feel you want it again?'

Eileen remembered the pain of the hand descending on her bare buttocks, the humiliation of being held in that exposed position, the defencelessness, the desire it aroused in her and the incredible release that her orgasm gave her. Yes, she thought, she probably would submit to punishment again – but not before her poor bottom had recovered.

'Yes, but not yet. So who is it going to be?'

Joyce looked at the other three women.

'We talked about this, haven't we ladies.' All three nodded.

'We decided that we should try out the, um, tools,' Edith said.

'So that means it has to be one of the boys,' Betty said glancing at the three men. Winston was impassive but Mick and Johnny looked at each other.

'Did you see how much Mick was enjoying Eileen's discomfort?' Joyce asked and Mick immediately turned the shade of a ripe tomato.

'He was pumping away at himself, as if it was the first time he'd had an erection,' Edith said describing what she had seen.

'Yeah, you were really going at it,' Johnny joined in.

'So, do we agree that Mick should be our trial victim?' Joyce said. The others agreed wholeheartedly. Mick looked around as if preparing to make his escape, but before he could move, Johnny and Winston pounced on him.

'There's no honour among thieves, or men,' Edith observed.

'He needs to be stripped,' Joyce said. Winston and Johnny complied instantly; dragging off Mick's training shoes, shorts, T shirt and pants. He stood naked; a very sad specimen with his flaccid penis dangling forlornly between his legs.

'Now fasten him to the stool,' Joyce commanded.

Mick was pushed into a kneeling position on the platform and Johnny pressed his shoulders forward so that his torso rested on the padded vinyl. Susan and Edith joined in fastening the straps tightly around his ankles, thighs and wrists. They stepped back to admire their handiwork.

Eileen looked on from her prone position on the floor. Even though he tried to wriggle, Mick was secured. His head hung down from the end of the stool and his muscular buttocks were raised up. His penis and testicles hung between his parted thighs.

'Are you comfortable?' Joyce asked.

'Uh, yeah, it feels OK, except I can't move,' Mick replied.

'That's the idea,' Joyce said. 'Now, who would like to start?'

Edith bent over and picked up the tawse from the floor. She examined the split leather strap.

'I remember this being used when I was at school, just after the first war,' she said, 'across the hand or over the bottom. It stung a lot.'

'Try it out,' Joyce urged.

Edith stood beside the punishment stool. She shuffled her feet into position and measured her reach. She raised her hand and the tawse dangled at head height. Then she swung her arm and twisted her body. The tawse descended on Mick's bottom with a loud slap. He yelped. A livid forked stripe appeared across the white skin. Edith bent forward to examine her efforts.

'It's a few decades since I saw that mark on skin,' she commented.

'Who's next?' Joyce called.

'The headmaster used a cane at my school,' Susan said reaching for the implement. She hefted it feeling its weight.

'Come on then, give it a go,' Joyce urged.

Edith moved aside and Susan took up her position. She raised the curved flexible stick and brought it down fast. It screamed through the air and hit Mick's bottom with a loud crack. An inch thick red strip appeared beside the previous mark across both the left cheek and the right. Mick shouted more loudly and complained.

'Ow, that really hurt.'

'Mr Winter warned about this.' Joyce mused.

'What's that?' Eileen asked.

'He said that the victims may complain about their treatment.'

'That's not surprising. What do you expect?'

'Well, it could put the disciplinarian off their stroke.'

'Yes, I suppose it could. What can you do?'

'Mr Winter recommended this.' Joyce reached into the box that contained all the punishment tools and picked out a strip of leather with plastic ball attached to it

'Ah, the ball gag,' Eileen said. Joyce went to Mick and fastened the strap around his head, pulling the ball between his teeth. 'He can breathe through the hole, but it will stop him making comments.' She stepped back admiring her handiwork, 'Now whose turn is it? Betty it must be you.'

Betty picked up the riding crop.

'I used to ride too when I was younger and thinner,' she said examining the leather binding of the crop, 'It was fun swishing one of these through the air.'

She stood close behind Mick, choosing her target carefully. Then she stepped to the side and did a quick flick of her wrist. The crop whistled through the air and struck Mick at the top of his left thigh. A gurgled cry emerged from Mick's gagged mouth. Betty bent to check her shot then stepped back and swung again. Another red stripe appeared slightly higher up on Mick's right thigh. He groaned again.

'He's getting warmed up nicely now,' Betty said, 'and look at his cock.' Sure enough, Mick's penis no longer hung disconsolately but was growing visibly and thrusting up under the stool. His ball sac had tightened too.

'Very good,' Joyce said, 'he's getting excited. Now it's my turn. I've really been looking forward to using this.' She picked up the whip. The knotted end dangled five feet from the raised handle.

'Do you know how to use it?' Edith asked.

'I've been practising,' Joyce said, confidently striding up beside the punishment stool. She stood a few feet from Mick's rear drew back her arm and swung her hand. The whip cracked and Mick yelped and jerked, even making the heavy stool shake. A new thin red line snaked across his buttocks.

Eileen got on to her knees and crawled to the stool. She reached out a finger to trace the pattern of red wheals on Mick's bottom. There was much less flesh than on a female posterior. The marks clearly identified the instruments that had been used. Her finger followed the wide band of the tawse, the long straight line of the cane, the short dark lines of the crop and the narrow curved path of the whip. Her fingers slipped into the crack between his buttocks drawn apart by the bonds holding his thighs to the wooden legs. Her finger circled his anus and she felt him tense. Air whistled as he exhaled through the gag. Eileen withdrew her hand.

'Are you going to give him some more?' she asked.

'Oh, I think another round will do, don't you,' Joyce said.

Edith stepped forward and delivered a blow with the tawse. Susan swung the cane and Betty wielded the crop. Finally Joyce lashed him. Each blow raised a muffled cry from Mick and he rocked the stool.

Eileen examined the results. Now his bum was criss-crossed with red stripes but even more interesting was his cock, fully erect, quivering with pent-up enthusiasm between the wooden uprights. She grabbed his ball sac with her right hand and pulled it back. His cock swung down and she took hold of it in her left hand. Gripped tightly the swollen knob glowed a different shade to his abused buttocks, more purple than red. She massaged the shaft as she would a cow's udder, her little finger flicking across the glans. It would not be long now, she guessed, because Mick was panting, his breath emerging from the gag with a sound resembling a steam kettle. She squeezed his testicles and tugged on his cock. A torrent of milky fluid poured out, pooling on the carpet. Eileen froze with both of her hands clenched tight, feeling the pulsations.

'Well,' she said, letting go of the slack penis and testicles, 'I think we've proved the value of discipline in providing pleasure. What's next?'

Chapter Eleven
Screen Stars

'What gives you pleasure when you are having sex?' Joyce asked the other four members of the Ladies' College for Erotic Arts. There was no reply for many moments. Just the tiny sound of a tongue lapping broke the silence. Eventually Susan, who was laid out naked on the bed, answered.

'I like it when someone is taking time to caress and excite me, particularly my breasts.'

'You mean like Mick is doing now?' Joyce said. The young man's tongue was circling around a nipple and a hand caressed the curve of the other breast.

'Yes. I could lie here for hours while he did this, feeling a little tingle all the time.'

'Susan's right,' Betty said from the sofa, with Johnny kneeling on the floor between her knees, 'having someone who knows what to do and when to do it and is prepared to give the time to satisfying you rather than just ramming his penis in. That's what I call pleasure. Ooh, that's right, Johnny.' Johnny's head was almost invisible buried deep between Betty's fleshy thighs but he was obviously busy with his tongue.

'It is useful when a man, or a woman for that matter, understands what excites you,' Edith said, 'but new experiences, new people, new situations can also bring pleasure.'

'Like when we visited the brothel,' Joyce said.

'Yes, of course. That girl, Cherry, was very talented and knew exactly how to give pleasure.'

'Control or the lack of it, can add to pleasure, I find,' Eileen said, stroking Winston's cock as he lay on the thick carpet.

'What do you mean?' Susan said.

'Perhaps it's me, but I like doing this.' She pulled back the foreskin exposing the glistening purple knob. 'It excites me to know that I can let Winston come, or not, and he'll let me do it.'

'Take hold of any man's cock and he'll say that he'll do anything,' Edith commented.

'Yes, but it makes me excited too,' Eileen added, 'and it also works in reverse.'

'What do you mean?' Joyce asked.

'If I have no control at all, I seem to feel things more intensely. Like when you had Winston beat me. The spanks were painful but because I couldn't move or escape and because my fanny was exposed for everyone to see I got really hot.'

'Well, I'm never sure what is going to turn me on,' Joyce said sadly. 'Sometimes familiar things work and at other times they don't at all. Then something unexpected, like when we visited the strip club, really gives me a high.'

'I suppose that's the thing about being a woman; our needs can change by the minute,' Edith sighed.

'It's simple for a man,' Betty said, straining to spread her legs wider.

'What do you mean?' Eileen said.

'If they get an orgasm they're satisfied,' Betty explained.

'And their cocks will make them do anything to ensure they get it,' Joyce added.

'At least they can learn,' Edith said. 'If they give a woman what she needs they'll usually get what their cock wants.'

'We're lucky to have boys who are willing to give us what we want,' Betty said tapping Johnny's head lightly.

'Luck's got nothing to do with it,' Edith said firmly. 'A woman's greatest skill is to train a man to provide her needs while allowing them to think they are satisfying themselves.'

There was an unfamiliar trill like a birdcall.

'What's that noise?' Betty asked.

'Oh, it's my new phone. Such a strange sound,' Joyce said, jumping up from the sofa and leaving the room. The others listened trying to make out her conversation, dividing their attention from their forms of stimulation.

A few minutes later, Joyce returned looking smug.

'Well, that was a surprise,' she said.

'What was?' Eileen said, pausing from sucking on Winston's knob.

'We've been invited to visit a film studio.'

'A what?'

'Film studio?'

'What did you say?'

'What are you talking about?'

The men were forgotten. Susan sat up pushing Mick's head from her chest. Betty hauled herself up in the sofa releasing a panting Johnny from between her legs. Eileen let go of Winston's cock. For a few moments it remained solidly upright before slowly sagging to lean like a living Tower of Pisa. Edith stared at Joyce.

Joyce sat down on a sofa and took a deep breath.

'That was Mr Mount,' she said.

'And who, pray, is he?' Eileen asked.

'He owns the film studio.'

'Right, we've got that. Why has he invited us to his film studio?' Eileen persisted.

'Well, it seems that he's been talking to Mr Threadman.'

'Who on earth is Mr Threadman?' Edith chipped in.

'He was the man who ran that club we danced at,' Eileen explained.

'You mean – the sex club; the fat guy with the cigar?' Betty asked.

'That's it. Well Mr Threadman apparently told Mr Mount all about us and now he'd like to see us,' Joyce managed to get out at last.

'Mr Mount would like to see us?' Susan repeated.

'That's it.'

'When?' Edith asked.

'Well, I said next Wednesday, if we can all make it,' Joyce replied. 'Susan you're the one with the most trouble. Can you get away all day?'

Susan nodded but Edith spoke up again.

‘Just a minute, why does he want to see all of us? What has Threadman been telling him about us? What kind of films does he make?’

‘That’s a lot of questions, Edith,’ Eileen said.

‘Yes, but I think they need to be answered,’ Edith insisted.

‘He said he has a proposition for us,’ Joyce said, ‘I don’t know what Mr Threadman said and I don’t know anything about his films.’

‘I think I can guess,’ Susan said quietly. The others looked at her. ‘If he’s friends with the manager of the sex club then he probably makes porno films.’

‘Pornography!’ Edith exclaimed.

‘Ooh, how naughty,’ Betty giggled.

‘Of course,’ Eileen said with a smile on her face, ‘This could be interesting.’

They argued about what the proposition might be for quite a while but agreed that it would make an interesting day out. Winston was roped in as minibus driver again and they went on to discuss what they should wear as film stars for the day.

The film studio turned out to be an old warehouse down a back street in the city. When Eileen mentioned the name Mount a security man unlocked a padlock on the gate to let them drive through. Winston parked next to a Rolls-Royce and they got out in their summer dresses and high heels.

In a small reception office a young woman with a very low cut blouse welcomed them.

‘Mr Mount is expecting you. He said to let you straight through.’ She pointed to a door. Eileen led them through into a large, dark space. Dark, that is except for the dozens of spotlights on gantries casting their light on a spot in the middle of the warehouse. The five women, with Winston behind them, headed for the light.

Joyce realised that it was a film set, the interior of which looked like a Victorian house. There were a couple of false walls covered in dark wallpaper with curtains and paintings. There were well-upholstered chairs, an occasional table, a glass fronted cabinet and a chaise longue, and on the chaise longue knelt a woman in ankle boots, thick stockings, a corset and nothing else. Her large boobs hung down while her ample bottom was raised high. Behind her a naked man stood with his cock thrusting into her fanny. Beside them was another man with a camera on his shoulder. He crouched down so that the camera lens was just inches from the woman's buttocks.

'Pull back, Roger,' a voice from the shadows said, 'let's see that entry again.'

The naked man pulled his hips back, and Joyce had a glimpse of a thick, long penis. Then it was rammed forward again and the knob disappeared into the woman's swollen red crack.

'That's it, Roger. Now pump away,' the unseen voice said. 'Not too fast, we don't want you coming too soon. That's it; a bit more. Pull out when you're ready for the come shot.'

The camera remained close while the man fucked the woman energetically. The woman moved her hips to meet each thrust and made eager groaning noises. Then the man pulled back, the end of his cock came into view and spurted creamy white semen across the woman's arse.

'Cut. Very good, Roger. Thank you, Rose. Take a break everyone.'

The figures on the set quickly disappeared into the shadows but a tall man in his late thirties emerged from the darkness. He wore black jeans and a tight white T-shirt. He approached Joyce and the ladies.

'Good morning. You must be the girls from the Ladies' College,' he said warmly. 'Come and join me in my office.'

He led them to a cabin built within the warehouse. Behind them the lights on the set went out. Inside the cabin there was a desk, a sofa, a couple of chairs and a large television.

'Have a seat. I'll get us some drinks, will champagne do?' He lifted a phone and called for the drinks. Joyce chose an upright chair close to the desk. Edith, Susan and Betty sank into the sofa, Eileen sat on the arm of the sofa and Winston stood beside the door.

'I'm Parry Mount,' the man said, shaking hands with each of them as they announced their names. 'I'm so glad you could join us today.'

'You mentioned something about a proposition but you didn't give any details,' Joyce said.

'That's right. I wanted to meet you all to discuss an idea I had after talking with Threadman.'

'An idea?'

'Yeah, for a picture.'

'You make X-rated films,' Edith said. Mount looked at the women taking in her grey hair and wrinkled face.'

'Used to. Supplied most of the adult film clubs across the country.'

'What did we just see if it wasn't an X film?' Eileen asked mystified.

'Ah, that was a scene in one of our takes on Dickens. Great Ejaculations. Follows on from the Prickwick Capers and Martin Nuzzletwat. But it's not a film.'

'What do you mean?'

'Film's old hat. This is the future.' Mount lifted up a black plastic box that lay on his desk, 'Soon every home will have a Sony Betamax video tape player. The potential market is huge and I intend to be a leading player.'

'You expect people to watch pornographic films in their own homes?' Edith was sceptical.

'Well, not every home, but in the privacy of their own home with something as easy to purchase and carry as a book you'll be surprised how many people will sit down to watch an adult movie.'

'I can imagine men who live alone wanting to do that,' Betty said, 'but what about married men with women at home?'

'The male market is important, but I think couples will happily snuggle up on a sofa to watch a bit of nookie. That's why you're here.'

'Oh. Why?' Joyce asked.

'Well for that part of the market the material has to be, how shall I say? – female friendly. I gather from Threadman that you are a bunch of women who are up for anything.'

'Well, it's true that we are open to ideas concerning our pleasure, Mr Mount,' Eileen said, 'but what are you suggesting?'

'I was thinking of a feature about you girls and your Ladies' College for Erotic Arts. That's what you call yourselves isn't it?'

'That's right,' Joyce said.

'I was thinking of calling it *School for Scandal* and showing the things you get up to. What do you think?'

'We'd be paid for doing this?' Susan asked quietly.

'Oh, yes, darling. I'm willing to make a substantial offer.' Mount examined Susan thoroughly. 'You, darling, could earn a fortune in adult features.'

'There is one thing, though,' Edith said.

'Oh, what is that?' It was Mount's turn to look mystified.

'What women want from a sex film will be different to what men want.'

'How do you mean?'

'Men will be turned on by naked flesh and the sight of a woman being fucked. Like we saw just now. What was it you called it? The come shot?'

'Yeah, the ejaculation is the climax of a sex scene. Shows that it's real. Gets guys really turned on. So?'

'Well, women need more. They need to identify with the characters, empathise with them.' Edith was in full flow, 'A cock fucking a cunt may give a man an orgasm but it won't do a lot for me.'

'You're saying that women need more characterisation and back story.'

'I think that's it.'

'Well, ladies, I'm even more convinced that you're the ones for this job. You can explain yourselves to the camera and get the women behind you.'

The girls from the reception office arrived with a tray of glasses filled with fizzy liquid.

'Ah, here's the champagne, girls.' Mount leapt up and took two glasses from the tray, 'Grab a glass and let's go get some practice shots.' He took Susan's hand, pulled her to her feet and gave her a glass. He tapped her bottom and guided her towards the door. The others followed.

As they crossed the dark warehouse floor, Parry Mount called out, 'Camera, lights. Roger, get your arse on set now.' There was a succession of loud bangs as the spotlights flashed on.

'Stay here, ladies,' Mount said at the edge of the set as he guided Susan across the cables snaking across the floor and on to the carpet of the Victorian drawing room, 'Take your clothes off, darling,' he said to Susan.

Roger stepped on to the set from the other side, easing a silk dressing gown off his shoulders and revealing his bronzed, muscular torso and already stirring cock. Joyce noted that his pubes were smooth and hairless and even his balls seemed to have a sheen as if they had just been oiled like the rest of his body. She began to fume as she watched Mount help Susan out of her sundress. Like everyone else surrounding the set she gave a little gasp as it was realised that she was naked underneath with no bra or pants. Susan's face turned pink.

'I didn't expect to be undressing under lights,' she said coyly.

'It's fine, darling. I like a girl who's ready for business,' Mount said, stepping back off the set. 'Sit yourself on the couch. Roger will do the rest.'

Susan sat on the edge of the couch. Roger stepped forward his cock quivering with eagerness. He pushed Susan's shoulders back gently and she fell on to her back. Roger put his hands under her knees and lifted her legs. Her legs bent as her thighs were shoved against her breasts.

Joyce found herself staring into Susan's fanny, a deep, dark channel. Roger edged closer. The man with the video camera on his shoulder bent down focussing on the cock locating the route to pleasure. The swollen purple knob passed between the red folds of skin. Susan let out a small gasp.

Joyce felt growing disquiet. Was this what they wanted as the image of what The Ladies' College for Erotic Arts stood for? She was considering the thought when Edith, standing at her side, suddenly strode forward on to the set.

'This isn't what we're about,' she shouted, dragging her light summer dress over her shoulders and revealing her all-encompassing white bra, the corset with the stockings attached to the suspenders and the full white briefs.

The cameraman stood up and swung around focussing the camera lens on Edith.

'I don't think you took any notice of what we said,' Edith went on, placing a hand on Roger's shoulder and pulling him back, 'It's female pleasure we're studying, not providing holes for men to fill with their cocks.'

Edith pulled Roger back on to his knees then went around to his front and pushed him. He fell back onto the carpet. Edith stood over him, unfastening her suspenders, pulling her knickers down, kicking them off.

Joyce wondered what Roger was thinking looking up at Edith's thin, blonde-grey pubic hair and the flaps that guarded her pussy. Then Edith bent her knees and began to crouch. Joyce was always amazed at how supple she was despite her age. Her fanny descended lower and lower towards Roger's face. His eyes widened, his mouth opened, his tongue moistened his lips. Now Edith was kneeling, stretching her thighs wide and pressing her cunt lips to Roger's mouth.

'Show me what you can do, lover boy. Make my juices flow.' She rubbed her clitoris against his nose. He gulped and sucked. The camera swung low recording it all.

'He's obviously enjoying it,' Betty said, observing Roger's vertical erection. She too tugged her dress off and dropped her knickers. She stepped on to the set and stood astride Roger's abdomen. She lowered herself until her dangling pubic hair brushed the head of the penis.

'Get another camera in there,' ordered Parry Mount's voice from the shadows. Another camera wielding man stepped on to the rapidly filling set.

Betty lowered herself onto the thick, erect cock.

'Ooh, he's wide this one,' she gasped but continued to engulf the penis. Back to back the two women moved in unison, Edith rubbing herself against the man's face with increasing urgency, Betty sliding up and down on the pole that was Roger's penis. His heels pressed into the floor, his legs straight and rigid; his arms beside his body, his hands also pushing against the carpet as he tried to thrust his cock up into Betty's substantial belly. Muffled moans came from his mouth pressed against Edith's quim.

Both cameras circled and zoomed taking in the action occurring at both cunts.

'Record their faces,' Eileen urged, 'Edith's and Betty's faces. Their pleasure; it needs to be recorded.'

'Do as she says,' Mount called from the darkness. Both cameras were lifted up to capture the rapture shown on both women's faces as Roger shook with the ecstasy of orgasm. His arms and legs trembled involuntarily. Betty opened her mouth and shrieked.

'Oh, yes!'

Edith arched her back, her mouth formed into a broad smile.

'Yes, indeed,' she whispered.

'Can someone give me hand?' Betty said, 'I can't get up from here on my own.'

Eileen leapt to Betty's assistance, offering an arm to haul her to her feet. Roger's penis plopped out and flopped between his legs. Edith rose smoothly on to her feet and stepped away from the prone body.

Parry Mount ran on to the set.

'That was great stuff, ladies,' he said gushing over the two women.

'I'm sure Betty and I gave your cameras something to film,' Edith said, 'but do you get the idea? Sex is not just about a guy fucking a pretty girl.'

Mount nodded enthusiastically. 'Yes, yes, I see what you mean. Older women can enjoy sex too.'

'But you have to pay attention to the woman's pleasure,' Eileen said, 'Cocks are useful tools but a man can be used in many ways to give a woman pleasure.'

Mount looked thoughtful.

'Hmm. Perhaps you ladies have got a message to put across.'

'Do you still want to make your proposal?' Joyce asked joining the others in the fake Victorian drawing room.

'Yes,' Mount replied eagerly, 'You've made me think. I'm

sure you women could put together a sure-fire winner. Perhaps I should hand over the storyboarding to you.'

'Good. I think we can manage that, can't we girls?'

The other four women voiced their agreement.

'Where had you thought of filming us?' Joyce asked again.

'Well, I had thought here,' Mount said, 'All our films are made here, but if you've got a better idea.'

'Our premises are big enough for your cameras and lights and more suitable for our activities.'

'Right, let's sort out the details then.'

'And the fee?'

'Of course.'

The following week a large van drew into the Old School's former playground during the afternoon and three men unloaded video cameras, lights, stands, reels of cable and various other boxes. Joyce and Winston stood and watched as the equipment was set up in the hall. The curtains were drawn and the king-size bed and sofas bathed in dazzling light.

In the evening the ladies arrived one by one. Johnny and Mick arrived on their bicycles and Parry Mount drove up in his Rolls with Roger.

Everyone assembled in the hall sitting comfortably on the bed, sofas and thick carpet. Joyce addressed the film maker.

'Now, Mr Mount, we've put together a programme for you. We have been using a certain book as our guide to finding pleasure in sex and we would like to give you a pictorial summary of what we have found out. An A to Z of female pleasure if you like.'

'That sounds perfect. The cameras will record everything and we'll edit the footage afterwards.'

'Don't forget to watch the faces. Women like to know that all the female participants are not only willing but are enjoying the activities.'

'We discussed that before. The lads know what to do.'

'Right. Girls and boys let's get started.'

Parry Mount stood and retired into the shadows.

'OK. Action!'

Chapter Twelve
Eileen Has an Urge

The "trim phone" gave its bird-like trill and Joyce hurried from the kitchen to pick it up.

'Hello?' she enquired.

'Hi, Joyce, it's me, Eileen.'

'Hello, Eileen. Is there a problem?'

'No, I was just wondering if I could borrow Winston this afternoon. I'm going shopping and he could be, um, useful.'

'Oh, yes, I'm sure. I'm not using him. I'll put him on.' Joyce held the phone away from her ear and called out Winston's name. The big, dark-skinned man loped down the stairs, 'Eileen would like to speak to you,' Joyce said and handed him the handset which seemed tiny in his hands.

'Hello? Eileen?' Winston spoke as if unfamiliar with using the telephone.

'Oh, Winston, good. Look I'd like you to join me on a trip to the shops in town this afternoon. Is that OK?'

'Uh, yes, I suppose so,' Winston said, a bit mystified. He wasn't usually invited to join women on their shopping outings.

'Good. I'll pick you up at two-thirty. Oh, and no knickers.'

'What?'

'Don't wear pants under your jeans.' The phone went dead and Winston was left holding the handset in front of his face, staring at it.

They parked in the town centre car park. Eileen dropped the car keys into the pocket of her short, white, shiny PVC mac. She did not have her handbag with her, Winston noted. They set off along the side roads that led to the High Street.

'Why are you wearing a raincoat?' Winston asked as they walked side by side.

'I thought it might rain,' she replied glancing up. It was a warm day, typical of August, but with a few white, fluffy clouds in the sky. 'Let's have a drink before we start,' she added.

They turned into a cafe, purchased two cups of coffee and collected a couple of tiny sealed cartons of milk. Eileen led them to the back of the long, narrow room and sat at one of the high backed booths. Winston placed his cup and saucer on the table and sat opposite her.

'You must be hot wearing that plastic mac,' Winston said, after sipping his steaming coffee.

'There is a reason for it,' Eileen answered. She undid the top button and leaned towards the table. The lapels stretched apart as her breasts moved forward. Winston saw the curves of her cleavage. Surely he shouldn't be seeing so much of Eileen's breasts. Then he realised. There was no bra confining Eileen's bosom, indeed no blouse or T-shirt or even a vest to be seen.

'You haven't got anything on,' he said astonished.

'Shh, don't let everyone know.' Eileen glanced around but the only other customers were sitting in the window seats a long way from them and the two servers were busy behind the counter.

'What about, um, lower down?' Winston whispered.

'No, nothing, not a thing. Just this raincoat. What about you? Did you do what I said? Undo your fly.'

Winston had become used to doing the bidding of the ladies so without hesitation he placed his cup back on its saucer and lowered his hands beneath the table. He found the zip fastener and eased it down over the bulge between his legs. There was a small clunk which he recognised as a shoe falling from a foot onto the tiled floor and then he felt a pressure on his knees pushing his legs apart.

Eileen's foot crawled up his thigh and pressed against his crotch. He looked at her. She was staring at him, her pupils flickering as she searched his face for emotion. Winston swallowed. Eileen's big toe wriggled, rubbing against his genitals through the thick denim until it found the gap between the two sides of the zip. He drew in a breath suddenly as he felt the skin of her toes against his penis and testicles. There was nothing he could do to prevent his erection growing. His penis unfolded, forcing its way out through the gap in his flies. He felt the air on his knob.

Eileen's big toe rubbed along the length of his shaft encouraging it to extend fully and harden. Her rubbing pulled his foreskin back and he could feel his swollen glans quivering. It bumped against the underside of the table. Wilson trembled with the tension. Much more of this and he could feel that he was going to spurt and spray come over the cafe floor.

Eileen's foot moved away.

'That's good,' she murmured. 'I don't want you to come here. You can put it away now.'

Winston let out the breath he was holding with an almost audible sigh. The feeling of relief was as if he had ejaculated. His cock sagged and slowly shrank. With some difficulty Winston stuffed it back inside his trousers and carefully pulled the zip up. One or two snags on hairs and the loose skin of his scrotum made him wince but eventually he was satisfied that he was decent again.

Eileen drained her cup and replaced the cup in its saucer.

'Right, it's time we got started. Now make sure you do what I say. No questions; just do it. OK?'

'What are we doing?'

'No questions I said. Just follow my instructions.'

Eileen did up the top button of her coat, got up and walked out of the cafe. Winston followed and noticed that she smiled sweetly at the young man who had served them. Back in the street she strode purposefully along the pavement. Winston was careful to keep close to her, just half a step behind.

They turned into the large department store. Eileen seemed to wander aimlessly among the counters of perfumes and cosmetics, amongst the women's clothes, upstairs through the kitchen utensils and on to the top floor. They lingered a little in the soft furnishings before they finally entered the displays of furniture in room settings. Lounge, dining rooms and bedrooms were separated by thin chipboard partitions showing off the sofas, tables, chairs, cabinets, dressing tables, wardrobes and beds in real-life contexts.

They reached a bedroom at the heart of the display. There was a king size divan style bed with a brown fake fur cover. There were partitions on all four sides with just a couple of door sized openings leading to adjacent rooms. Eileen unfastened the top button of her raincoat.

'Get your trousers down,' she said, undoing the second button.

'What?'

'Drop your jeans,' she undid the third and last button and threw the coat off her shoulders. It fell to the floor. She kicked off her shoes.

Eileen was naked. Winston's eyes opened wide

'Quickly, we won't have long.' She leapt on to the bed, lay flat on her back and spread her legs. Her hands rubbed her crotch pulling her labia apart

Winston stared at her fanny. The channel was red and swollen and already glistening with the juices flowing from her crack. It was as if his brain suddenly got into gear. So this was what it was all about; she wanted him to fuck her here, now, in this shop. He reached for his belt, unfastened it, undid the brass button, pulled the zip down. Already his cock was straining for release. He pushed the jeans down his thighs. His balls swung free and his cock sprang out.

Eileen stretched out her hands towards him.

'Now! Quick! Fuck me,' she urged. She raised her knees and pulled them back raising her pussy to him. She pushed her thighs wide. Winston stared into the gaping dark chasm and felt the rush of blood that made him flush. He knelt on the bed, his trousers around his knees. He pulled his foreskin back and leaned forward. His knob touched the shining, wet cunt.

Eileen gasped, 'Yes! Do it.' Winston shoved his pelvis forward and his cock slid into the crack. He supported himself on his arms either side of her tits and looked down seeing his shaft disappear. He glanced at Eileen. Her eyes were fixed on his penis, watching as he entered her. He pushed in until his balls slapped against her perineum. She arched her back and her mouth opened in a silent cry. She began to rock.

'Come on. Finish it,' she urged. Winston moved his hips and thighs backwards and forwards. His cock withdrew and thrust in again and again. He felt it thicken, harden, fill her hole. She was breathing in rapid pants as she moved to his increasing tempo.

Just a few more thrusts and the contractions began, sending a wave of pleasure through his abdomen and up to his skull. The tide of semen spurted from his cock.

'What's going on there?' The voice came from one of the rooms nearby. Winston leapt backwards, his cock, still almost firm, flopping from the hole. His feet found the floor and he stood up. His hands fumbled for his trousers pulling them up his thighs.

'My coat! Pick it up,' Eileen shouted. Winston bent, one hand gripping the waistband of his trousers the other reaching for the PVC mac.

'Hey! What are you doing?' The voice was closer, in the next room. Winston headed for the exit on the opposite side and began to run. He ran and he ran.

Eileen crawled off the bed, got to her feet. Spunk trickled down her thigh. Winston was already gone. She went to follow him.

'Good heavens. She's got no clothes on.'

Eileen didn't look at the owner of the male voice, but he was in the bedroom display, just behind her. She ran this way and that, around beds and sofas and dining tables. She didn't know where she was going she was just trying to keep ahead of her follower. His cries were just behind her, she could hear his intakes of breath. Now there were two voices, two pairs of shoes stomping on the floor.

She reached the last of the rooms; ahead was the open floor of the carpet department. Now she could run in a straight line but more people were shouting and chasing her from the left and in front. Eileen turned to the right. Her foot caught on the edge of a heap of fluffy rugs. She sprawled forwards arms and legs flailing.

She landed on the soft rugs, rolled on to her back, started to get up but they were on her. Arms reached for her, grabbing her arms, grasping her legs, feet, thighs. An arm encircled her waist. Hands fell on her breasts and were withdrawn as if she was burning. She was lifted up, carried, arms and legs spread. She wriggled but the arms and hands held her firmly. There was talking, shouting, exclamations.

Then she was in a small room. She was lowered to the floor on her back. The arms and hands left her. She struggled to get to her feet and make her escape but they clustered together backing out through the narrow door.

'Keep her here.'

'Call the police.'

'Lock the door.'

They shouted at each other as they squeezed through the doorway. The door was pushed shut and Eileen heard a key turn in a lock. It was quiet.

She looked around herself. They had dumped her in a small store room. There were piles of boxes some of which were open revealing reams of receipt and order forms. There was a single light bulb hanging, unshaded, from the ceiling, but no windows. The floor was covered by thin, ribbed carpet and there was no furniture at all.

Eileen sat down again on the floor leaning against the pile of boxes. She tucked her knees up under chin and wrapped her arms around her legs. This was not supposed to happen. After they had fucked, she and Winston were supposed to have got dressed quickly and made their escape from the store. Had he got away? What would he do? She hoped he had her coat with her purse and car keys and that he'd drive back to Joyce. The store security may treat him roughly if they caught him – a man acting indecently and from an immigrant family as well. She suddenly realised that she might have got Winston into a lot of trouble. They'd be gentler with a woman, wouldn't they? She hoped Winston was safe. It was her predicament she had to find a way out of. She didn't have any ideas. She was naked. She had no identification on her. Perhaps staying silent was her best move, at least until she could work something out.

Minutes passed. No one opened the door. Eileen sat rocking slightly. It had been fun though. She recalled the pleasure of Winston's entry into her, the frenzied lovemaking and her orgasm at the moment that Winston's balls had emptied inside her. Her fanny felt wet. She realised that Winston's semen was still dripping out of her. She shuffled her position and grinned when she saw the large sticky, damp patch she had made on the carpet. Whatever they did to her she would have the memory of having sex in the shop.

There was a fumbling in the door lock. The door opened and a young policeman entered. The door closed behind him. He stood by the door and looked down at her. He wore a cap rather than a helmet. That means he has a car, Eileen thought, he isn't a bobby on his beat.

'Well, what do we have here?' he said in a kind of sigh. Eileen decided to keep quiet and anyway it was hardly a question that deserved a reply.

'Giving the beds a bit of a try out, were we?' That too didn't require an answer.

'Looking for the most comfortable, were we?' He grinned at his attempt at a joke. Eileen treated him to a thin smile.

'Where's your boyfriend, love?' Obviously she couldn't answer that but the question suggested that Winston had got away. She didn't reply.

'What's your name, darling?' She wasn't going to answer that. She must remain anonymous for as long as possible. There was no way they could identify her if she kept quiet – not unless they examined her teeth and checked dental records, but that would take days. Nevertheless she ought to make some response before he became upset.

'Sorry, love, can't tell you that,' Eileen said with a smile.

'Ah, at least you can talk.' The policeman crouched down so that he was at the same level as her. She saw him examining what he could see of her body. She tightened her arms around her legs.

'Having a bit of fun, were we? A bit of exotic sex. Did he put you up to it? Doing it in public?'

Eileen smiled. Most of his deductions were correct except it was her urge not Winston's. He could be a detective one day.

'Possibly,' she said adopting a coquettish tone. He rocked back on his bottom and crossed his legs. Eileen relaxed her arms lowering her knees into cross-leg, lotus position, revealing her breasts and crotch. Despite her being considerably older she was pleased to see that the young policeman's eyes widened as he took in parts of her naked flesh.

'You know you shouldn't do that, don't you?' he said. To which bit was he referring, Eileen wondered. 'You know, public indecency is a criminal offence.' Ah, it was that.

'I know,' Eileen said sounding as contrite as she could, 'I don't know what came over me. I couldn't resist doing it.'

'Do you often come shopping wearing nothing but a coat? You were seen wearing a white plastic coat.'

'No, Officer, it's not something I make a habit of.'

'Well I'm glad to hear that. A woman like you shouldn't put herself at, um, risk.'

'A woman like me?'

'Well.' Eileen noticed a flush creeping up from the collar of his jacket. 'I can see you are a mature woman but one that is, er, still attractive.'

Eileen graced him with a broad smile, wriggled a little to make her breasts wobble and relax her legs a little.

'Thank you, Officer, you are kind.' The blush rose into his cheeks.

'I think I had better get you out of here and take you to the station for questioning.'

'Oh good. I was beginning to think I was going to be left here in the hands of the store security.'

'No. You have committed a public order offence and so it is my responsibility. I'll get them to give you something to cover yourself with, then we'll go to my car.' He got to his feet, went to the door, opened it a crack and called out. He spoke quietly to someone and then waited in silence as a minute or two passed. A hand thrust a grey blanket into his. He turned and gave it to Eileen.

It was a rough woollen blanket of the sort that might be used to cover furniture during a removal. Eileen stood up, unfolded the blanket and wrapped it around her.

'Are you going to arrest me?' she asked.

'We'll caution you down at the station,' the young officer replied.

'What if I try to escape? Shouldn't you handcuff me?'

Their eyes met and some kind of understanding passed between them.

'I suppose I should.' He unclipped the handcuffs that dangled from his belt. Eileen held out her hands with her wrists close together. The blanket slipped down her arms revealing the top half of her breasts again. He clipped the metal rings around each wrist, the chain preventing Eileen from separating them by more than three or four inches. He tugged the blanket up on her shoulders then pushed her towards the door.

There was just one man outside the storeroom. He wore a suit with an engraved badge that marked him as the floor manager.

'Are you going to charge her?' he asked as soon as they passed through the door.

'I am taking her to the police station for questioning,' the officer replied in a formal voice. 'We'll let you know if charges are made.'

'She's disgusting. Fornicating in public. She should be locked up – and the man she was with.'

'That will be for the courts to decide, sir. Now if you please, show us to the staff entrance. We don't want to create any more disturbances being seen by members of the public.'

'Oh, no, of course. This way.'

The manager strode off with Eileen behind and the policeman by her side holding her elbow. They passed through a door on to a stairwell with narrow, tiled stairs and a steel banister. The police officer held Eileen firmly as they travelled down. The steps were cold on Eileen's feet. At the ground floor the manager stood by a door that opened on to a loading area. The police car stood a few yards away. Eileen was rather disappointed. It wasn't a Jaguar or even a Rover or Ford Cortina but a small Austin Allegro painted in pale blue and white.

'It's a panda car,' she said sadly.

'I'm sorry if you expected something grander or speedier, but it's what they give us to get round our beat,' the officer said with a tone of regret.

The tarmac was rough on the soles of Eileen's feet but it was just a few paces to the police car. The manager remained at the door watching them. The police officer opened the rear door and helped Eileen into the seat. She shuffled to make herself comfortable on the cloth seat and rested her handcuffed arms on her lap. The policeman closed the door and went around the car to get into the driver seat. He took off his cap and placed it on the passenger seat then looked around at her, smiled when he saw that she was comfortable, turned and started the engine.

'Right. Off to the station then,' he said.

'Do we have to?' Eileen said. 'I feel embarrassed covered just with this old blanket.'

The policeman laughed.

'That's wonderful coming from someone who was happy to strip naked and have sex in the middle of a department store.'

'That was different. Having sex is pleasurable. Being marched into a police station is not.'

'Hmm. Well, I suppose we could get you dressed before going to the station. Where's your home?'

Eileen named a village some way out into the countryside.

'That's quite a way,' the officer said.

'It doesn't take long. I'll direct you,' Eileen said chirpily.

'OK then.' The police officer put the car into gear and they drove out on to the road.

Eileen directed them out of the town and then down narrower and narrower lanes until they were driving along a track barely the width of the car with grass growing in the middle of the road.

'Are you sure, this is the way?' The policeman asked as they stopped at a gate at thc cntrancc to a woodland.

'Well, we might have taken a wrong turning somewhere,' Eileen replied. The police constable turned in his seat to glare at Eileen. The blanket had fallen from her shoulders and with her hands on her knees her top half was uncovered. Eileen smiled sweetly, rolling her shoulders back so that her breasts rose. He was mesmerised by the firm, dark, nipples that she thrust towards him.

'You did that deliberately, didn't you?' he said.

'What? Got us lost?'

'No. Showing me your tits. What are you after?'

'What could I possibly want other than my freedom,' Eileen replied holding up her bound hands, 'I don't want my neighbours to see me with these on.'

'You practically asked me to cuff you.'

'Well, I'd like them off now. Can't you unlock them?'

'Of course. The key's here.' He took a bunch of keys from his jacket pocket.'

'Please,' Eileen wheedled.

'Well, all right.' He got out and moved around to the rear door, opened it, put one knee on the seat and bent over towards Eileen. He inserted the key in the lock on each wrist and released Eileen's arms.

'Thank you,' she said. 'Now perhaps I can release you.' She leaned over and quickly and expertly undid the waistband of his trousers and lowered his zip.

'Hey!' he called, but it was too late. His trousers were down and Eileen's hand was cupping his testicles. She tugged drawing him towards her. Before he could recoil, her other hand whipped his white, policeman's underwear down and grabbed the growing cock. She pulled him towards her while wriggling in the seat to shed the blanket and turn to face the policeman. She spread her legs, hooked one over the back of the rear seat and the other over the driver's seat. She was pleased to see that his eyes were grabbed by the tuft of hair between her legs and the red slash.

'Come on my Bobby. You know you want it,' she whispered, while rubbing the end of his cock with her thumb and massaging his balls. The response was satisfying. The penis grew and swelled in her hand. He dropped the handcuffs beside her and scrambled on to the seat resting his knees between her thighs.

'Suck my tits,' she urged, 'they need a bit of attention.' His head lowered and his mouth enclosed her nipple. Eileen was surprised at how her body reacted. It was as if she hadn't been touched for days. The sensation rippled from one breast to the other, down to her crotch and up to the top of her head. She felt the muscles in her vagina clenching. He turned his attention to her other breast and more delicious feelings coursed through her. She kept rubbing his cock, feeling its firmness and an increasing slickness to the knob. She directed it down to her crack and he responded willingly. She inserted the tip into her hole then released it and grasped his buttocks. She pulled and his cock slid in. Eileen gasped.

'Yes. That's it, Copper. Give it to me.' As a good officer he obeyed the authoritative order and began to thrust. Eileen found herself unable to contribute much to the movement with her heels hooked out of the way but the policeman was energetic enough for both of them. The seat springs squeaked as the car rocked to their rhythm. Eileen delighted in the thick rod sliding in and out of her tunnel and his balls slapping against her arse. He was young, experienced but very eager. Eileen gasped as she felt him explode inside her. He groaned and began to subside on to her. She reached behind her head feeling for the catch of the door. Found it, tugged. The door opened and she pushed her feet against the other side of the car. She shot backwards tumbling out of the car as the policeman collapsed.

Eileen was on her feet. She leapt over the gate and ran into the trees. She kept on running across a carpet of soft pine needles, deeper and deeper into the wood. There were no sounds of a chase but she dared not pause to look behind until she was quite out of breath. She hid behind a thick trunk, panting hard and looked around. There was nothing to see except trees. There was no birdsong and no noise of a rampaging, angry policeman. She waited until she had recovered, looked again then set off at a fast walk. A few minutes later she came to a path which she followed right up to the gate at the back of the Old School.

Joyce answered the knock on the door. Her mouth dropped open.

'Don't keep me here, someone may see,' Eileen pushed past her into the hallway.

'Eileen! Where are your clothes?'

'I haven't got any. Is Winston here?'

'Yes, he got back over an hour ago in your car. He wouldn't say where you were.'

Winston appeared at the bottom of the stairs. His face was creased with worry.

'You got away,' he said.

'Eventually.'

'Got away from where?' Joyce asked, 'What have you two been up to?'

'Get me a cup of tea and a dressing gown and I'll explain,' Eileen said, taking herself into the lounge and falling onto the sofa.

'Really, Eileen, what is it with you?' Joyce sighed as Eileen finished her tale, her tea cold in its cup, 'Why do you have to do all these risky escapades?'

'I don't know, but have you seen that Woody Allen film?'

'Bill and I never went to see any of his films. Which one do you mean?'

'*Everything you wanted to know about sex* – or something.'

'I think I've heard of it. What's it got to do with you?'

'I saw the film a couple of years ago and one scene is about a woman who only gets an orgasm when she has sex in a public place.'

'Such as a shop.'

'Yes. Well, you know it takes a lot for me to have an orgasm so it's stuck with me. I wanted to see if it would work.'

'And did it.'

'Oh, yes. It was a quick fuck and no time for pleasuring all the senses but when Winston came, I did too.'

'Good for you. But in the film, did the woman get arrested'

'Well, no, not really.'

'So, having sex in public is more risky in real life than in films.'

'Sadly, I suppose it is,' Eileen said, biting her lip.

Chapter Thirteen
The Mistress

Joyce was in heaven. Not the sort of heaven she had been taught about at her school many years ago. This wasn't a vast white place filled with chanting angels and hordes of people shouting hallelujah. No, this was her own personal heaven of wave after wave of delicious sensations travelling from her abdomen to the back of her head and she wanted it to last for eternity.

She shouldn't really be comfortable, flat on her back on the thick rug with her thighs drawn back and her calves resting on Mick's shoulders, her toes touching behind his head – but she was. She couldn't move; Mick was doing all the work, but she had felt in control. Well, up to the point when her orgasms had started.

Mick had proved to be a good learner. He had lost the excitability of inexperience and now was prepared to use his stamina to satisfy her. He rocked up and down on his knees, slipping his delicious long cock in and out of her vagina; but it was more than just that. He twisted and rotated his hips so that his hard knob struck each of her pleasure points. Meanwhile his hands caressed her breasts, his fingers tweaking her nipples.

He was beginning to breathe in short pants. Joyce knew that not even a fit, young man like Mick could keep up this effort for more than a few minutes let alone for ever. She decided to allow him to come.

'Yes!' she cried, 'finish it!'

She wriggled her bottom from side to side and exercised her newly acquired control over her vaginal muscles. It's amazing what regular sex does for muscle development, she thought. As

Mick thrust, she squeezed. It was all he needed. The extra friction brought him to his climax. Joyce had the additional experience of paradise gained as she felt him spurt inside her.

The doorbell rang. Joyce groaned but was in no mood to terminate her enjoyment to leap up.

'Can someone get that?' she called in a wavering voice. She heard mutters and feet moving. Slowly the trembling in her fanny subsided. Mick pulled out and rocked back on his heels, his cock flopping on to his thigh. He took hold of her ankles and gently lowered them to the floor. He sat there panting. Joyce folded her legs under her and pushed herself up on her arms.

Winston entered the hall followed by two extraordinary characters. Joyce glanced around and saw that all her friends were staring at the visitors. She looked too, taking in their striking appearance.

First was a woman with short black hair cut in a severe fringe. She had bright blue eye shadow and dark red, almost black, lipstick on her full lips. She wore a full-length leather coat despite it being a warm late August. The coat, however, was open, revealing shiny, black boots that reached up to her thighs contrasting with the naked white skin above them. Her torso was encased in leather moulded to her full bosom, squeezing her middle and forming a sharp V down to her crotch. There was a wide belt around her waist with a big silver buckle and various rings from one of which a bunch of keys dangled. On her pubis was a silver ring attached to a zip. She looked tall, but that may have been her high heels, and she was young, barely into her thirties, Joyce guessed. In her gloved right hand she held the leather loop of a lead that was attached by a chain to the thick leather collar fastened snugly around her companion's neck.

The companion had a completely different appearance. She looked about the same height but was also wearing high heels. These were part of golden sandals fastened around the girl's ankles by straps with small brass padlocks. She had bare, pale, smooth legs and a skirt of frayed, worn denim so short that it barely covered her slim hips and bottom. Her translucent pink, nylon blouse revealed that a corset was at least partly responsible for her narrow waist. Her breasts were contained by a plain white bra which Joyce found surprisingly modest, considering the rest of her dress, as it revealed no cleavage whatsoever. Her bare arms were restrained behind her back. Were they tied or locked in handcuffs, Joyce wondered. Her head was fascinating. A pale face with long black eyelashes and pink lipstick was surrounded by a cascade of blonde curls tied with little pink bows. Large gold rings pierced her ear lobes.

In the moments that Joyce took all this in she got to her feet. Both the guests seemed oblivious to her nakedness with no emotion showing on their faces.

'You must be …' Joyce began.

'The Mistress,' the leather-clad woman interrupted.

'Yes. Mrs Glover did say that was your title when I asked for her advice about bondage. May I take your coat for you? It's quite warm isn't it.' Joyce found she was talking for the sake of it not wanting to take her eyes off their two guests. The Mistress took off the coat revealing kid gloves covering her arms beyond her elbows. She passed the lead from hand to hand and gave the coat to Winston.

'Please, take a seat,' Joyce said, indicating a vacant sofa. The Mistress lowered herself carefully, sitting upright on the squashy cushions. She crossed her legs giving Joyce a flash of the silver zip that circled her crotch.

'And this is …?' Joyce asked nodding at the timid companion at the end of the chain.

'Daisy, my slave,' The Mistress replied without hesitation, giving a tug on the lead. Daisy folded her legs to sit at her feet on the floor. Joyce was impressed that she could move so gracefully despite her very high heels and her wrists fastened behind her back. 'She knows her place,' The Mistress added.

Joyce sat at the other end of the sofa and her fellow members of the Ladies' College for Erotic Arts took up positions on the other two sofas with the men on the floor. It amused Joyce to note that their guests were the only clothed ones present, not counting Edith's basque.

'Bondage is just one of my skills,' The Mistress said in her quiet but powerful voice, 'It is just one aspect of the art of domination.'

'Mrs Glover did mention that and said that you have trained some of her girls.'

'That is true.'

Joyce could see Susan eager to say something.

'You are a dominatrix,' she blurted out.

The Mistress smiled.

'That term is used, but I find it rather a clumsy word. I prefer Mistress not in the sense of being courted by a man but as a woman in authority, with power and knowledge.'

'And you exercise that power over Daisy,' Eileen said with, Joyce noted, a gleam in her wide-eyes.'

'Amongst others,' The Mistress replied.

'You have more slaves?' Edith asked.

'Oh yes. I have many. Some come to me for a few hours, a few days, a few weeks. Others I keep for longer. Daisy is one of my two indefinites.'

'Indefinites?' Betty said.

'Yes, they are mine until I tire of them or someone makes me an offer which it would be disadvantageous to refuse.'

'Don't they have a choice?' Eileen asked.

'Daisy and the other have been presented to me for an indefinite period. As my slaves they do not have choices. Temporary slaves are contracted for a fixed period during which time they are mine to deal with as I wish.'

'Dealing with your slaves gives you pleasure?' Joyce wondered what these contractual arrangements had to do with erotic pleasure such as she had felt a few minutes before.

'Indeed yes. Domination is all about control. I enjoy being in control. Training my slaves to perform as I wish gives me great pleasure both mentally and, ah, sexually. The mental pleasure is akin to exercising any skill well, such as training a dog or a horse.'

'You consider dominating your slaves to be like training a horse?' Edith looked flushed and attentive.

'Of course. We forget that humans are animals. I keep humans like other people keep dogs and cats and parrots and horses. Not as pets mark you, but as animals that have some purpose like sheep dogs or guide dogs or horses trained in dressage or to pull a carriage.'

'But humans are people. We are intelligent.' Betty was indignant.

'It is only a matter of degree. I have known some extremely intelligent dogs. Nevertheless it is true that humans need particular treatment in order to train them for whatever purpose is desired.'

'How do you train one of your slaves?' Joyce said wondering if it was a question she dared ask.

The Mistress was quiet for a moment. She uncrossed her legs and passed the lead from her left to her right hand. Daisy was looking up at her expectantly.

'It varies from one subject to another of course. They each have different characteristics, different inhibitions, different pressure points. Of course being human they are able to understand instructions and can easily learn by example but getting their complete obedience requires the use of three techniques.' She paused to take a breath and compose herself. Joyce and the other ladies leaned forward to listen.

'First there is restraint; bondage if you like. Removing a subject's freedom to move any part of their body, or to perform bodily functions, or the ability to use their senses; these give the Master or Mistress immediate control. Restraint provides a constant reminder that the slave no longer has the right to make choices. Release may be a reward for performing some task or merely at the whim of the controller.'

Joyce looked at Daisy sitting on the floor with her wrists bound and the chain fastened to her neck resting in The Mistress's hand.

'Daisy is being trained?' she said.

'Oh, yes. She has been mine for over two years and she has taken her training well but while she is under my control there will still be more she has to learn and I will keep her under restraint especially when we are out like tonight.'

'Two years,' Susan gasped.

'Yes. It was difficult at first. We had to start from the

beginning – no movement, no senses, removal of control of her bodily processes. But that was a long time ago. Now she does what I ask of her and she is learning new skills.'

'You said there were three techniques,' Eileen prompted.

'Ah, yes. The second is discipline. You probably know what I mean.'

Eileen certainly did. She recalled the spanking she had received.

'You beat your slaves,' Betty said with a note of horror in her voice.

'I don't like the word "beat". It sounds as if it is carried out with anger on the spur of the moment. Discipline is not like that. It is planned and controlled. The point is that pain can be used to alter behaviour. If you touch something that is hot, the pain teaches you not to touch it again. Using a crop or whip or electricity judiciously can bring about the desired behavioural change in the slave. It is very effective I can assure you. Isn't it, Daisy?' The slave nodded.

'And the last method?' Joyce asked.

'That can loosely be described as humiliation; removing the slave's dignity. Dignity or pride is the great inhibitor. It holds people back from new experiences and in the case of slaves makes them disobedient. Simply it means placing them in situations that they have not chosen for themselves, often partly or wholly naked or in bizarre costumes that may accentuate their genitalia. We often dream of being in a public place without our clothes and are embarrassed. In training a slave it happens for real.'

Joyce noticed that Eileen's face had turned a bright red. She knew all about being naked in public.

'Alternatively, it can mean offering the slave for the sexual pleasure of others in ways that they may not have experienced or desired. Or they can be made to perform chores, that they may consider beneath them, in a humiliating manner.'

The Mistress paused and Joyce realised that she had not offered any refreshment. She signalled to Winston to bring drinks and he departed to the drinks cabinet in the shadows at the end of the hall.

'You've listened to me enough,' The Mistress said, 'I'm sure you want to see some of the results of training.'

The ladies nodded and Joyce wondered what The Mistress intended.

'Daisy has one very useful attribute,' The Mistress went on, 'Show them Daisy.'

The slave rose up on to her knees to face the ladies and stuck out her tongue. Joyce observed that it was remarkably long and at its tip it was pierced with a pair of small gold balls.

'Daisy's tongue is remarkably manipulative and can reach places few others can. I have trained her to make use of her extraordinary gift.'

'And the stud? What is that for?' Edith asked.

'Its purpose is two-fold. First as an instrument of restraint; I can clamp it and Daisy will be unable to move her head. Very useful if I want to keep her still. Secondly it provides extra friction. Would you like to see?' She reached down and unclipped the lead from Daisy's collar. 'Go on Daisy, show the lady what you can do.'

Daisy got to her feet and walked towards Edith. She knelt in front of her, with her wrists still locked behind her. She bent her head. Edith sensed what was required of her and parted her knees. Daisy pushed her head between her thighs. Edith gasped and lifted her hips, shoving her pelvis forward.

'Oh, gosh, yes,' she cried.

'What is it? Tell us,' Betty demanded.

'It's wonderful. I've never felt a tongue so deep. She's right inside me and yes those studs; they press in all the right places. Ooh …'

Joyce watched the rapture take Edith while the slave worked patiently at her crotch with just her mouth and that amazing tongue.

'She can do each of you, if you like,' The Mistress said, taking a glass from Winston's hand.

Edith sank back exhausted but by the look on her face, supremely happy. Daisy simply shuffled sideways to Betty and again bent to her task.

Joyce had a question that she was itching to ask.

'How did you get into this?'

The Mistress took another sip of her drink and smiled at Joyce.

'I felt the need to be in control and discovered I had a talent for it.'

'Oh.'

'That's a glib answer. The story is a bit more involved. I was top of my year at school, a first class graduate at university. I was confident, assured. At least I thought I was. Then I met a man. I felt we were in love. We had satisfying sex – this was the sexual revolution, after all. He gave me romantic presents. We got married and I thought I would be happy for ever. I wasn't. Once he had the certificate saying that I was his wife he changed. He wouldn't let me go out to work or meet my friends. He kept me short of money, shut up in his house.'

'How did he do that?'

'He kept me in chains. We'd got into a bit of light bondage before we were married, but afterwards I found myself locked up day and night. He would move me from room to room depending on the tasks he had for me.'

'How awful,' Joyce said.

'Then he began beating me and forcing me to have sex when he wanted it in ways that he chose.'

'How long did that go on for?' Eileen enquired.

'A couple of years. I had become subservient, compliant. I obeyed him meekly, completely.'

'What happened? How did you escape?' Joyce was intrigued.

'I discovered that he had taken a lover. On the evenings that he locked me in a cupboard with my hands and feet bound and mouth gagged, he was out playing the romantic with another woman. When I found out I was furious. I'd almost forgotten what it was like to have feelings. That's when I started to plan my escape. One evening I managed to get him so drunk that he became unconscious. I took his keys and got away.'

'What did you do?' Eileen asked.

'I had nothing. I certainly couldn't go to my parents' home – he'd find me. I went on the streets, sold myself. Madam Glover found me and realised that I had potential. I was adamant that I would be in control from then on. Madam supported me, helped me get an apartment where I began to offer bondage and training. Soon I was able to purchase my present house. It's on the edge of town, with a large secluded garden for outdoor activities, plenty of rooms and a cellar that provides a sizeable dungeon.'

Betty had been reduced to a quivering heap of blubber with a look of rapture on her face. Daisy moved on to Susan who opened her thighs readily. Joyce wondered how much Daisy enjoyed exciting women to orgasm.

'Was Daisy a lesbian when you, um, started to train her?' Joyce asked.

The Mistress laughed as if she had heard a good joke.

'I'm very pleased that my training is so successful. Daisy, stand up.'

The slave pulled back from Susan leaving the woman with a sad look on her face. Daisy stood and faced The Mistress.

'It's time for you to remove your clothes, Daisy,' The Mistress said, 'Turn round.'

Daisy did as she was told revealing the large padlock that passed through silver rings attached to a wide leather cuff around each wrist. The Mistress unclipped the bunch of keys from her belt, selected the appropriate key and removed the padlock. The slave swung her arms and rotated her hands rubbing each of her wrists. Then she stepped into the centre of the semicircle of sofas and faced the ladies. Looking at each in turn she began to unbutton her blouse, then slipped it from her shoulders. It floated to the floor. Then she tugged on the torn miniskirt, pulling it over her hips. It fell down her bare legs and she stepped out of it. Joyce was surprised to see that she was wearing large knickers of rather thick material that covered her buttocks and pubic area. Along with her bra they seemed rather lacking in sexual allure.

Reaching behind her, Daisy unclipped the bra, then held the cups and pulled them away from her chest. Joyce was not the only one to gasp. Daisy did not have breasts. The bra cups were filled with fake boobs. Her chest was hairless, smooth and manly. The truth came to Joyce like an electric shock, but Betty expressed it.

'Daisy's a man!'

Joyce looked at Daisy's smooth, made-up face and saw that her nose and jaw line were quite masculine and she had a prominent Adam's apple. They were features she hadn't noticed before, fooled as she was by Daisy's long, curly, bowed hair and feminine dress.

Daisy let the bra and rubber tits fall to the floor and began to roll down the hem of the heavy knickers. She or he (Joyce was unsure how to think of her now) tugged them down to her thighs and let them drop. Daisy stood before them, naked except for her high-heeled sandals, waist-clinching corset and dog collar. Her body was white and hairless and, given a quick glance, lacking in genitals. Then Joyce observed that her penis and testicles were tucked between her legs giving her an almost smooth crotch.

'How does she, he, I don't know which, keep her tackle out of sight?' Edith asked.

'Turn round and bend down,' the Mistress commanded. Daisy obeyed drawing another gasp from the ladies. Her buttocks and back were criss-crossed with a tracery of red lines, many faded but others darker and a half dozen still livid. Her arsehole was blocked by a silver sphere the size of a tennis ball and the pink knob of her penis had a gold ring through it which was attached by a padlock to another ring that passed through her perineum. Her testicles were squeezed between her thighs either side of her cock.

'She has been whipped – a lot,' Betty said.

'Yes,' The Mistress agreed, 'As I said, it is part of the training programme and Daisy can still be disobedient, even after two years. I discipline her from time to time. It's important to keep it a surprise and whip her when she least expects it.'

'Is that comfortable?' Susan asked, pointing to Daisy's contorted genitals

'I'm not interested in comfort,' The Mistress said indignantly, 'I said that restraint involves denial of control of bodily functions. Daisy pisses and craps when I allow it and she is not permitted to have an erection. She cannot pass as female with a prick and balls dangling to the fore so they must be out of sight and her anus must be stretched. Let me show you. Come here, Daisy.'

Joyce and the others watched open-mouthed as Daisy knelt on the floor with her backside to her owner. The gloved hand of The Mistress grabbed hold of the silver ball and tugged. There was resistance for a moment and Daisy tensed. Then with a slurp the ball moved and a silver dildo some eight inches long was drawn slowly out of the slave's anus. Daisy gasped as the tip emerged from her hole.

'There. That will go back in before we leave,' The Mistress said to her audience while placing the dildo on the floor. She selected another key from her bunch and reached between the slave's buttocks. She undid the padlock and released it from the perineal ring, then snapped it shut. The weight of the lock pulled the penis down, stretching it between Daisy's thighs. It swung backwards and forwards.

'Now, back to your task,' The Mistress said in her commanding voice. Daisy crawled to Susan and once again pushed her head between the young woman's legs. Joyce was surprised that the slave's penis hadn't become erect having been released from its confinement. It dangled, pulled taut by the heavy padlock, but not engorged. Then Joyce noted a thin gold ring underneath the circumcised knob. It constricted the shaft and would obviously cause considerable pain if the penis attempted to become erect. It was a clever device, Joyce thought, to ensure that the slave never became aroused.

'How did, ah, Daisy, come to be your slave?' Joyce asked, 'Was she a transvestite?'

The Mistress laughed.

'On the contrary. Daisy's femininity is a result of her training. A little over two years ago she was an arrogant, brash male with a very well-paid job. He was selfish and profligate with no regard for women other than to use them as a means to an orgasm. He was a regular at Madam Glover's. All he wanted from a woman was a cunt or mouth or arse to fuck.'

'He sounds a very unpleasant character,' Edith said.

'He was, but his luck changed. He lost his job. He had no real friends and no woman would go near him without payment. He was broken. Madam Glover suggested that if he wanted a fresh start he should come to me. I said I would only take him on if he contracted to be my slave indefinitely. He agreed and his training began. At first I deprived him of all movement and senses for a month. After that I was able to start building a new persona. Given his previous attitude to women I decided that he should learn what it was like to be one. That meant I had to deny him the pleasure of the male orgasm. Erections are not allowed. Strangely the humiliation of being dressed and paraded as a female quickly passed; he actually relishes being a woman. I've decided to let it go as far as it can. Perhaps soon he will have my permission to receive breast implants and to have the cock and balls that he no longer needs removed.'

Joyce and her friends listened in stunned silence except for the gasps and whimpers from Susan as she reached a body-shaking orgasm. Daisy withdrew and turned her attention to Eileen.

'But what was the dildo for?' Betty asked.

'Betty really! You're so naive. Ooh,' Eileen was interrupted by the insertion of Daisy's tongue into her vagina. Her face took on an angelic expression.

'Anal dilation is part of any slave's training,' The Mistress explained, 'First as part of the restraint programme it shows that I own the whole of the slave's body. The inside as well as the out. Then for humiliation. For most new slaves anal intercourse is outside their experience. Daisy was a straight male and had never contemplated being sodomised but as a female she had to experience being penetrated. Perhaps one of your men would like to demonstrate.'

Joyce looked at Johnny and noticed his cock twitch.

'Go on, Johnny. You know you'd like to.' she said. Mick shoved Johnny in the back urging him forward. The young man coated his growing penis with a liberal quantity of lube from a tube which happened to be lying nearby and then crawled to the rear of the slave who had not paused in his/her exploration of Eileen's cunt.

Johnny lined himself up with his knob at the gateway to Daisy's back passage. Then gently he thrust forward. There was a muffled groan from Eileen's crotch and Daisy arched her back pushing her buttocks back against Johnny's thighs.

'Oh, it's easy,' Johnny sighed as he sank his full length into Daisy's anus. He began a rhythmic piston movement. From the sounds that Eileen was making, the slave's tongue was continuing its work inside her.

The others watched intently, but Joyce turned to The Mistress.

'What type of people come to you to be made into slaves?'

'All sorts; men, women. There's something about giving up all control that attracts them. I even have married couples come to me for days or even weeks. They're bored with regular sex and want to spend some time without all the responsibilities of marriage. Some come back time after time.' Joyce was incredulous at this revelation.

'You said you had another, um, indefinite, slave?'

'That's right, a real girl. She was my first long-termer. I've had her four years now, since I had my first apartment. She had no family and a poor job that bored her to death but she was dreadfully shy and rigid and totally scared of sex. She's called the Slut now.'

'Oh! Where is she?'

'Back home, strapped to a frame, being fucked by six men. They'll be seeing to her until I get back.'

Next to Joyce, Johnny, Daisy and Eileen were grunting and crying in harmony. Johnny's buttocks tensed as he thrust into Daisy driving her head hard into Eileen's fanny. Even Eileen must be getting close to a climax now, Joyce thought. She glanced back at The Mistress who was surveying Winston's dark-skinned body.

'What about you?' Joyce asked

'What do you mean?' The Mistress turned to look at Joyce with a mystified expression.

'You said you enjoy being in control, training your slaves, but what gives you pleasure? What gives you a muscle trembling orgasm?'

A flash of anger passed across The Mistress's face. Oh, oh, thought Joyce, she doesn't like being put on the spot about her own desires. Then the look passed and the dominatrix smiled.

'Planning a training programme and carrying it out does give me a real thrill and I feel confident when I am in authority over other people but from time to time I do like to have a real hard cock up my pussy and the strong arms of a man around me.'

Joyce glanced at Winston who was watching and listening avidly.

'I'm sure Winston would oblige. He's a very considerate lover.' She signalled to Winston to get on to his feet. He hauled himself up to his full impressive height with his shiny dark cock at attention. The Mistress smiled and stood up.

'You do seem to have your men well trained,' she said to Joyce.

'Oh, we don't control them,' Joyce said laughing, 'they do what they like, but we have taught them a thing or two.'

The Mistress reached down to her mound, took hold of the silver ring and carefully tugged on it. The zip undid round her crotch and up the crack between her bum cheeks. She advanced on Winston pulling her glove off her left hand. She grasped his penis and squeezed. Winston grinned.

'Yes, I do like a firm cock,' she said, walking him backwards to the bed. The mattress caught Winston behind the knees and he fell backwards. Immediately The Mistress was astride him, lowering herself onto his vertical penis. His knob parted the zip-trimmed leather and slid between the protruding red lips of her fanny. She allowed herself to drop, crying out as the shaft slid into her. Winston arched his back lifting her bodily and driving his penis even deeper. She urged him on. Winston grabbed the white moons of her buttocks and bucked. The Mistress rode him laughing aloud.

Joyce's attention was drawn by simultaneous sighs and groans from Eileen, Johnny and Daisy. Johnny pulled out his flaccid penis, dripping cream. Daisy lifted her head gasped for air then without pause crawled between Joyce's legs. Joyce saw Mick's eyes fixed on Daisy's rear.

'Come on Mick, your turn,' she managed just before her

breath was taken away. Daisy's tongue had flicked across her clitoris, before plunging into her vagina. The little gold studs rubbed against the walls of her quim sending electricity coursing along her nerves. She was vaguely aware of Mick approaching Daisy's raised arse and of his quivering penis being aimed at its target but then her vision clouded and she was deluged by the sensations from the tongue feeling and probing deep inside her. This too was paradise.

The Mistress and her slave had left. Daisy's dildo, restraints and clothes had been restored and she had been led out to the large old Humber that the dominatrix drove. Joyce was amused to see that the slave did not have the comfort of a seat but was bundled into the boot which The Mistress ensured was locked.

After their guests had driven away, the ladies and their men retreated to the hall for a drink.

'Well, what did you think of that?' Joyce asked.

'Well, I like to be in control,' Eileen began, 'but it was all too planned and technical for me.'

'Too cruel,' Susan said screwing up her nose.

'Too serious,' Betty said shaking her head.

'I want a slave,' Edith announced.

Chapter Fourteen
Viva Espana!

At last they had reached the front of the queue and the five ladies squeezed up to the Crown Airlines desk. The dark haired clerk in her pale blue uniform gave them a welcoming smile.

'Good morning, ladies,' she said with a hint of Spanish in her voice.

'Hello, we are going to May-orca,' Joyce said handing over the five passports, three of which had only arrived from the Passport Office the previous day.

What a rush it had been to get that little task sorted. It was less than a month since Joyce had waved the cheque from Patrick Mount, the film producer. It was the first payment for the filming of *School for Scandal*. He'd included some publicity photos from the film.

'Gosh, Susan, you look just like Marilyn Monroe,' Betty said. Susan blushed.

'I don't think she was ever filmed sucking cock,' Edith said.

'I bet she did it for President Kennedy though,' Eileen giggled.

They discussed what they should do with the money, several hundred pounds, with more to come when the video tapes started to sell.

'I know. Why don't we all go on holiday,' Joyce announced suddenly.

'All of us? Together?' Eileen asked.

'What about the boys?' Betty wondered.

'Just us,' Joyce said, 'Winston can visit his parents and Mick and Johnny will have college.'

'They can entertain each other while we're away,' Eileen said, 'those boys like giving each other one.'

'Susan, could you get away for a week? What about your little girl?' Joyce asked.

'I think so. Mum would look after Hannah.'

'Wouldn't she wonder how you're paying for a holiday?' Edith asked.

'Oh, she's getting used to me having more money. I've told her I'm doing more hours at the salon on the evenings she babysits,' Susan explained.

'What are you doing?'

'I'm going to Mrs Glover's.'

'Oh, that sort of work. You take it steady, my girl,' Edith warned, 'the life of a whore can be exhausting.'

'I know but Mrs Glover chooses my clients very carefully.'

The thought of a September holiday seemed popular so next day Joyce visited a few travel agents in town and took the brochures to her friends.

'Mal-lorca looks lovely,' Susan said.

'It's pronounced Madge-orca,' Betty disagreed.

'No, in Spanish it's May-orca,' Joyce corrected, 'it will still be lovely and warm there in September.'

Mallorca it was. Luckily, a hotel in Magaluf was able to give a booking for all five of them and then there were just Betty's, Susan's and Edith's passports to get.

'Can we all sit together?' Susan asked, 'I don't want to sit on my own for my first flight.'

Joyce peered at the plan of the aeroplane on the clerk's desk.

'Yes, we can. Look there are five seats in a row, two on one side and three on the other.'

'Oh, it's a one-eleven we're flying on, is it,' Edith said standing on tiptoe trying to see over Joyce's shoulder.

'How do you know what plane it is?' Betty asked.

'Oh, my Stanley was always keen on aeroplanes. When we were young we often cycled to an airfield to watch them take off and land. Mind you we also used to get up to some other things lying in the grass beside the runways – that was what kept me interested.'

With the tickets grasped in her hands, Joyce turned away from the desk.

'Let's go girls, we're off to Spain.'

They set off for the duty-free shops, arm in arm. Betty broke in to song, 'We're going off to sunny Spain,' and the others joined in.

'Y Viva Espana.'

Susan had the window seat with Joyce next to her and the other three were across the aisle. Soon the plane was taxiing and the jet engines at the rear roared. Susan leaned closer to Joyce.

'You've flown before, haven't you, Joyce.'

'Yes, Bill and I flew to the south of France a number of times.'

'Do you know about the Mile High Club?'

'The Mile High Club! You mean the club for people who've had sex on a 'plane?'

'That's right. Have you done it?'

'Definitely not. Bill wasn't adventurous like that. Do you want to?'

'It would be exciting wouldn't it?'

The engines reached a deafening loudness and Susan and Joyce were pressed back into their seats. In a few moments Susan could see the airport receding from them and then they were into the clouds.

'How are you going to do it?' Joyce resumed the conversation as the BAC 111 levelled off, 'All the male passengers seem to be with wives and children or they're retired, and there are no male stewards. The only eligible men are probably in the cabin flying the thing.'

'Does it have to be intercourse with a man? Or does having an orgasm count,' Susan whispered loudly.

'I suppose you could do it anyway you like.' Joyce realised what Susan was thinking, 'Do you want me to help?'

'Oh, yes please.' Susan lowered the tray on the back of the seat in front onto her knees. Then she took hold of Joyce's hand, tucked it under the hem of her sun dress and placed it between her thighs. The touch of the soft, smooth skin on her fingertips produced a tickle in Joyce's tummy. Gently, she explored further up Susan's legs. Despite the cramped seating Susan managed to open her legs a little. Joyce's finger reached Susan's crotch and felt short curly hair.

'Susan! You haven't got any knickers on,' she hissed.

'No,' the young woman giggled, 'I thought it would be a thrill to go without.'

Joyce's finger found the crack and slipped inside. Her inner labia were slick with juices and hot. She probed deeper with two, three fingers. She found the little bud and when she rubbed it Susan threw her head back and moaned.

'Susan! Act as if nothing's happening,' Joyce warned. Susan recovered herself but her cheeks were flushed.

'Oh, please carry on. That's lovely,' she said.

Joyce pushed her fingers deeper into the hole and began to rub. She could feel Susan's vaginal muscles tensing and relaxing. The more she rubbed the more the pulsations increased in tempo. Despite Joyce's entreaties, Susan sighed loudly.

'Would you like a drink, madam?' Joyce looked up to see a stewardess addressing her.

'Oh, yes, a white wine please.' It was too late to withdraw her hand from under Susan's drop-down table. Let the stewardess think what she liked.

The hotel was comfortable though not completely built yet and there was a gaping hole next to it where an army of Spanish men were busy on another. At least their rooms on the fourth floor had a view of the Mediterranean Sea. Joyce shared with Eileen; Edith and Betty were together and Susan, as the youngest, had been given the honour of the single room.

'It's more of a cupboard really,' Susan said, 'and the bathroom only has a loo and a shower.'

The ladies went out for a quick exploration of the sea front. Then it was time for their dinner in the hotel. After a few drinks in the bar afterwards they all said they felt tired from the travelling and headed to their rooms.

Joyce was up bright and early for breakfast. It looked like being a wonderful hot, sunny day and she was impatient to get by the sea. Eileen joined her and soon Betty and Edith came down wearing brightly coloured sundresses.

'Where's Susan?' Edith asked.

'No sign of her yet,' Joyce replied, 'probably enjoying a morning without having to get her daughter up.'

With breakfast finished and still no appearance from Susan, Joyce knocked on her bedroom door. There was no reply and Joyce was about to go away when the door opened a crack and Susan peered out. She had a towel wrapped around her. She looked as if she'd just woken up.

'Oh, hello Joyce.'

'Good morning, Susan. I was just checking if you were OK. We've all had breakfast and are heading off to find the sun, sand and sea. All the esses. What about you?'

'I expect I'll join you soon.'

Joyce saw a movement behind the young woman. The door to her shower room opened and a man stepped out. He was dark haired, young, Spanish and naked.'

'Oh, I see. Quick work. You've managed the other ess already.'

'What?'

'Sex.'

Susan giggled, raised her hand to cover her mouth, dropping her towel and revealing her nude body.

'Yes. I've hardly had a wink of sleep. Look he's got to go to work soon. I'll catch up with you and tell you all about it.'

'His name's Carlos. Our eyes met when he was serving us dinner last night. Didn't you recognise him, Joyce?' Susan was lounging in a deckchair on the sandy beach beside her friend.

'I only had a glimpse of him in your room and it wasn't his face that caught my eye,' Joyce replied rubbing suntan lotion into her arms and shoulders, 'Mind you, all these young Spanish men look the same with their floppy, shiny hair.'

'When we went to the bar after dinner I kept seeing him and

he was looking at me. When you went off he was in the foyer. Instead of taking the lift I followed him out to the swimming pool. He lit a cigarette, saw me and started talking. I don't know any Spanish and the only English he knows are "beer" and "fish and chips" – that's all English people ask him for.'

'But you managed to communicate?'

'Oh yes. We didn't need many words.'

'I can imagine.'

Susan giggled.

'Well, there was one other word he knew – fuck. We understood each other. We had a kiss and a cuddle by the pool and then I decided to take him up to my room. He was pretty keen.'

'I bet.'

'Carlos has so much energy. He kept me at it all night.'

'And?'

'And what?'

'Did you enjoy it?'

'Oh, God, yes. He was so keen to satisfy me. First he kissed me again and again on my lips, ear lobes, neck. Then he undressed me. He was very pleased to find I had no knickers on. He put me on the bed and started to lick and kiss me all over. His lips on my breasts sent me into a frenzy. I pulled his clothes off and tried to drag him on top of me, but he wouldn't come. He kept saying, no, no, no, and carried on kissing me. Eventually he got down to my fanny. He sucked on my hair, licked my thighs, kissed my bottom and stuck his tongue in my arse, then he slowly licked all the way around my crotch until he got to my clit. I was thrashing around by this time of course, coming time after time, but he held my thighs in his arms and just carried on sucking my pussy lips and jabbing his tongue into my hole. I don't know how long he kept at it. It could have been seconds or hours. At last though he pulled his head out and stuck his cock in. I hadn't even seen him up to then as he'd been doing such wonderful things. It didn't feel as big as Johnny's but Carlos knew how to use it. He twisted and turned and lifted me up so that it rubbed against every bit of my vagina. I just kept coming and eventually he did too.

I was ready to doze off then, but he wasn't. He pulled his cock out; it was still half erect and covered with cream. He wanted me to suck it.'

'Which, of course, you did.'

'Of course. He tasted salty and fishy. Just like the sea. He was hard again in no time. I'd woken up again so I treated him to what he'd given me. I sucked and nibbled his knob and his shaft and his balls and licked his arse until he was pleading with me to finish it. I understand that bit of Spanish. Then I rode him till he came.

I thought that might have been enough, but we'd barely started. We fucked in every way we could. On the bed, on the floor, in the shower, leaning out of the window. He had me from behind, on top, up against the wall, until I finally just fell asleep. I think it was beginning to get light at that point.'

'So what next?'

'Well, he had to go to work. He serves lunch and dinner.'

'Are you going to see him again?'

'I hope so. We sort of made an arrangement to meet by the pool again this evening when he gets off.'

'Well, I hope he keeps making you happy.'

As the sun sank towards the blue horizon the ladies trudged from the beach carrying their hired deckchairs. They returned them to the attendant, an old man with a dark, whiskered face and arms like tanned leather.

'Gracias Senora,' he said to Edith who handed over the last of the chairs, 'You are English?'

'Yes, I am, do you speak it?'

'A little, not good,' he said with the last half inch of a cigarette stuck in the corner of his mouth, 'I learn from good friend in the war.'

'The Second World War?'

'No, the Civil War.'

'Oh. Which side were you on?'

He glanced up and down the promenade and stepped closer to Edith. He was barely the same height.

'I was communist. I am communist,' he whispered.

‘You don’t think much of Franco then.’

He spat out a gob of tobacco-coloured phlegm.

‘I glad he dead at last.’ He looked over his shoulder.

‘My Stanley was a communist in the 1930s. He got over it after the war.’

‘This Stanley is your husband? Is he still alive?’

‘Yes, but in a home.’ Edith tapped her head and grimaced.

‘I understand.’

Edith noticed that the other four had walked on ahead to the hotel.

‘Look we must have a chat. I’d like to hear about your experiences. Stanley fought in the war, the world war that is. What time are you here till?’

‘Till it’s dark and everyone has left the beach. Then I collect all the chairs that haven’t been returned.’

‘Well I’ll see you later, ah …’

‘Juan. Your name is?’

‘Edith.’

Later after dinner, Edith made an excuse and left her friends in the hotel. She met Juan just as he was finishing securing the deckchairs for the night. He invited her to walk with him to his home. They linked arms and walked along the promenade. Edith was surprised to find that Juan lived in a tiny, tin shack amongst the building sites of the new hotels. When they were inside he lit a paraffin lamp and hung it from the ceiling. Edith looked around noting the bed, the small table and single rickety wooden chair and a book shelf packed with books.

‘You have no electricity or water. How do you manage?’

‘I have friends in the hotels. They let me use their servicios. Everyone knows old Juan.’

‘But why do you live like this?’

‘I have no money. Franco wouldn’t let me have a job except looking after beach chairs.’

‘But why not? You’re obviously an educated man.’ Edith pointed at the books.

‘Perhaps now that the old dictator is dead things will improve but the government has a long memory. They remember which side I was on in the war.'

Edith found herself filled with admiration for the poor, old beach attendant. She looked at him closely and realised that beneath the sunburnt, unkempt appearance there was still an attractive man.

'Do you have a family?' she asked.

'Not since the war,' he replied. His eyes filled with tears.

'We're both alone,' Edith said sadly. 'My love has lost his mind and yours is gone.'

'Enough,' Juan said brightly, 'life goes on. Let us drink and be happy.'

He pulled out a wine bottle without a label from under the bed and poured the dark red liquid into two plastic cups. He offered one to Edith.

'Cheers,' he said. As there was nowhere else, Edith sat on the bed and sipped the wine. It was cheap but not too rough and once she had drunk one cupful she was eager for another. Juan sat beside her and it wasn't long before his hand fell on her bare knee and began to travel up her thigh. She knew she could have stopped him there and then, left him in his hut and walked back to the hotel, but she didn't want to. His fingers found their way to her satin knickers. Edith sighed and pulled her dress over her head. In deference to the temperature of the Mediterranean she had ditched her body-hugging basques and corsets in favour of a secure and all-encompassing bra. The hooks didn't stymie Juan for long.

Even after the months of playful sex at the Ladies' College for Erotic Arts, Edith found that the act of sprawling on the rough blankets in the dim, light of Juan's shack gave her a thrill. She was naked in front of a man her own age who she barely knew. Juan pulled off his rough trousers, cotton shirt and grey, holey pants. He knelt at her feet feasting on her body, wrinkles and all.

His testicles hung in a hairy scrotum like two walnuts but Edith was pleased to see his penis swell and grow into a fine firm rod. He fell on her, devouring her tits and stomach and cunt with his gap-toothed mouth. His unshaved chin rasped her skin, but Edith didn't care. His wine-lubricated tongue excited her, making her own juices flow in her channel. She reached for his cock, squeezed it and rubbed the skin back and forth until he begged for her to stop. Instead, she guided him to her hole and slipped it in.

With his crotch pressed against hers, Juan stopped and rested on his arms. Edith loved the feeling of his cock filling her vagina, not moving but just from time to time giving a gentle throb. She felt filled and content. Juan nibbled her ear and she giggled like a schoolgirl when his tongue tickled her. After what seemed like a delightful eternity Juan began to move inside her, maintaining his erection. She responded, moving against him, forcing his cock deeper still, the friction exciting her. There was no explosion of youthful energy but he tensed and froze suddenly. Then she felt his gentle ejaculation as hotness pooling inside her. Edith too was satisfied. They wriggled until they lay together, face to face, his penis still resting just inside her cunt. Juan dozed off first and Edith feeling comfortable found her eyes becoming heavy.

She awoke to find the paraffin lamp still burning and Juan still beside her with his eyes open.

'You are beautiful woman,' he said softly.

'And you're not so bad yourself. Do you think you can do it again?'

'Two times in one night? In my youth I did it five, ten times a night.'

'But we're not in our youth are we; neither of us.'

Edith rolled him on to his back and started to softly massage his cock and testicles. She was impressed to see how quickly he began to stiffen and when she glanced at his face his expression told her that he was surprised too. She climbed on to him and gently rode him. His hands reached for her breasts and massaged them in time with her rocking motion.

It was a long time before he came again and Edith slid down beside him again ready to drift into deep sleep.

'I don't know where Edith is,' Betty said at breakfast with Joyce, Eileen and a yawning Susan, 'I don't think she even slept in her bed last night.'

Just then Joyce spied Edith mounting the steps to the hotel. She joined them in the dining room and told them of her night with old Juan.

'Well, I shouldn't be shocked,' Joyce said, 'but you and Susan have been quick off the mark.'

'What are we doing today?' Eileen said, changing the subject. 'Do we have to eat here again? I'm tired of fried bacon and eggs and grilled steak and chips.'

'It's what they think us English tourists want, so Carlos says. Chips, chips and chips,' Susan said imitating a Spanish accent.

'Juan said he was going to take me to a genuine Spanish bar this evening,' Edith said, 'why don't you all come too?'

So, after another day by the pool and on the beach they all met up with Juan after nightfall. They walked along the promenade, past all the modern hotels and entered an old part of the town. They came to a lime washed stone building with a roof of curly ceramic tiles. Inside there were just a few candlelit tables, only one of which was occupied. The four old men glanced up then returned to their card game. Tinny but rhythmic flamenco music played from a small cassette player and there was the delightful smell of fresh cooking on a griddle. Juan was greeted by a fat man with a stained apron over his bare torso and old dark trousers. The two men kissed and then Juan introduced the ladies. Their host welcomed Susan, Joyce, Eileen and Edith warmly but then he saw Betty. He took a step back to look her up and down.

'Ah, an English woman after my own heart. You obviously like your food.'

Betty nodded, embarrassed by the fuss made of her. She had struggled and strived to reduce her weight but she knew she was still tubby.

'Now, ladies, you want sangria?' He clapped his hands and beckoned to the young and thin, bar girl, then showed them to one of the vacant tables. The girl brought a tray bearing a large jug of orangey-red liquid and six tumblers. She filled each one.

'Drink,' the bar owner urged. 'It is my own recipe, handed down by my father and his before him.'

Joyce took a sip. The drink was sweet and very pleasant.

'Don't be fooled,' Eileen warned, 'it may go down easily but it is very alcoholic.'

'Now, I, Pedro the chef, bring you tapas.' Pedro departed into a kitchen but returned moments later with the first of many small plates which he placed on their table. Back and forth he went until their table was full and he started on the adjacent table. Each plate contained a different dish which Pedro named proudly – *patatas bravas, gambas, chorizo, mancego, ensalada, jamon, tomates, calamares*. The list went on and on and the ladies ate and ate, and drank sangria. Eventually all but Betty could not eat more, but still Pedro plied her with tempting morsels.

Susan made her apologies – Carlos was awaiting her. Edith and Juan offered to walk her back to the hotel and then Joyce and Eileen decided that it was their bedtime too.

'Are you coming Betty?' Joyce asked.

'No, no, I have more for you to try. I look after you,' Pedro appealed to her. Betty giggled and swayed in her chair.

'I don't think I want to go anywhere just at the moment,' she said with a burp.

Eileen looked at Joyce and winked. They left Betty being served a brandy by Pedro.

Betty was enjoying herself and her worries about her waistline had disappeared along with the contents of the plates of tapas and jugs of sangria. The old men finished their card games and left, swiftly followed by the young bar girl. Pedro turned off the music and blew out the candles.

'Come,' he said pulling Betty to her feet. Swaying dangerously he guided her to the back room. It was lit only by the moonlight pouring in through the wide open veranda doors. There was little in the way of furnishing, just an unmade bed and a large wardrobe. Pedro lowered Betty on to the bed, and untied his apron. He let it drop to the floor.

'I cook no more,' he slurred. 'Now I make love to a beautiful woman.' He unfastened the string holding his trousers up and eased the waistband over his protruding belly. Betty giggled as she saw his flesh and struggled to pull her sundress over her ample bosom.

Pedro stood naked before her, his cock and balls obscured by the folds of flab hanging from his abdomen.

'Come here, tiger,' Betty urged. 'Let's see what you've got under that fat.'

He crawled ponderously on to the bed like a beached seal. Betty pushed him and he subsided in a heap of blubber. She loved his odour of olive oil and all the foods and spices he had fed her, the salty tang of the seafood, the heat of green chillies, the zest of oranges and lemons. She pushed his legs apart and burrowed into the flesh. She found his cock dangling like a little pink pepper and lowered her head towards it. At first it flopped limply between her lips but she nibbled on it with her teeth and gradually it swelled to the more attractive proportions of a chorizo sausage. Pedro made contented groaning noises as Betty continued to work on him, taking his knob deep into her mouth and squeezing his balls in her fist. When she was sure that he was ready she released his erect penis and turned, presenting him with her elephantine rear. She pulled on her buttocks revealing her pendulous pussy lips and dripping channel.

'Fuck me?' she appealed.

Pedro hauled himself to his knees, and bent over her back. His stomach slapped against her bum as he negotiated his entry. Betty sighed with relief as he slipped into her. The springs of the bed complained bitterly as Pedro pounded her.

It was all over too soon for Betty as Pedro spurted his spunk into her cunt. Then he collapsed onto the mattress beside her and began to snore. Betty, however, was content. She had found a man who could satisfy the desires of her stomach and fanny.

'We're a fine pair, aren't we?' Eileen said, between sips of her fresh orange juice.

'What do you mean?' Joyce said.

'Well here we are, just the two of us at breakfast on our last full day.'

Joyce dug into a slice of melon, 'I see what you mean. Susan has her randy waiter, Edith her energetic war hero and Betty her amorous chef.'

'And here we are, the two founders of the Ladies' College for Erotic Arts, not getting any action.'

That wasn't strictly true, Joyce reflected. The twin beds in their shared room had not been pushed together to make more floor space. 'I've enjoyed it – a complete rest. What do you want to do?'

'Let's take a walk down by the harbour. Perhaps there's a boat trip we can go on while the others make the most of their last day.'

There were indeed offers of boat trips available but Eileen didn't fancy crowding on to a boat with lots of other tourists. Then she noticed a sign on the pontoon that read, "boat for hire" and alongside, a small fishing vessel. A swift gesticulated negotiation resulted in Joyce and Eileen hopping aboard. The boat sailed out of the harbour and headed north. The helmsman was a grizzled fisherman with a fag in his mouth and cap at a jaunty angle. His crew was a smooth-faced young lad. Neither seemed to speak much English.

Eileen and Joyce laid out their towels on the boat's bow deck and settled down to enjoy the trip in the bright clear sunshine. The young crew man sat in the shade against the front of the cabin and pulled out a magazine from his back pocket.

'Have you seen what he's reading?' Eileen whispered.

'No, what is it?'

'It's a girlie mag.'

'Naked women?'

'Yes.'

'Well, he's a young man. He may not have seen much of it.'

'Let's give him something real to see. Come on, Joyce, put some suntan lotion on my front.' Eileen unclipped her bikini top and let it drop. Then she lay back on her towel. Joyce poured some lotion from the bottle and proceeded to rub it into Eileen's breasts.

'Is he watching?' Eileen asked.

'Oh yes, he's moved to get a better view.'

Eileen giggled. 'When you've finished I'll do you.'

'You do realise that our fisherman has a good view out of his wheelhouse.'

‘He should be happy he’s being well rewarded for the hire of his boat.’

They motored through the water for over an hour. The gentle swell lulled Eileen and Joyce into a doze while they lay on the deck with their bosoms exposed. They were woken when the engine note changed to a slow chug. They looked up and found that the captain had manoeuvred into a narrow cove with tall, dark cliffs around a small sandy beach. The crewman threw an anchor over the side and the captain cut the engines. He emerged from his little cabin.

‘You go skinny dip?’ he said with a broad smile.

‘Is he suggesting that we swim in the nude?’ Joyce said to Eileen.

‘I think so.’ Eileen made a face to show she didn’t understand. The captain pointed to the deserted beach.

‘No people look. You swim; no clothes.’

‘Oh, I see,’ Eileen nodded her head and turned to Joyce, ‘I think he’s brought us here because you can’t get to the beach from the land – look at those cliffs – and because of our little game with our bras he thinks we’re nudists.’

‘Well, there’s no one to see us.’

‘Right, let’s do it.’ Eileen pulled her swimming bottoms down. She stood on the side of the boat and stepped off. She made a big splash as she entered the clear blue sea but soon surfaced and swam on her back looking up at the boat. Joyce gazed down at her golden body with a dark tuft of hair at her crotch.

‘Come on, it’s gorgeous,’ Eileen called. Very swiftly Joyce divested herself of her swimming costume and leapt into the sea. The water was like swimming in a hot bath. Joyce paddled alongside Eileen.

‘Oh, look the boy’s coming in too.’ Eileen pointed to the boat. The young man stood naked on the gunwale, his long cock dangling down between his thighs. He dived and sank into the water with barely a splash. He disappeared from sight. Joyce looked around but couldn’t see any sign of him.

There was a tickle on the bottom of her foot and she instinctively kicked out. There was a thrashing and eruption of water and the boy surfaced with water streaming down his face and black hair stuck to his head. He grinned.

'You!' Joyce laughed, 'I thought it was a jelly fish or something. You tickled my foot.'

The boy laughed, 'I chase you.'

'What, oh, all right.' Joyce struck out for the beach, thrashing the water with her arms and legs. The boy followed effortlessly behind, with Eileen following.

They reached the gently shelving beach and Joyce rolled exhausted on to the sand with the small waves breaking over her. The boy crawled out of the sea and stood gazing down at her body.

'You have no hair,' he said pointing at Joyce's pubic area.

Joyce looked where he was pointing. She barely thought about her smooth, naked mound these days; it was what she was accustomed to now. Eileen came splashing out of the water.

'He thinks you're a strange creature without body hair,' Eileen said. 'No Spanish girl would think of shaving off her pubes. Why don't you ask him to feel how smooth it is?'

Joyce grinned at her, knowing what she was thinking. She reached out for the young man's hand. He resisted at first but then allowed her to tug his hand to her crotch.

'Feel,' she said, 'Nice isn't it.'

The palm of his hand rubbed gently over her mound then his fingers took over searching down between her wet thighs. Joyce parted her legs. Small waves lapped against her fanny and his fingers slipped between her lips. Joyce looked at him so intent on exploring her that he didn't seem to notice his cock inflating like a large sausage balloon.

Eileen knelt in the wet sand beside him and ran her hand over his buttocks, down his crack and took hold of his pair of testicles in their large, wrinkled sac. He glanced around then, saw Eileen smiling and resumed his task of examining Joyce. Eileen reached further between his legs and took his shaft in the palm of her hand.

'You like fuck,' he said.

'Yes,' Joyce replied. 'I like fuck.' She pressed her heels into the sand and raised her pelvis towards him. He lowered himself aiming his penis towards its target. Eileen kept hold of the shaft guiding it into Joyce's hole. As the cock disappeared so Eileen gradually released her grip.

His thrusts pushed Joyce into the soft sand but she arched her back and pressed against him. Eileen ran her fingers up and down his bum crack then rested her forefinger against his hole. As he pulled his cock back so Eileen's finger was forced in; a little more with each thrust. The rhythm increased. Joyce cried out, urging him on. He grunted and groaned and wriggled his hips. His cock pistoned in and out of Joyce's cunt while Eileen finger-fucked his arse. He came with a juddering climax and white foam oozed out of Joyce's hole to float away on the water. Eileen and the boy pulled back and lay on their backs in the sea.

There was a rough grating sound of wood on sand. Joyce looked up to see the boat owner in a small rowing boat. He stowed the oars, jumped over the side and pulled the boat a few feet up the beach. Then he reached inside and lifted out a wicker basket.

'Eat now?' he said, 'or more fuck?'

'Oh, I think there's plenty of time left to eat,' Eileen said rising to her feet and advancing on the sailor. 'I think you need to get your clothes off and some seawater on your skin, don't you?' He looked a bit confused by her words, but fully understood her actions when she reached for the belt of his jeans.

Later, quite a while later, they sat on the dry sand drinking cheap wine straight from the bottle and eating fresh bread and fish grilled by the fisherman on a fire of driftwood. In the Anglo-Spanish chat that accompanied the refreshments the ladies discovered that their sea-captain was called Hernando and his crewman, Diego.

'I always wondered what it would be like to make love in the sea or on a beach,' Joyce said.

'Well, there you are, that's another mystery solved,' Eileen said brushing sand off her thigh, 'Mind you, this dry stuff gets in all the cracks.'

'I wonder if they want more?'

‘What food or sex?’

‘Oh definitely sex.’

‘From the way that Hernando and Diego keep looking at us and the way their cocks keep bobbing up and down, I think that’s a certainty. Come on we’ve only got one afternoon left.’ Eileen jumped up and grabbed Diego’s hand, dragging him down the beach to the lapping water’s edge.

Chapter Fifteen
An Inspector Calls

She really ought to get out and do some shopping before lunch, Joyce thought, but this was just too pleasant. She caressed the long dark cock that hung in front of her face. The skin was stretched taut so that it gleamed like glass and yet when her encircling fingers squeezed there was just the tiniest amount of give before the hard core resisted. She smoothed her fingers along the shaft and touched the contrasting purple knob. It always amused her how it twitched when she flicked it as if it had a mind of its own. At the root of the cock, Winston's testicles swung like two hard-boiled eggs in a polythene bag. The skin of his scrotum was smooth and hairless now she had encouraged him to shave. She liked to see his balls naked and shiny.

It was Winston's tongue that gave her the most pleasure, roving around her cunt, licking her lips, pressed against her clit or probing into her hole. He'd had her on the edge of orgasm for minutes now and it was only the hard arm of the sofa on her neck that made her wish it would be over sometime soon.

The doorbell rang.

'Dash, who can that be?' Joyce said. 'I suppose I'd better see. It could be a parcel delivery or something. Get off me, Winston.'

The young man lifted his head from her crotch and put a foot down on the floor. He rose, turned in one graceful movement and offered a hand to pull Joyce up.

'Thanks.' She grabbed her housecoat and hurried into the hall. She fastened the third popper as she passed the wall mirror and glanced to see if she was decent before opening the door. A small, thin man in a dark grey suit stood on the doorstep holding a clipboard in one arm and a leather briefcase with his other hand. His dark hair was slicked across his head with Brylcream and a short moustache sat on his upper lip. He looked at her disapprovingly. Joyce had the impression that this was his normal expression and not one that he had put on especially for her.

'Mrs Blandford?' he said. It was part question, part statement.

'Yes.'

'You are the owner of this property?'

'Yes. Well it used to belong to my husband but he's dead so now it's mine.'

'May I come in? We have an important matter to settle.'

'Oh? And who are you?'

'Healey. Rates Inspector.' He spat it out as if on a roll call.

'I see.' She didn't actually. 'And what is this important matter?'

'It is about your rate assessment. I need to come in if you please.'

Joyce opened the door and reluctantly invited the little man into her home. She led him into the lounge where she was glad to see that Winston had had the presence of mind to don his dressing gown.

'This is Winston,' Joyce said. Winston held out his hand but Mr Healey did not drop his briefcase or clipboard in order to take it.

'A lodger?'

Joyce thought quickly. Why was a rates inspector here? Would it mean anything if she had a lodger? 'No, Winston's a friend, staying for a while.'

Healey glanced at the paper on his board and nodded.

'I see.'

'Would you like a seat?' Joyce offered Mr Healey the sofa which had so recently borne her naked bottom and dripping pussy. Mr Healey sat carefully, placing his briefcase by his foot and his clipboard on his lap. Winston backed out of the room.

'What is this all about? I pay my rates,' Joyce said.

Healey glanced down again.

'Ah, yes, I see you have been making payments to the Council. The question is more to do with the status of the property.'

'Status?'

'Yes. At the moment it is registered as a private dwelling, having previously been an educational establishment. You have been paying rates calculated according to its rateable value as a residential property.'

'Uh, yes, that's true.'

Mr Healey straightened his back and drew himself up. 'It has recently come to our notice that this property may be being used for commercial purposes and hence should be registered for business use, thereby attracting the business rate.'

'Commercial? Business?' Joyce was flummoxed, 'Where did you get that idea from?'

'I am not at liberty to divulge our sources. However, it is imperative that I carry out a full inspection to ascertain the truth of the information provided to us.'

Anger welled up inside Joyce, but she just stopped herself being rude to the little man.

'Well, you'd better do your inspection and see that this really is just my home.'

Mr Healey stood up picking up his briefcase and his clipboard.

'Lead on, please.'

Joyce took him back into the hall through the dining room and the kitchen. They came to the door leading into the old school hall.

'What is through that door?' Mr Healey asked.

'It used to be the assembly hall when the school …'

'Let me see, please.'

Joyce opened the door and stood aside for Mr Healey to step through. She saw him taking in the thick rugs, heavy black curtains and red decor and the large painting on the end wall with its unrestrained representation of naked bodies. I hope he doesn't recognise me, Joyce thought. Instead, his eyes were fixed on the king size bed

'A strange bedroom,' he commented.

Joyce tried to think of a response. How could she describe what went on on that bed and the sofas?

'Uh, some friends and I are rehearsing a little play. The bed is part of the set ...'

'I see. Show me upstairs please.'

They visited all the bedrooms, disturbing Winston lying on his bed, and even called in the bathroom. At last, they returned to the front door.

'Thank you, Mrs Blandford. I shall see that you are informed of the result of my investigations.'

'You can see there's no business going on here, can't you?'

'I shall be the judge of that. Thank you.'

He stepped outside and was gone. Joyce closed the door and leaned against it. Now what was all that about? Who had reported that she was running a business? What did people know about what went on at The Old School?

That evening was a meeting of the Ladies' College for Erotic Arts. Betty was strapped to the whipping stool and crying out at every blow delivered by Edith with the paddle. Edith was dressed in her new sleek leather basque with red stitching and suspenders.

'Yes, again, Edith. Punish me for putting on weight.'

Splat!

'Ow! Oh yes. It was Pedro's tapas that did it, but it serves me right.'

Splat!

'Ow.'

Already Betty's enormous globes had taken on a rosy glow and with her legs stretched wide apart her pendulous pussy lips hung swollen and red. Edith had put on quite a sweat but was relishing her task. She swung back her arm for another swipe.

Susan's nose rubbed in Johnny's pubic hair, his hard cock rammed down her throat. With Mick's tool thrust up her hole also she felt as if the two rods were going to meet somewhere in her stomach. Mick pulled out and she lifted her head letting

Johnny's shaft slide past her lips until she caught the knob between her teeth. She sucked in a quick lungful of air before Mick shoved his dick in again and she tipped forward swallowing the cock. Johnny groaned and arched his back.

Eileen rode on Winston's penis using the bed springs like a trampoline to give her all the motion she wanted. The friction between his glans and her vagina was sending such powerful signals that she felt the elusive orgasm was not far away, not far at all.

Joyce sat on the sofa vaguely watching and thinking. She heard a clatter. What was that noise?

'Did you hear that?'

No one replied, they were all too intent on their business.

Joyce stood up, wrapped her housecoat around herself and crossed the room. She turned the key in the lock of the back door of the hall, the main entrance for the school's former pupils, and stepped out. She looked to the left into what was once the playground, now used for car parking, and right, along the wall of the hall. A stepladder lay on its side and beside it a man pushing himself on to his knees, trying to stand. Joyce recognised him at once and strode up to him.

'Mr Healey, what do you think you are doing?' She grabbed his arm and hauled him upright. He seemed somewhat dazed.

'Pursuing my inspection,' he said shakily.

'You were spying on us.' Joyce dragged him towards the door.

'Just doing my job,' he said, sounding a little drunk.

'You were peeking through the curtains to see what we were up to.' She shoved him into the hall. He staggered, found his feet, stopped, straightened up. Joyce took hold of his arm and pulled him towards the sofas.

'Look what I've found, snooping around outside,' Joyce announced.

'Who is it?' Eileen asked sitting on Winston's crotch, her knees stretched wide apart either side of his hips.

'What's he been up to?' Edith said, the paddle paused above her shoulder.

'I can't see, what's happening,' Betty said, unable to move.

Susan's eyes looked up but her mouth was still filled with Johnny's cock.

'It's Mr Healey, that Council nosey-parker I told you all about. He was trying to see what we were doing.'

'And I can see now, thank you,' he said, apparently having regained his composure. 'A house of ill-repute. I shall have you in court.'

'On what charge?' Eileen demanded dismounting from Winston and striding up to the little man. His wide eyes stared at her naked body.

'We're not doing anything illegal. We're all consenting adults,' Joyce said.

'Living off immoral earnings,' Mr Healey tried again. 'I knew there was commerce taking place.'

'Not at all,' Eileen said standing right in front of the man and thrusting her breasts into his view. 'We're all friends here, there are no business arrangements.'

'Keeping a disorderly house.'

'Nonsense, we make no noise and we're not disturbing the neighbours.'

It took a struggle but Mr Healey tore his eyes away from Eileen's bosom only to see Johnny's cock plopping out of Susan's mouth and Mick's slipping out from her vulva, much reduced in size. He turned away.

'I must go and make my report. You will be hearing more of this.'

He took a step but Joyce and Eileen grabbed an arm each.

'Oh, no you don't. You're not going anywhere,' Eileen said.

He struggled but the two women held on to his arms.

'Release me this instant,' he asserted.

'What shall we do?' Joyce asked.

'I don't know but we can't let him go. He'll spread gossip about us.'

'How do we stop him?'

'Let's get him on the bed. Winston come and help.'

'Let me go or I will report you to the police,' Mr Healey cried.

With the large black man's help they got the wriggling

official on to the bed. Susan joined in and together they held him down.

'Edith, get some more of those cuffs and rope,' Eileen ordered. Edith was ready in moments and while the others kept Mr Healey still, Edith fastened his wrists and ankles to the bars of the bedstead.

'Stop. Let me go. You can't do this,' Mr Healey screamed.

'Oh, put a sock in it,' Eileen said, 'Edith, gag him so we can hear ourselves think.'

Edith stuffed a ball gag in his mouth and pulled the strap tight behind his head.

'Are you going to let me off this thing so I can see what's going on,' Betty wailed.

'Coming, Betty. Hold on,' Edith said.

'Well, I'm not going anywhere,' Betty replied.

They all stood around the bed looking down at the bound and gagged rates inspector. At least he had stopped struggling and moaning.

'What can we do?' Joyce said, 'He could have us for false imprisonment now. We could all go to gaol.'

'We've got to make sure he doesn't talk,' Eileen said.

'You mean do away with him,' Edith said.

'No, of course not. We're not in a gangster movie, Edith,' Eileen shook her head.

'We've got to embarrass him,' Susan said thoughtfully, 'So he won't say anything.'

'We've got to get him so he doesn't want to give us away,' Betty said.

'That's it,' Joyce said, 'We've got to make him one of our boys.'

'What?' Eileen said staring down at the scrawny, middle-aged weakling of a man, 'you want to fuck that?'

'Yes,' Joyce said, 'For the College. We've got to give him a night he'll never forget and will want to repeat.'

'Hmm, this'll be a pleasureless task,' Edith said.

'Yes, well the sooner we get started,' Joyce said, 'Let's get his clothes off. Winston, Johnny and Mick; you go, you needn't be part of this.'

The three young men sauntered off without much complaint.

'Now, ladies, we'll have to do a bit at a time.'

By unlocking each of the cuffs around his ankles and wrists in turn they divested Mr Healey of his highly polished shoes, knee-length woollen socks, trousers and braces, jacket, tie, shirt, vest and Y-front underpants. He lay on the bed with his arms and legs stretched out looking not unlike a plucked chicken, Joyce thought. He gurgled through the gag but she had no idea if he was complaining.

'It's not very appetising, is it,' Eileen said lifting his limp prick between her finger and thumb. She released it and it flopped back down between his thighs.

'Pitiful, actually,' Edith said.

'Shall I see what I can do?' Susan said.

'Might as well,' Eileen said, 'Mind you I would have thought all this naked female flesh would have given any man a hard-on.'

Susan climbed on to the bed and knelt between Mr Healey's legs, facing him. Her firm breasts hardly wobbled. She leaned forward brushing her nipples against his abdomen, over his hollow chest and back again. No result. She repeated the movement. Still no sign of life below. Susan rested on her thighs and bent her head down to his crotch. She took the flaccid penis between her lips and tugged. The short, thin prick stretched like an elastic band. She opened her mouth and it flopped back, shrinking into the wrinkled sac nestled between his thighs.

'I don't know,' Susan said. 'I've never failed before.'

'Let me have a go,' Betty said, 'perhaps he prefers a big woman.'

Betty took Susan's place on the bed. She turned to face his feet and lowered her paddle-reddened buttocks on to his face, pressing her crotch against his nose and gagged mouth.

'Don't smother him,' Joyce warned.

Betty shuffled her ample behind, 'No, I'll let him get some air.' She looked down between his legs but still there was no flicker of response.

‘Do you think he’s a homosexual?’ Eileen asked.

‘No, I don’t think so,’ Joyce said. ‘He didn’t show any sign of interest when he saw the boys’ big cocks.’

Betty clambered off the bed and stood looking at the little man’s inadequate tackle with disgust.

‘He’s a little English twerp, isn’t he?’ Edith said thoughtfully.

‘Yes, but how does that help?’ Joyce asked.

‘Well, he was probably a mummy’s boy, disciplined if he soiled his pyjamas or pants with a wet dream. Put across her lap when he needed to be taught a lesson,’ Edith went on, fantasising.

‘You’re just making it up,’ Joyce said.

‘No, Edith, you could be right,’ Eileen said. ‘He’s just the sort of inhibited wimp who fondly remembers the spankings he got from his mother.’ She bent close to the man on the bed, ‘What would Mummy think of you showing off your little willy to these lovely ladies?’

There was a stirring between his legs, the merest stiffening, a little lengthening, a half-hearted effort by the penis to raise its head.

‘It’s working,’ Susan said.

‘We need to give him a reminder of how a mother treats her naughty little boy,’ Eileen said, ‘Put him over someone’s knees and give him a good spanking.’

Mr Healey obviously heard Eileen’s words because his penis gave a little twitch and grew another centimetre.

‘I’ll do it,’ Betty said rubbing her hands with enthusiasm, ‘there’ll be no problem putting him over my knees.’

‘Right, let’s get him off the bed. Tie his wrists and ankles together so he can’t escape.’ Eileen gave instructions.

Trussed like a chicken with his hands tied behind his back, Mr Healey was lifted from the bed and carried to Betty who had sat herself down on a sofa. He was draped over her ample thighs with his bony buttocks uppermost. There was more gurgling.

‘Do you think we should remove the gag? He may choke,’ Susan said.

'Let Betty get started and then we'll take it off to see what he has to say for himself,' Eileen replied.

'Do you want to use the paddle, Betty?' Edith offered.

'No thank you. I'll start with my hand. See if I can make a handprint on his cheeks. He's a bag of old bones.'

'Where's his cock and balls?' Joyce asked bending down to look beneath Betty's legs, 'They're not squashed against your leg, are they?' Betty opened her legs. 'No, there they are. He looks a bit more excited than he was. He's obviously eager for you to start, Betty.'

'Right then.' Betty pushed his head down with her right hand so that his feet dangled off the floor. She raised her left hand, palm flat. 'Who's been a sly boy then, listening to nasty rumours?'

Her hand came down and hit the left buttock with a sharp smack. There was a muffled grunt from the gagged mouth. Betty raised her hand again.

'Who's been spying on the nice ladies?'

Her palm came down on the right buttock. There was an audible whimper.

Another slap to the left and again to the right. There were four bright red marks of palm, four fingers and a thumb.

'You've been a wicked boy,' Betty said and gave two hard smacks to the back of his thighs. A nasal cry emerged from the blocked mouth.

'Shall we see what he has to say for himself,' Joyce said. The others nodded and Joyce bent down to remove the gag. She noted also that Mr Healey's prick had grown to more acceptable proportions and was thrusting into the flesh of Betty's thigh.

He coughed and spluttered.

'I'm sorry, please let me go,' he appealed in a high pitched voice.

'Oh, I don't think Mummy would let you off so lightly when you've been so naughty,' Betty said, smiling broadly as she brought her hand down again on his left buttock.

'Ow,' he screamed. 'I said I'm sorry.'

'Sorry isn't good enough. What are you going to do about it?' Betty raised her hand again. The other four ladies watched, wondering how Mr Healey would respond. The hand came down adding another mark to those already covering the right cheek.

'Oof. What do you want?'

'You're going to be a good boy, aren't you?'

'Yes.'

'And you're going to forget about investigating Mrs Blandford's rates, aren't you.'

'Uuh.'

The hand came down again with a resounding splat.

'Yes, yes.'

'Are you sure?' Another smack.

'Yes, all right, I'll do what you say, please stop.' He was beginning to sob but the ladies could see that between Betty's legs the flow of blood aroused by the spanking had pumped his cock to full readiness.

'I think he should do something with that,' Edith said.

'It's a bit tiddly for my liking,' Susan said.

'I think he should show what he does with his own erection,' Eileen said.

'What do you mean?' Susan asked.

Eileen stepped forward and undid the cords binding his wrists together.

'Tip him on to his knees, Betty,' she instructed. Betty twisted and Mr Healey slipped on to the floor.

'Ooh, the boy has got a hard-on,' Betty said, observing his purple knob poking from his foreskin. 'Mummy doesn't want to see that, does she? You'd better get rid of it.'

'What do you mean?' The man said trying to cover his erection with his hand.

'She didn't mean cover it,' Edith said curtly. 'She meant wank it off.'

'That's right,' Eileen said, 'unless you want a few more smacks.'

Reluctantly he gripped his shaft in his left hand and began to move it slowly up and down.

'Harder than that,' Edith urged. 'Or you'll lose it and we'll have to start all over again.'

His hand moved a bit quicker, less hesitantly, growing in urgency. His mouth dropped open and his eyes began to lose their focus. A strange moan came from his throat. He was masturbating hard now, his attention totally on his cock, oblivious to the five pairs of female eyes watching him with amusement.

Semen spurted from the tip, forming a pool of white on the rug.

'Naughty boy. Disgusting,' Betty said, 'Don't leave your mess on the floor. Lick it up.' Obediently he leaned down and stuck out his tongue. He licked the rug sucking up his ejaculate.

Joyce put down the Polaroid camera and examined the prints she had collected. There were some good shots of Mr Healey over Betty's knee, of him kneeling naked on the floor with his cock proudly erect, of him abusing himself and lastly licking the semen up. She held them up for him to see.

'Now I am sure you wouldn't go back on your word, would you?' she said. The man had turned a pretty pink from his neck upwards. 'But just to make sure we'll keep these photos and if we hear anything from the Council about changing our rates then I'm sure there would be some people interested in seeing these pictures.'

'That's blackmail,' he whispered uncertainly.

'That's not a very nice word,' Betty said. 'Do you want Mummy to punish you again?'

A variety of expressions passed across Mr Healey's face – fear, anticipation, pleasure. Joyce recognised what that look signified.

'We're not getting anything out of it,' she said. 'On the contrary, if you would like to check that we still have the photos, I am sure "Mummy" here,' she indicated Betty, 'would be willing to provide correction once a week for any misdemeanours you might have committed.

'Once a week,' he said weakly.

'That's right. Every week you'll get what you deserve.'

He looked at Betty with his head lowered.

'Thank you, Mummy,' he said sheepishly.

Chapter Sixteen
False Alarm

'Oh, hello, Joyce. Hear you had a bit of bother the other night,' Miriam, the post-mistress said.

Joyce stood at the head of the queue with a package in her hand.

'A bit of bother?' She had no idea what Miriam was referring to.

'Yes, Wednesday evening. We saw the fire engine go by with its lights flashing. Mr Evans says he was on his way to the Plough and saw it stop at the Old School. That's your place isn't it?'

'Oh, yes, that.' Joyce could feel her cheeks warming. 'It was nothing really.'

'Nothing! Mr Evans said that the fire engine was still parked outside on his way back.'

Joyce was struggling now. How could she explain what had happened?

'Yes, well it was a false alarm really, but since they'd come out all that way I couldn't let them go without a cuppa, could I. They were in no hurry to get back to the station.'

'I suppose you had all your friends there, didn't you?'

'All my friends?'

'Yes, Wednesday evening. Isn't that when you have your little theatre group?'

Golly, what does this woman know, Joyce wondered

'Of course, yes, we were all there. It was quite a party.'

Joyce handed over the money for the stamps as quickly as she could and got out before Miriam cross-examined her any more. What rumours were going around the village as a result of the visit of the fire crew?

It was Winston's fault. The evening was just getting underway when he decided he needed a slice of toast, and then of course Johnny and Mick said they were hungry too. Winston put a few slices under the grill and came back into the hall. That's when Susan started to work on him. Once his cock was having some attention his brain appeared to switch off. Susan was soon licking his shaft and massaging his balls so he was far gone. No one else gave a thought about the toast.

It was Eileen who screamed out that the house was on fire. She ran to the hall saw smoke in the kitchen and grabbed the phone. She'd dialled 999 and summoned the fire brigade before anybody else got into the kitchen.

The smell was beyond burned toast and the kitchen was full of grey smoke but it wasn't as bad as it looked. Joyce covered her face with her hanky and luckily remembered where the mains switch for the cooker was. Then she pulled the grill pan out. There were only a few bits of flaming charcoal left. Edith opened some windows and that was when the firemen arrived. One look told them there was no fire to put out but the chief, Pugh, had a good look around and checked that the cooker was OK. The kitchen was a bit of a mess with black soot on the walls and surfaces but a good wash would see to that.

The men really weren't in a hurry to drive back to their station. They had the whole night on call ahead of them with nothing much to do until their radio summoned them to another emergency. Joyce offered them a cuppa.

There were five of them and as soon as it was clear they weren't going to need to unroll their hoses they looked around to see what was happening. There was quite a lot to open their eyes. There was Winston of course, running around naked, Edith in her dominatrix style leather and Susan just in a G-string. Johnny and Mick had had time to pull on their tracksuit bottoms but were bare-chested. Betty had found time to put her dress back on but without her bra her big boobs rolled around like two cats in a sack. Eileen had been down to her bra, suspenders and stockings so gave the men a lovely view of her bush, but Joyce had pulled on her housecoat which was almost decent.

Joyce made the tea and ushered everyone into the hall. By that time the firemen had been whispering and nudging each other and had a pretty good idea of what was going on. The sofas, the great big bed, the whipping bench and the huge painting of the ladies and the boys in the all together and engaged in various uninhibited activities, was sufficient information to say nothing of the dildos and other little toys that happened to be lying around.

It was Susan who got things underway. Not the shy young thing she had been, once she had her clothes off she was a seductress and keen to start the action. Pugh looked a bit reluctant when she climbed on to his lap but a brush of those firm breasts across his lips had him melting, and when she got a hand in his flies he was undone in more ways than one. She soon had his waterproofs off followed by his trousers and pants and was stroking his cock into a fine erection.

The team were quick to follow their leader even if the rest of the ladies weren't apparently such delectable youngsters as Susan. Edith cornered Barney, the driver and oldest of the crew. Grey-haired and in his early fifties he wasn't put off by Edith's age – the shiny black leather made sure of that. She had him stripped off in no time and she knelt over him rubbing her crotch over his face.

Betty chose the youngster of the team, Tom Cuthbert. He looked terrified as she descended on him, tugging off her dress and wobbling her tits at him. She forced him to the floor and tore off his protective clothing – not that protective in this respect. Joyce thought he was in danger of being smothered as she wrapped her thighs around him and buried his face between her buttocks but when he came up for air he looked as though he was enjoying himself, especially as Betty was nibbling on his knob by then.

Eileen and Joyce fancied Fireman Harold Dibble. He was the other mature member of the crew, a very fit forty. The two ladies worked together like a team. Joyce stripped his top half while Eileen took the bottom. Then while Eileen sucked his balls and massaged his cock Joyce gave him a taste of her fanny.

That left Gerry Grubb, a thin man in his late twenties. He seemed shy at first, the way he hung back watching what was going on. Joyce thought it was just nervousness and lack of experience but the truth soon became clear. Winston, Mick and Johnny had nothing to do for once. Winston wandered off – to clean the kitchen, Joyce hoped. Johnny and Mick sat together on a sofa and as often happened when they weren't involved with one of the ladies, they started to play with each other. They had quite lost any shyness of fiddling with each other in the ladies' presence. In fact, Joyce found it quite educational to see two boys exciting each other.

First Johnny tugged Mick's tracksuit down to reveal his cock and balls and then Mick returned the service. While Joyce enjoyed the feel of Dibble's tongue licking her pussy she watched what was going on. Grubb's eyes widened as he saw Johnny and Mick handling each other's cocks. His hand went to his own crotch and started to rub vigorously. Johnny wasn't so far gone that he didn't notice. He left Mick to wank himself and knelt at Grubb's feet. The last Joyce saw, before Harry Dibble took all her attention nibbling her clit, was Johnny lowering his mouth onto Gerry's knob with a look of expectant astonishment on Gerry's face.

The firemen showed off their stamina but Joyce was proud of her friends' response. Quite a time had passed before they all surfaced and lay around the floor pretty well all naked.

'Blimey, girls, is this how you pass your time?' Pugh said.

'Surprised?' Edith asked arching her eyebrows.

'Not 'arf,' Pugh replied.

'Because we're old biddies, Susan excepted?'

'No, no,' Pugh replied laughing. 'We just don't get many callouts like this.'

'Well, don't go dousing this fire; you'd better make the most of it,' Betty said bustling up to the fire chief.

And so everyone moved around, like musical chairs. This time, though, the men were more confident, more in control of their equipment and prepared to give as good as they got.

Gerry Grubb had got over his shyness and seemed to be having a great time with the boys. Joyce watched him enthusiastically sucking on Johnny's cock while Mick eased himself into his arse. Gerry opened his mouth wide and arched his back as Mick's grease-slicked tool slipped into his anus but he soon clamped his lips around Johnny's knob and resumed his chewing. Joyce was impressed by the rhythm he got going so that it seemed he was sliding back and fore along one stiff, pink rod.

Joyce was receiving attention from young Cuthbert. He seemed to have got it into his head to give her an all over tongue wash, starting with her boobs. Joyce considered that they must teach them well in the fire brigade because he made a good job of it. His warm wet tongue circling her nipple sent beautiful tremors down her middle to her pussy. Meanwhile his fingers were caressing her smooth mound. Despite being a modern man and up to date with fashions he was apparently fascinated to find that she had shaved her pubes.

While he was pleasuring Joyce in all the right ways she was able to follow what else was going on. Susan and the very fit Dibble were trying a position Joyce couldn't have contemplated in a month of Sundays. A sort of fireman's lift. He'd picked Susan up and supported her buttocks on his palms while she had wrapped her arms around his neck and her legs around his waist. At some point, Joyce didn't see when, he had inserted his not insignificant cock into her hole so that they were slotted together. Even though Susan was a slip of a girl Joyce was still amazed at how he managed to hold her up, while bending his knees to get a rhythm into his thrusts. Joyce supposed that running up and down ladders with distressed ladies over his shoulder must do wonders for the strength in his calves and thighs. Susan was evidently enjoying the experience and shouting encouragement. Harry's face got cherry red and sweat was pouring down his back. He came with a loud grunt and they tumbled together into a sofa with Susan laughing her head off.

Edith and Barney were still together. Edith was introducing him to the joys of discipline. He had taken up the position over the whipping bench and she was belabouring his bum cheeks with a riding crop. Eileen assisted her by sitting beneath the contraption tugging on his prick and balls. She separated the two testicles with a forefinger and thumb around each loose sac and happily pulled them apart. Despite her age Edith had some strength in her arm and she produced some livid red stripes on Barney's white arse but he seemed to be loving the attention and encouraged Edith and Eileen to keep at it.

That left Betty, on her knees with her head resting on her folded arms and bum thrust up in the air. Pugh was behind her thrusting his tool into her fanny. He looked as if he was bouncing on a space hopper except that although her thighs were nicely tanned from the week on Majorca her cheeks were virgin white. Pugh was giving Betty a good seeing to because his knob appeared before each thrust when his shaft disappeared and his balls slapped against her mound.

By this time Cuthbert had worked his way down to Joyce's fanny. She encouraged him to come astride her so they could sixty-nine. Joyce liked sucking on a cock while a tongue and lips were working her over. Cuthbert may have been new to it but he was thorough. He didn't just chew on her clit, but he licked and sucked on her lips and dug his tongue deep into her hole. Joyce knew her juices were flowing well and he lapped them up like a kitten at a saucer of milk.

Although it was a short time since his first orgasm it was not long before Joyce's efforts brought reward. As she licked around the little hole in his knob, and pressed her lips against the silky softness of the skin she could feel his cock stiffening and throbbing. His legs stiffened and he pushed his cock into her. His semen gushed into her mouth. The eggy aroma filled her nose and she tasted the saltiness on her tongue. Joyce swallowed and sucked every last drop from his shrinking penis as she tipped over into her own climax. Her thighs squeezed his head pushing him even deeper into her vagina as pulse after pulse of contractions gripped her. She had almost strangled him by the time she relaxed and they parted, panting on the rug.

All lay in a tangle of limbs and genitalia getting their breath back. As far as Joyce was concerned she was finished for the evening but not those energetic firemen. They had aroused passions in Susan and they were happy to stoke the fire. She announced that she would like three of them at once. Were they up to the challenge, Joyce wondered? Of course they were.

It wasn't long before she had Dibble, Cuthbert and Pugh salivating at her with their pricks as long and hard as ever. She made Pugh lie on the floor and mounted him. The look of pleasure as his cock slid into her channel was something to behold. Then she got Cuthbert to kneel behind his boss's head and she leant forward to take his knob between her lips. Dibble, the experienced one, knew what was required of him. He lubricated his penis then knelt behind Susan and parted her bum cheeks. The tip of his dick pushed against the pink rose of her arse. He eased forward, Susan relaxed and the tip slipped inside. The sphincter tightened around his knob and he paused. Then he pushed a little more and a few inches of his shaft eased into her backside. Now Pugh began to move, arching his back and thrusting his cock upwards. Cuthbert rocked to and fro, sliding his penis between her lips. Dibble alone held still his cock gripped tightly by her ring of muscle.

Afterwards Susan said she could feel the two rods almost touching inside her abdomen. She was at the mercy of the three men but they were gentle, keeping their urge to stampede to their own orgasms in check while bringing Susan to her climax. She said that she couldn't keep a count of the number of times she thought she'd reached a peak. As it happened each of the three men came close together. White froth oozed from Susan's cunt, arse and mouth almost simultaneously and the three men let out a chorus of exclamations. They unplugged from Susan in turn and lay together with their arms wrapped around each other.

Meanwhile, Gerry Grubb had lost any semblance of innocence of gay sex by enthusiastically buggering Mick while Johnny urged him on. Edith and Betty soothed Barney's abused buttocks with kisses and took his mind off the stinging weals by coaxing his cock to another erection taking it in turns to use it to fill their cunts. Winston returned in search of some action which Eileen happily provided, presenting her backside for him to insert his eager cock in her fanny.

Joyce felt quite exhausted by watching all that went on but that proved to be the last round of play. Chief Pugh decided it was time for the crew to leave and they stiffly pulled on their uniforms and safety gear. Before they left they stood in a line, saluted then marched down the driveway back to their fire engine.

'Well that was an evening to remember,' Betty said as they returned to the hall for a few minutes relaxation. Susan was so exhausted that she was fast asleep.

'A pretty good response to a 999 call,' Edith said.

Chapter Seventeen
The Flasher

'We've got a flasher,' Betty announced as she waddled into a meeting of the Ladies' College for Erotic Arts.

'What do you mean – *we've* got one?' Joyce said, pausing in the act of pulling Johnny's tight nylon knickers down over his bulging cock and balls.

'The village has. Audrey Sparrow told me in the shop.'

Betty had attracted their attention now. Joyce completed her task of releasing Johnny's tool and sac from the constricting cloth. She turned and sat at his feet as he lowered himself on to the sofa. She lifted a hand and gently caressed the quivering piston.

'Come on,' Edith urged while Mick helped her out of her dress and revealed her tight leather basque, 'you've got to tell us more.'

'Well, Audrey said that at least three people have seen him, all women.'

'Where?' Eileen asked from the bed where Winston was already fucking her energetically

'On the common,' Betty replied. 'A lot of people use the path across it to get from the new houses to the shop and the pub.'

'I think I know where you mean,' Eileen said thoughtfully, as Winston pumped his cock into her. 'It's not like a village green, is it. The grass is pretty long and there are shrubs and bushes.'

'That's why it's a common and not a green,' Joyce said, 'Sheep used to graze on it.'

‘I knew people who got up to all sorts of things in the long grass – no one could see you,’ Susan said from beside Johnny, rubbing her tits and examining her dark red nipples. The others nodded as if they knew what she meant.

‘Right, so we know where. What else is there? Come on, Betty.’ Edith was showing impatience. Mick knelt at her feet and smoothed his hands up her silk-stocking-clad legs.

‘Audrey says he’s a young man; wears one of those long parka things. He waits for a woman to come along when there’s no one else about and then leaps out from behind a bush and shows off his tackle.’

‘You mean he doesn’t have anything on under his parka,’ Susan giggled.

‘That’s right. Not a stitch except for a pair of Wellingtons.’

‘Was there a description of his “tackle” as you call it?’ Edith asked again.

‘Well, no, I wouldn’t expect Audrey to give me a full description – she does the flowers in the church.’

‘What’s that got to do with the price of fish?’ Eileen said, gasping as Winston gave her an extra deep thrust. ‘I bet there are plenty of vicars who have some hanky-panky behind the pews.’

‘Really, Eileen, just because you like fucking in unusual places doesn’t mean that everyone gets up to it,’ Joyce said in mock horror.

‘No, I mean it. You hear lots of stories about randy clergy.’

‘Did Audrey say anything else?’ Edith asked trying to get the conversation back on track while Mick nuzzled his face into her mound.

‘She did mention that the flasher, well, she said “touches himself”, but I think she means …’

‘Wanks off,’ Eileen said firmly as Winston came with a prolonged groan.

‘Well, yes, I expect so,’ Betty agreed.

‘When does this happen?’ Joyce asked.

‘Oh, late afternoon, early evening, when it’s getting dark,’ Betty replied.

‘Getting a bit cold, this time of year, to be getting your

privates out,' Edith observed widening her stance a little so that Mick could push his tongue between her thighs.

'Those parkas are surprisingly warm,' Joyce commented, 'and they're edged with fake fur.'

'They're not warm if you go round flinging them open with nothing on underneath,' Eileen said, 'I'm surprised he keeps warm enough to get a hard-on.'

'The thought of exposing himself must be arousing, I suppose,' Joyce said.

'Well, we can't let it go on,' Eileen said firmly, pushing Winston on to his side and twisting to sit up on the side of the bed.

'Why not?' Susan said. 'It's nothing to do with us.' Her hand fell from her breasts to finger the blonde hairs at her crotch.

'Oh, yes it is,' Edith replied. 'Just think. People in the village getting all worked up about sexual shenanigans; the police being called in to question everyone; a watch kept on the common; newspaper reporters taking an interest. It'll be all over the papers. We won't have any peace.'

'Edith's right,' Betty said, at last removing her raincoat. 'It's just the kind of story that newspapers love to print and there'll be policemen everywhere.'

Despite her gentle ministrations Johnny's penis had gone a little limp in Joyce's hand. Her mind had been on the flasher.

'What can we do about him?' Susan asked, sliding a finger between her pussy lips.

'We can catch him,' Joyce said, taking such a firm grip of Johnny's cock that he gave a little yelp.

'What!' the others exclaimed together.

'Why not? We know when and where he does it,' Joyce went on. 'We can act as decoys, attract his attention and then the boys can jump out and grab him.'

'And how do we "attract his attention"?' Edith asked with a note of scepticism in her voice.

'By playing him at his own game,' Joyce said, smiling proudly as she thought of her plan.

'You mean showing our bodies to him,' Susan said coyly

with two fingers in her fanny.

'Exactly. We walk across the common. He'll see us as typical, middle-aged, uptight women. Then when he approaches us and opens his coat, we do the same. I am sure the sight of a naked woman will be the last thing he expects.'

'It could work,' Eileen nodded in agreement.

'Just one thing,' Edith said.

'What's that?' Joyce asked.

'What do we do with him when we've got him?'

'We'll bring him back here and teach him a lesson so he doesn't do it again. I'm sure you will have some ideas about that, Edith.'

It was agreed and so the five ladies and the three men made their plans.

The next day Winston hid amongst the bushes on the common early in the afternoon, before the flasher was expected to begin his activities. He settled in for the prolonged vigil. It was a relatively balmy day for November but Joyce made sure he was wrapped up warm. By four o'clock the sun was sinking below the tall poplar trees at the edge of the common.

Joyce took the first walk along the path from the village shop. She had her long mink coat wrapped around her and knee-high boots covering her lower legs. She didn't dawdle but neither did she walk too briskly. The crossing of the common was completed without seeing another soul. Joyce was disappointed but not surprised that they'd failed on the first run. A few minutes later, Eileen followed, similarly attired but wearing a woollen coat rather than fur. Then Susan in thigh boots and a knee-length PVC mac came next. There was a pause as a couple of ladies from the small housing estate hurried to catch the shop before it closed. Once they had cleared the path it was Edith's turn and then Betty's. None of them saw so much as a rabbit sticking its bright white tail above the grass let alone an exposed penis.

They repeated their lone strolls in the other direction but again without result. By this time it was dark and it was getting difficult to see more than a few feet on either side of the gravel track.

'I think that's it for now,' Joyce said, 'I'd better call Winston in.' She gave a low call, a bit like an owl, but not much.

There was no sign of movement but a few moments later Joyce leapt in the air with a whoop. Winston had goosed her.

'I didn't see you,' Joyce said.

'That was the plan,' Winston laughed. 'There's one advantage of being dark.'

They returned to the Old School and resolved to do it all over again the following evening, with Johnny as the one to lie in wait.

The next afternoon was cloudy and cold but nevertheless Joyce said they must go ahead with the plan. Johnny was despatched to the common and just before four o'clock they began their walks. It passed much the same as the previous day until the light had almost faded and Joyce was beginning to think it was time to give up.

She began her second traverse of the common. Her feet crunched the gravel and she looked ahead trying to look natural. She was about halfway across when a figure appeared in front of her. One moment the path was empty, the next he was there walking towards her. It was him; she could tell by the dark grey parka he wore. They approached each other until he was less than ten feet from her when with a sudden sweeping movement with both arms he opened his coat wide revealing his naked torso. Joyce stopped and stared. His penis was erect with a curious upward curve and his testicles were tight against the root as to be almost invisible. He had little body hair and his skin almost glowed with its whiteness. Joyce found that she was so intent on examining the flasher's equipment that she forgot what she was supposed to do. He obviously wasn't prepared for her lack of reaction.

'Well?' he said in a thin plaintive voice. The sound brought Joyce back to consciousness. She grabbed the edge of her fur coat and opened it up in the same manner as the young man.

'Snap!' she said, immediately aware of the cold air on her privates. She had often wondered what gobsmacked meant but she imagined the look on his face was a good definition. 'Get him!' she called.

The flasher didn't move. He stood gazing at the wonders of Joyce's naked body with his own fully exposed. The tableau lasted for a few seconds when with a yell Johnny flattened the young man with a flying rugby tackle.

The other ladies were running down the path behind her but their help was not needed. Johnny was already on his feet with his captive held in an arm lock. Joyce buttoned up her coat.

'Come on,' Joyce urged. 'Get him home before anybody else comes along.'

The struggling flasher was half dragged, half carried to the edge of the common where the Rover was parked. Joyce opened the boot and the young man was tipped inside. Joyce slammed the boot-lid shut and hurried to the driving seat. Johnny, Edith and Betty got in, while Susan joined Eileen in her Escort.

Joyce drove the short distance back to the Old School aware of the thumps and muffled shouts of the prisoner in the boot. She hoped they didn't pass any villagers who might wonder at the noises.

Back at the Old School, Winston met them and helped Johnny lift the young man from the car and carry him, still wriggling into the hall. He was dumped unceremoniously on the floor between the sofas and the bed and surrounded by the five women and three men.

He rolled on to his back and lifted himself on to his elbows. His parka fell open revealing his body again but now his penis had shrunk to miniscule proportions.

'Wot you doing? Why'd you bring me 'ere?' he asked, looking up at them.

'To teach you a lesson to stop you exposing yourself in public,' Joyce informed him.

'You can't keep me 'ere. That's false imprisonment,' he complained.

'That may be so, but we'll keep you until you have decided to behave.'

'Wora you gonna do?' He'd begun to look a bit scared of the frowns of the people looking down on him.

His hair was matted and dirty, his unshaven face marked by grime, and his ribs poked through his thin frame. Young he most certainly was, but definitely not looked after, Joyce thought.

'First we're going to punish you for frightening those poor ladies you have shown yourself to. Let's get that filthy parka and those muddy boots off him,' Joyce said.

Hands descended on the young flasher and despite his struggles he was completely naked in moments with his arms and legs held motionless.

'What now?' Winston asked.

'On to the bench,' Joyce ordered. The young man was carried to the whipping apparatus, draped over it and his wrists and ankles strapped into place.

'Who wants to go first?' Joyce asked.

'Me, please,' Edith said. She had become the leading disciplinarian of the group and skilful at wielding a whip or a cane. She took off her winter coat revealing herself in full dominatrix wear. She drew a stout cane from the box of instruments of punishment and positioned herself behind the flasher's rear.

His thighs were drawn wide, parting his bony buttocks. His cock hung limply but his balls were still held tight. He flexed the muscles in his legs but he was unable to move an inch. Edith's arm swung down; the cane made a delightful swish and hit him firmly on his right cheek. He yowled. Edith shifted her position and another blow fell on his left cheek. A V-shaped weal appeared at the apex of his anus which tensed and opened involuntarily. He pulled at the bindings on his wrists and ankles but the leather straps held him so firmly that he was unable to move any limb at all. He sagged over the bench resigned to his fate.

'You do realise that what you have done is wrong,' Joyce said, bending down to see his tear-lined face.

'Yeah,' he sobbed, 'it was just a lark.'

'It wasn't a lark for those poor traumatised women not used to seeing a young, smooth, stiff cock,' Joyce recalled its pleasing curve and pink, flawless skin, 'nor seeing a man wanking himself off in front of them.'

'I'm sorry,' he cried.

'Sorry isn't enough. You have to take your punishment.' Joyce nodded to Edith and two more red lines formed on his bum.

'You do agree you must be punished?' Joyce asked.

'Yeah, yeah,' he said obviously hoping his agreement would end the torment.

'Good.' Joyce stood up and looked around. 'Who else would like a go?'

'Oh, yes, please.' Eileen stepped forward with the handle of a long whip in her hand, 'I've wanted to try this out.' She stood six feet from her target and flicked the whip. It made a satisfying crack and a thin dark red line joined the others on the young man's backside. He yelped again.

'A few more Eileen, then we'll see what he can tell us about himself,' Joyce said standing back.

Eileen obliged with three more lashes that brought shouts and tears from the bound boy.

'Good,' Joyce said and Eileen laid the whip down, 'Now, young man, tell us your name.'

'Wha–?' he said through a sob.

'What are you called?'

'My da' calls me "wanker" and "prick" and "knob".'

'Probably very apt names, but what is your real name?'

'William or Willy.'

The ladies chuckled and Joyce went on

'How old are you, Willy?'

'Twen'y.'

'Good. Now where do you live?'

'Nowhere.'

'What do you mean, nowhere? Everyone lives somewhere.'

'I hafen' got nowhere. My ol'man chucked me out. Tol' me to get lost.'

'I see, Willy, I'm sorry. So what have you been doing?'

'I bin on the common, found some bits of corri-gated iron and cardboard lyin' round.'

'So you are homeless. Why did your father throw you out of

your home?'

'He caught me wanking. Said I was a layabout and I should gera job, not spend my time looking at tits and cunts and pulling myself off.'

'You like looking at women's private parts do you, Willy?'

There was a pause.

'Answer, please, Willy.'

'Yeah, I s'pose so.'

'Come on, Willy, be honest or I'll ask Eileen or Edith to punish you again.'

'No, please. Yeah, I like looking at wimin.'

'Has a woman ever allowed you to fuck her, Willy?'

'No,' he replied in a forlorn tone of voice.

'Or ever held your cock?'

'No.'

'Well, perhaps if you behave yourself you'll get some attention.'

Eileen coughed. 'If you are thinking of giving him some behaviour therapy, something nice after the punishment, Joyce, I'm not touching his bits while he's so filthy. Look at him. I don't think he's had a bath for a month.'

Joyce could only agree. Now under the hall's spotlights, streaks of dirt could be seen marking his pale skin.

'If he is homeless I don't imagine he has many opportunities for a good wash,' she said.

'Now don't go feeling sorry for him,' Edith said. 'He's a lazy good for nothing.'

'Oh, that's a bit harsh,' Betty declared. 'I'm sure he's not really bad.'

'Well, I think Eileen is right,' Joyce said. 'Before we give him any more treatment I think he needs cleaning up. Boys if you could see to it please. Put Willy in the shower and make sure he washes himself thoroughly – everywhere.'

Willy was released from the punishment bench and carried out in the strong arms of Winston and Johnny.

'Now, ladies, what are we going to do with Willy?' Joyce asked.

'We can't let him go back to sleeping rough on the

common,' Susan said.

'Why not?' Eileen said, 'If his family don't want him, why should we be bothered?'

'He'll go back to exposing himself if we let him go now,' Edith stated, 'I think it's going to take some training to change him.'

'Training, that's it,' Joyce said. 'Edith, you said a while ago that you'd like to have a slave to train.'

'I did?' The passage of various thoughts was evident on Edith's lined face. 'I did.'

'Do you think you could manage him? We'd help out, of course.'

'Hmm, yes. I have a spare room at the back, and my house isn't overlooked by neighbours. It'll be quite a project taking on that little wanker.'

'You'll do a good job on him, Edith. Do the rest of you agree?' Joyce looked around at Eileen, Betty and Susan who nodded enthusiastically.

'Make sure he earns his keep,' Eileen said.

Joyce stopped the Rover outside the red brick cottage surrounded by trees. Joyce noticed that the foliage obscured the view of the upstairs windows and formed an archway to the front door.

'I didn't realise how secluded Edith's place was,' she commented to Eileen.

'It will help to keep Willy from disturbing the neighbours.'

They left the car and approached the front door. A few moments after ringing the doorbell it was opened by Edith wearing a pinafore over her dress.

'Hello, come on in. He's upstairs.'

Joyce and Eileen followed Edith up the narrow stairs to a landing and then into the rear bedroom. Winston had helped Edith make some alterations in the last couple of days. The only furniture was a large iron bedstead. Steel rings had been screwed in to three of the walls and the ceiling. Thick linen curtains hung from poles across the window.

'Hello, Willy,' Joyce said. There was a muffled response

from the former flasher. He lay on the bed naked but for the leather collar around his neck fastened by a chain to the ring on the wall behind the bed. His wrists were handcuffed and connected by a short chain to the collar. There was a gag strapped across his mouth and his ankles were bound to the posts at the foot of the bed.

'He looks tidy,' Joyce said.

'Yes, he cleaned up nicely, didn't he, but he's dreadfully thin,' Edith said. 'I'm going to have to feed him up a bit.'

'You have his hands on a short chain,' Eileen noted.

'I had to do that,' Edith said, 'to stop him playing with himself. Any chance he gets his hands are round his cock, rubbing away. I've got to get control of his erection if I'm going to get him to obey me.'

'Oh, so that's why you've got his penis in that, ah, contraption,' Joyce said. The young man's manhood was enclosed in a stainless steel tube that was locked to metal rings that encircled his testicles and the base of his genitals.'

'It's a chastity device. Mr Winter supplied it to me.'

'Mr Winter?' Eileen said, confused, 'Oh, the sex toys salesman, I remember.'

'He said it's a special product. He doesn't sell many.'

'I'm not surprised. Who wants to restrict a cock from extending to its full length,' Eileen said leaning down to examine the apparatus carefully.

'Have you made any progress, Edith?' Joyce asked.

'Oh, yes. I think he understands that he will only get a taste of the crop if he disobeys me and he seems pleased that he's being kept warm, fed, and relatively comfortable. I think he considers the loss of his freedom a good deal. Of course he lost all his dignity by flaunting himself in front of those women.'

'So what's next?' Eileen asked.

'Well, having stopped him wanking for over a day now I want to start showing him how he can give pleasure.'

'And be rewarded?'

'Of course.'

'Do you want me to give him some practice?' Eileen asked.

'Yes, if you like,' Edith said, 'see how good he can be with his tongue and I'll manage his dick.'

While Eileen took off her coat, skirt and jumper – she wasn't wearing underclothes – Joyce unfastened the gag from around Willy's face and Edith undid the chastity apparatus. The young man's eyes widened when he saw Eileen's body and his cock twitched and grew.

'A quick response,' Joyce noted. Eileen climbed on to the bed and placed her knees either side of his shoulders. She lowered herself to his mouth.

'Now, Willy,' she said gently, 'all you have to do is open your mouth and stick your tongue out. When you feel me just move it in a circular motion. And don't forget that Edith will have your cock and balls in her hands, so don't try anything stupid.'

She spread her knees wider and pushed her pelvis forward until her fanny touched his lips. He shivered but obeyed her instructions and stuck out his tongue. Eileen felt its warm, wetness touching her lips and she trembled.

'Phew,' Edith whistled. 'That's an erection. He's rock hard.'

Eileen rocked forward an inch and felt his nose rub against her clit. It sent electric currents up through her abdomen. His tongue continued to circle around her hole. She could feel her juices running. She pressed down.

'Try pushing your tongue deeper,' she instructed. Immediately she felt his stiff tongue extending into her channel. She sighed with pleasure and jogged up and down.

'Oh-oh,' Edith said, 'I think he's going to come.'

Eileen felt his body stiffen beneath her. His legs tensed and strained at the bonds holding his legs apart. He arched his back and thrust his face deeper into her quim. He groaned.

'A fountain!' Joyce exclaimed.

The young man subsided, his muscles relaxed and his tongue withdrew. Eileen sighed; she hadn't quite got to her climax. She dismounted and stood by the bed looking at the cream fluid that soaked the mattress cover between his thighs and coated his shrunken cock.

'Well that was interesting,' Eileen said. 'His mouthwork has potential and he has a good long probing tongue, but you're going to have to do something about that response Edith. You can't have him gushing the moment he touches a female.'

'He is rather over-eager despite all the masturbation,' Edith agreed.

'He's young,' Joyce said. 'Plenty of spunk in him and plenty of time to learn.'

'I think you're going to have to keep his cock cage on until he learns how to give pleasure for longer,' Eileen said. 'But a good start.'

'Well, I'm ready for a cup of tea,' Edith said, wiping semen from her hands with a towel, 'how about you two?'

Chapter Eighteen
Assignments

The Ladies' College for Erotic Arts
The Old School
1st December

Dear Fellow Students,

It is nearly the end of the year and quite a while now since we came together for the first time to discover the art of pleasure. We have taught ourselves a great deal, and had a lot of fun. Now I suggest it is time to show what we have learned. I challenge you to develop your skills still further and stretch your inhibitions to the utmost. At our meeting early in the New Year we will each report on our exploits and reveal how we're feeling about our journeys of self-education.

I wish you all well. Good fucking,
Joyce.

Susan

She peered between the curtains, looking out for the car that he'd sent to pick her up. The house was dark and quiet, especially so now that her mother had called to pick up Hannah. Her daughter had got quite used to spending nights at her grandmother's house – two or sometimes three times a week. Susan felt torn. She felt responsibility for her little girl and loved her more than anything or anyone, but, and it was a big but, she was enjoying her new life. No longer did she spend days worrying how she would pay the rent or the electricity bill.

She had money to spend now on the necessities and treats for Hannah, and herself. Did Mother realise where the money was coming from? Susan suspected that she did.

'Strange to be having a training course over a weekend just before Christmas?' she'd said before leaving with Hannah a few minutes ago, 'and I wouldn't have thought you would be expected to dress up in your best new outfit.'

Susan regretted having changed into her new Biba dress before her mother had left. It was black and short with a wide gold collar; hardly the gear to wear for an evening with other beauticians in a cheap hotel. But of course that wasn't the plan at all and her mother's sideways look said as much. Did she guess that Susan was earning hundreds of pounds as a sought after and exclusive whore?

'Look after yourself,' she'd said as she stepped outside the door with Hannah in her arms.

'I will, Mum,' Susan had replied.

A large car, a Bentley, slid slowly between the two rows of parked vehicles edging the narrow street. It stopped outside her door. This must be it, Susan thought, letting go of the corner of the curtain and picking up her overnight bag. She pulled the door closed behind her wondering if any of the neighbours were looking out.

The chauffeur stood holding the rear door open. She climbed in, seduced by the smell of leather, the thick padding, the space. The driver got back in and silently the car moved off, increasing in speed smoothly when they turned on to the main road.

Where were they going, she wondered? He'd only said that it was a hotel, a rather special one; special, because this was their first weekend together. He'd been her regular client for about a month now. Once a week he had arrived for his appointment with her at Madam Glover's establishment. Almost from the first session Gerald had treated her differently to the others. Perhaps it was because he was younger than most of the men that could afford to purchase Madam's merchandise. He was relaxed, made love to her because he wanted to not because he needed to show off his male dominance. She had wondered why he chose to pay for her services when he could have had any of the young modern girls who would willingly throw themselves at his feet. He didn't want an acolyte, he said, and he couldn't be bothered to seek out a woman that wasn't after his money.

The Bentley turned off the A road and drove up a long drive to what had once been a stately home. It still was stately except it was now a very exclusive hotel. A step up even to a Hilton Susan thought. The car pulled up at the porticoed entrance. One footman opened the door, another collected her bag and another escorted her into the entrance hall. She didn't have to do anything so mundane as register; a bellboy guided her straight up the broad, grand staircase.

They know precisely who and what I am, Susan thought, but each servant treated her as the lady she looked like and not the impostor she felt herself to be.

A wide, tall door was opened and she was ushered into the room. No, not a room, a suite, an apartment. The foyer was bigger than her house and beyond was a vast sitting room with sofas, chairs, grand piano, huge TV and thick, thick carpets.

He was there, standing by the fireplace, dressed as usual in jeans and T-shirt, stroking his short but scruffy beard. He never did conform to the expectations of dress for a man of his wealth. In many ways he still looked like the nerdy teenager he'd been just a few years before when he'd started on his road to riches.

The footman carried her small case into the adjoining bedroom and then stood waiting for a tip. Gerald dug into his tight pockets and pulled out a coin. He dropped it into the servant's hand.

'Thank you, Mr Henson,' the young man said and withdrew.

Gerald looked Susan up and down with admiration.

'My, you look good tonight,' he said with the voice of an eager youth. He stepped forward and kissed her on the lips. Susan felt his tongue searching, pressing. She opened her mouth and let him in. His tongue explored while his hands were also busy. He lifted the hem of her dress above her waist, finding the waistband of her tights. He yanked the tights down and ran his hands over her bare bottom and down her crack. One hand migrated to the front and cupped her bush, a finger questing between her already moist lips.

His hands released her and returned to holding her dress. His mouth parted from hers and then with one sweeping movement he pulled the dress over her head and flung it into a corner of the room. So much for my expensive new dress, Susan thought. She hadn't worn a bra so now his eyes were caught by her pert breasts and cherry red nipples. He gathered her up in his arms and carried her the few feet to a low padded coffee table the size of a small divan. He laid her down and dragged off her tights and knickers. In a few moments more he was also naked and crawling between her legs, planting a kiss in her navel.

There was a polite knock on the door.

'Ah, that'll be dinner,' Gerald said as he leaped up and approached the door quite unconcerned by his erection that went before him. He opened the door and without speaking to the knocker returned to Susan. A maid pushed a trolley bearing silver dishes into the room. Susan noticed her eyes glance at her and her lover but her face displayed no reaction at seeing two naked guests. She retreated leaving the trolley in the centre of the lounge.

Gerald lifted various lids and examined the contents.

'Great, just what I ordered. I'm sorry, love, I didn't give you a choice but I've ordered a special dinner for us this evening. I chose every dish.'

'Oh, should I get up and dress again?' Susan asked rising on to her arms.

'No, love. Stay there. You're part of it. You'll see.'

Gerald selected one of the silver pots and carried it to where Susan lay. He lifted off the lid and picked up a pineapple ring. He placed it over Susan's left breast with her nipple in the centre. Another ring was located over her right breast.

'So, I'm to be the table for this meal, am I?' Susan asked, giggling.

'Not the table, the crockery. We're going to start with a fruit cocktail,' Gerald replied scooping up a handful of melon balls. He placed them carefully in her navel. Susan gasped and giggled.

'Ooh, they're cold and they tickle. The juice is running down my side. It's going to stain the material on this whatever it is.'

'Don't worry about the furniture. If we spoil it I'll replace it for them. Now raise your knees and lie still.' Susan did as she was told, wondering what Gerald was going to do next.

He went to the trolley and returned brandishing a large banana. It was bright yellow and almost straight. He snapped open the end but did not peel it. He knelt on the floor at her feet and pushed her legs apart.

'What are you doing? Aaah.' Susan found the answer to her question as Gerald parted the lips of her fanny and placed the end of the banana between them. He pushed gently sliding the fruit into her vagina. Susan raised her head to see what he was doing but careful not to dislodge the pineapple rings or melon balls. He stopped when just the curved end that he had split open was visible.

'Is that comfortable, love?' he asked as he climbed on to his feet and retrieved from beside a sofa a large camera with an electronic flash gun attached.

'Um, yes, it feels a bit strange but not uncomfortable. It's softer than a dildo.'

'You've had a dildo up your cunt then.'

'Oh yes.'

'Good, I like it.' He moved around her taking photos at various angles. Then he put the camera down and knelt beside her. He lifted one of the pineapple rings up in his teeth and moved it to Susan's mouth. Together they chewed on the sweet fruit until their lips met. He repeated the action with the other ring then licked the juice from both breasts. Susan sighed; she was enjoying this way of eating fruit.

Gerald moved to her navel, leaned down to take a melon ball in his lips and transferred it to Susan's mouth. One by one the balls disappeared leaving just a little pool of juice in her tummy-button. He lapped it up drawing more giggles from Susan. She wriggled and felt the banana move in her vagina.

'What about the banana?' she asked.

'Don't worry. I haven't forgotten it,' he said crawling

around to kneel between her legs. He parted the open end of the skin exposing the white flesh. He lowered his head, opening his mouth to surround the tip of the fruit with his lips. Susan felt the pressure of his mouth against her fanny through the cool skin of the banana. He tugged and pulled the banana an inch from her hole. He chewed and tugged again, using his fingers to part the strips of skin. Bit by bit the banana emerged from her vagina and he chewed it all.

'Sorry you didn't get any of the banana,' he said, swallowing the final bit.

'It doesn't matter, I enjoyed watching you,' she replied feeling excited by his strange behaviour.

'The main course is next. Nothing exotic, but my favourite – bangers and mash.' From the trolley he collected two silver dishes. He opened one to reveal a heap of brilliant white, creamy mashed potato in which he stuck a finger.

'Good, not too hot and just the right consistency.' He began to ladle the mash onto Susan's body, covering her breasts and tummy right down to the triangle of hair on her mound. When she was completely covered he collected a bottle of ketchup and squirted it over the potato to mark her nipples, navel and pubes. He stood back to admire his handiwork.

'Just, don't move,' he ordered, 'or it will all slide off.'

Susan giggled but tried to do as he said.

'What about the sausages then?' she asked having the beginning of an idea of what he intended.

He lifted up the second dish and revealed a pile of unusual sausages. Well cooked and glistening with fat, they were larger than the standard butcher's banger in both length and girth.

'I had to get these specially made,' Gerald said. 'No one makes British sausages this size normally.' He held one up and Susan estimated it to be the size of a penis, Gerald's penis, in fact, about seven inches long and one and a half in diameter.

'I think I can guess where that's going,' Susan joked. She wasn't wrong. He knelt between her legs and slid the greasy meat rod into her cunt. Susan felt it stretch her vagina and its warmth spread through her abdomen. When the whole length of the sausage was inside her Gerald gave it an extra push. Susan felt her vulva close around it.

'I'm going to let it marinade for a few minutes,' Gerald said moving around her clicking away with his camera, 'so let's tuck into the mash.' He put the camera down and picked up a spoon. He ran it up the middle of her body scooping up the potato. He ate some and put some in Susan's mouth. Spoonful by spoonful they ate all the mashed potato that covered her, then he returned to between her legs.

'Right push, love, as if you were giving birth.' Having had Hannah, Susan knew what he wanted. She squeezed her pelvic muscles and felt the sausage ooze through her lips. He bent forward and licked the tip.

'Oh, yes, a wonderful flavour – partly pork fat, partly you, my love.' He bit into it and chewed, then lowered his head and pulled another inch from her hole. He gobbled up the whole banger.

'Don't I get any?' Susan asked.

'Of course,' he said, picking out two sausages. 'But first I'll put another away to prepare.' He pushed it into her as before then brought the other for her to nibble on.

Susan hungrily devoured the sausage.'Can't I nibble on your other one?' she said nodding towards his tool which bobbed fully erect between his legs.

'Of course, love.' He knelt astride her and lowered his cock to her mouth. She welcomed it in comparing its size and texture to the cooked meat that filled her quim. She sucked avidly and was delighted when he came with a rush, filling her mouth with delicious creamy semen. He withdrew and she swallowed.

'Good I needed a drink after the sausage,' she said, laughing.

'Right, well it's time I had my second,' he said twisting around to kneel astride her stomach. He lowered his head to her fanny placing his lips on her and inserting his tongue to lick around the buried tip of the sausage. Susan knew that her juices were flowing and she was becoming desperate for an orgasm herself but it seemed that he was not ready just yet. He ate the whole sausage pulling it a little at a time from her hole and savouring every bite. When it was all gone he licked around her pussy and thrust his tongue as deep inside her as he could manage. She trembled and quivered but didn't quite come.

He leapt off her and hurried to the trolley.

'Now for the dessert,' he announced returning with a huge bowl of strawberries and whipped cream. Ignoring the mess he made of the Dralon-covered divan, he ladled the fruit and thick cream onto her pelvis, pushing the large strawberries between her fanny lips. Every other scoop he offered to her mouth letting her eat her fill. Then he put the bowl down and after taking a few photographs buried his face in the white foam between her thighs. He bit into the strawberries, sucked the cream from her pubic hair and licked it from her thighs.

'Push, love,' he urged, and one by one she popped strawberries from her vagina into his waiting mouth.

'I hope you were keeping count,' she said, 'I don't want to find you've left one up inside me.'

'All accounted for,' he said, licking the final drop of cream from the crack between her buttocks and sucking her clitoris for good measure. He got to his feet.

'Just one more thing,' he said.

'You're not thinking of serving cheese and biscuits from my bum crack, are you?'

'Now that's an idea I didn't think of.'

'Or hot coffee from my navel?'

'No, but how about a glass of wine from your cunt.' He picked up a bottle and swiftly removed the cork.

'I had thought of champagne, but since that has to be served cold, I thought you might complain.'

'You bet I would.' Susan didn't want to contemplate an icy liquid filling her up.

'So this is a sweet dessert wine at room temperature. Lift up your bottom so I can get at least some of it into you.'

She drew her feet back and put her hands under her buttocks and raised her hips. He stood with the bottle between her legs. She felt the cold neck of the bottle pressing against her crack as he slowly tilted it. The wine started to flow out. Most of it flowed down between her buttocks adding to the mess on the Dralon but she felt some of the cool liquid flow into her. He paused, moved the bottle away and lowered his head to her again. His placed his lips at her hole and sucked. There was a loud slurping noise as he lapped at her.

The effort of keeping her bottom raised became too much and Susan relaxed. That was a signal. Gerald dropped the bottle and leaned forward. His penis, revived and hard, pressed against her, demanding entry. She threw her arms around him and drew him in rejoicing in the feel of his warm prick as he entered her. She thrust against him already feeling that peak that she had spent the evening climbing towards become attainable.

He withdrew and rammed into her again. She cried as she felt him come, filling her with his spunk. It was the final thing she needed to climax with a muscle pulsating burst of electricity.

'Well that was a different way to have dinner,' she gasped as her body began to relax.

Betty

The doorbell rang and Betty hurried to answer it, just pausing to pick up her coat and handbag from the stand beside the door. On the doorstep stood a little man, his hair slicked down. He smoothed his moustache.

'Good evening, madam,' he said, dipping his head.

Betty pulled her coat on.

'Hello, Trevor. It's very kind of you to take me out.' She pulled the door closed behind her and Trevor Healey guided her to his brown Hillman Avenger.

'It is my pleasure. To be out with as fine a woman as you was once beyond my wildest dreams.' He helped her into the passenger seat and seated himself behind the wheel.

'It's so nice to be with a polite gentleman who appreciates me,' Betty said. Trevor Healey, the council rates inspector was certainly a change after her salesman husband, Tom. At least *he* was out of her life at last. He had called home one night last week to collect a suitcase full of washed and ironed clothes and she had sent him packing, telling him he could shack up with his floozies in Plymouth, Southampton and Birmingham if he wished but to expect nothing more from her. Tonight would be a much more pleasurable affair with the solicitous Trevor.

They went to a Berni Inn where they dined on prawn cocktail, well done rump steak (Trevor) and breaded plaice (Betty – she was endeavouring to control her weight), with black forest gateau to follow, washed down with a bottle of Black Tower and finishing with coffee in wine glasses with floating cream. While the conversation was pleasant Betty did sense that Trevor was eager to complete the meal and return to her house.

He parked carefully, held the car door for her as she got out, and stood obediently behind her as she put the key in the lock.

'I shall go upstairs to change into something a little more comfortable,' Betty said in her schoolmistress voice, 'and I want you to go into the living room and prepare yourself. Off you go.'

Trevor, doing as he was told, went into the living room. Betty hung up her coat and climbed the stairs, smiling in anticipation of what was to come. She quickly took off her polyester dress, slipped off her knickers and wrapped a nylon dressing gown around her rotund body. Then she made her way back down to the living room.

The main ceiling light was on filling the room with brightness. Trevor stood beneath the pendant light, naked with his hands clasped over his privates. A muscle in his thin buttocks twitched.

Betty pulled out a dining chair from the table, turned it around and sat down facing Trevor.

'Now, Trevor. Have you been naughty this week?'

He hung his head.

'I'm afraid so,' he said in a quiet, trembling voice.

'Tell me.'

'I sent twenty cases of non-payment of rates to the prosecutions department. I ogled the young girls in the typing pool and wanked myself off in the washroom.'

'Dear me, Trevor. You have got a lot to be punished for. Did you masturbate just the once?'

Trevor's chin dropped lower and he spoke in a whisper. 'No, it was three times. Once on Monday and twice on Wednesday.'

‘Gosh! What got you so excited on Wednesday?’

‘I caught sight of the top of a pair of stockings when one of the typists went up the stairs.’

‘Well, well, what a hussy. Fancy wearing stockings to work in this day and age; and how wicked of you to look up her skirt. Right, we had better get on. Are you ready, Trevor?’

‘Yes,’ he said almost inaudibly.

‘Speak up and move your hands,’ Betty ordered. Trevor moved his hands to the side of his thighs revealing his shrivelled little prick and wrinkled balls. ‘Tell me what I need to do to you, Trevor.’

‘I need to be spanked,’ Trevor said and his tiny penis quivered and grew a little.

‘Bend over.’ Betty pressed her knees together and Trevor leaned over them. Betty shuffled him into place, pushing his head down to the floor so that his skinny bottom was raised and he was balanced on the tips of his toes. She pushed his legs apart and grabbed his prick and balls, tugging them out then letting them flop against her thigh.

She examined the bottom on her lap. There was no sign of last week’s punishment so she raised her right arm and brought her hand down with a resounding thwack. Trevor, jerked and cried. His buttocks shook. Now there was the bright red outline of her fingers and thumb. She repeated the action again and again, until his bottom was a livid crimson and each hand-mark overlaid another. Each blow brought a cry and a sob but Trevor did not struggle. Betty paused and checked the progress between his legs. She was pleased to feel that his cock had grown to a reasonable length and was as hard as iron. His balls, warmed by the heat in his buttocks, had slackened and hung freely. She was puffing slightly after her exertion and perspiration trickled down between her breasts.

‘There you are, Trevor. Now show me how grateful you are.’

He slid off her knees and knelt in front of her. She opened her legs and as usual was delighted by the expression on Trevor’s face as his eyes gazed on her massive thighs constrained by her stocking tops, and the suspender belt and straps that framed her pubes. Betty wriggled forward on the chair and opened her thighs wider. Trevor buried his nose in her bush and breathed in deeply. He pushed his narrow, weaselly face into her quim and lapped at her. Betty placed her hands on his head and pushed him in deeper and squeezed her thighs against his ears. She imagined pushing his head right into her vagina and feeling his tongue licking around inside her.

It was minutes before she remembered he needed to breathe. She opened her legs and pushed him away. He gasped and sucked air into his lungs. She thrust him on to his back on the floor, his penis vertical like a, short, flagpole and she sank onto it relishing the little rod of iron that penetrated her.

She rocked up and down, exhilarating in the exquisite feel of his cock sliding in and out of her until she could feel her orgasm coming and he was begging her to finish him off.

It was a matter for conjecture which of them came first. His come spurted into her as she was racked by contractions that vibrated her rolls of fat. She collapsed forward burying his head once again, this time in the soft flesh of her bosom.

Edith

Edith was glad that she was no longer the only one in the house. She still missed Stanley tremendously but she knew that he was gone from her for ever. Her daily visits to the nursing home had become painful because he didn't even recognize her now. All memories of their courtship and marriage had been erased. Each room in the house had become a reminder of what she had lost.

Not any more. Her time was filled with training Willy to be her sex slave. It gave her something to do or think about every minute of the day and, as she allowed Willy out of his bedroom, slowly each room took on new memories.

He still spent a lot of time chained to the bed but now she only gagged him when she felt it was time to go to sleep. Still, she had to prevent him from reaching his cock and balls with his hands so his wrists were bound and either locked to the collar around his neck or to the upright bars of the iron bedstead. Most of the time she kept his penis locked in the chastity device that prevented him from having an erection but now for an hour a day she gave it its freedom. She enjoyed watching it almost burst from its constriction, growing to its full curving length in an instant. At first he ejaculated almost as soon as his cock was erect, but gradually she had gained control so that now his first orgasm only occurred when she touched the purple tip or caressed the smooth shaft.

Edith had begun to let him get up for more than the obvious daily necessities. She guided him around the house, naked of course but for the shackles, and taught him the chores that she desired of him – clearing and laying the coal fire in the living room; washing up after meals; preparing the clothes washing (hers of course) for her old Hotpoint; dusting and vacuuming the house with her old Hoover Junior; polishing the silverware (not much of that), Stanley's medals and photos of them together (plenty of them).

Willy seemed to be an eager learner and tried hard to please her by doing a good job even with his ankles chained together and his wrist movement constrained, but he made some errors. Edith punished his mistakes and misdemeanours with frequent and capricious use of the riding crop, her favourite instrument, but occasionally she used a cane or tawse as the fancy took her. He also received rewards for work well done and he seemed to appreciate the well-cooked meals that she fed him. Edith was pleased that his body had lost the gaunt, malnourished appearance and his skin had taken on a healthy texture and colour.

Once all the daily tasks were completed the remainder of the time was taken in training Willy as a lover. This was difficult as he had no experience of women, their desires or their private parts other than in the pictures in porn magazines. His indulgence in self-abuse had reached such an extreme that, until Edith set to work on him, every moment of his free time, and he had had plenty, was spent tugging on his cock, handling his balls and repeatedly wanking to orgasm.

Even after a few weeks, the moment that she released his hands they automatically moved to grasp his manhood. Only repeated punishment had made him start to think and halt the action. There was more to his training than simply preventing masturbation. She had begun to teach him the use of his hands and mouth to pleasure a woman. In this respect he had not been a slow learner. From his experience in manipulating his manhood he knew how to stroke and caress. It took just a short time to show him how to carry out these actions on her breasts, the skin of her inner thighs, her buttocks, and, of course, her quim. He didn't seem at all bothered that her body, though fit, betrayed her years, not that she appeared naked in front of him. There was always the protective covering of corset or basque to hide her wrinkles and silk stockings to cover her varicose veins. Still, she was getting to enjoy his fingerwork.

Now she was making a start on his mouthwork training. She lay on her bed with her legs wide apart. He knelt between them with his wrists locked behind his back, his ankles joined by a short length of chain, his cock in its steel cage, and the chain to his collar held firmly in her hand.

'Now lower your head with your lips pursed until you touch my mound,' she instructed. He did as he was told. Edith gasped as his soft lips brushed her thin, grey pubes.

'Circle around the whole area, spiralling in till you touch my labia,' she continued. His lips moved accordingly, sliding down the crease between her left thigh and groin to her buttock, across her crack and up the right thigh back to where he had started and then again but now around the ellipse of her pussy until finally he reached the centre of her senses. His lips skimmed over her clit and she gasped. Then he came to rest against her lips.

Edith's breath came in small gasps.

'Gently poke out your tongue. Feel me, taste me, explore me.' She anticipated the touch but it still made her cry involuntarily. His warm, wet tongue, reached out and slid between her lips. She was unable to give further instructions; it was down to him now to use his own initiative. Edith was pleased to discover that he had some. The tongue moved around finding the folds of her inner and outer lips, measuring the length of her crack, discovering her clitoris, investigating it, and then probing into her hole. He sucked her juices, swallowed, licked and sucked again, returned to her little knob, nibbled, sucked, tugged. She came with a juddering orgasm that clamped her legs around his head and pulled on his chain so that he gurgled in his throat.

Gradually she relaxed and released him.

'Very good, Willy,' she said, drawing up her legs and twisting around. 'Now I will give you your reward.' She reached into the drawer of her bedside table for the key to the chastity device. 'I'll show you how a lady shows her appreciation of a competent cunt licker.'

Joyce

'I really think you deserve something special,' Eileen said forcefully.

'Why?' Joyce replied.

'Well in addition to providing us with the use of your house you've spent so much time organising things for us to do, looking after the boys as well as us ladies. Really the Ladies' College for Erotic Arts would not exist without you, Joyce.'

'Yes, but I've enjoyed it. We've got up to some really naughty things, haven't we?'

'That's right, and tonight we have decided that you should have the services of all three of the lads for your exclusive pleasure.' Eileen clapped her hands and into the hall came Winston, Johnny and Mick, each naked with their cocks at the ready.

'Oh! Well, if you are sure.'

'We are. So now I'll leave you in their good hands. They have their instructions to give you a night of absolute and extreme pleasure. I'm sure you'll enjoy it.' Without another word, Eileen turned and left. The three young men stood in front of Joyce, eager and alert. Joyce decided that she would fall in with Eileen's plan, after all she hadn't thought of a better way of spending the evening.

'Well, boys, you'd better do as the lady says,' she said, wondering what she was in for.

'We have a bath waiting for you,' Winston said, taking her

hand and drawing her upstairs. She almost didn't recognise her own bathroom. The electric light was off but the room was lit by the yellow glow of dozens of candles on every horizontal surface. Nearby, soft music was playing. The bath was filled with water, much fuller than she usually had it especially after last year's drought, and scented foam floated on the surface.

Hands were pulling on her clothes, undoing buttons and zips. She found herself naked and Johnny's hand holding hers as she stepped into the bathwater.

'We've checked the temperature so you won't be scalded,' he said reassuringly.

She sank into the welcoming water. It was just right. Mick offered her a glass and underwater hands gently caressed her body with soft sponges. She took a sip of the wine; it was sweet and sparkling Asti Spumante, her favourite.

'This is very decadent,' she said, enjoying it immensely.

'This is just the start,' Winston said, winking. 'As Eileen said, we want to give you a real treat.'

Joyce relaxed and closed her eyes for a minute or two as the hands continued to stroke her. She finished her glass and decided that perhaps she shouldn't lie about for too long.

'That was lovely but I'd like to get out now,' she said. She noticed that Mick already had her largest and fluffiest towel in his arms ready to wrap around her. Winston offered an arm to help her out of the bath. She was enveloped in the towel and tapped and padded all over so that she was dried in no time. The towel was removed and she was powdered like a baby. Her dressing gown was offered to her. Then the young men led her to her own bedroom where just the bedside lamps shone.

'I presume you want me on the bed,' Joyce said anticipating what was going to come.

'Yes, please,' Winston replied.

Joyce dropped her gown to the floor feeling warm and comfortable after the bath. The room was warmer than usual; the boys must have turned the central heating up. She scrambled to the middle of the double bed and spread her arms and legs out in a star shape.

'Well, here I am,' she said, almost dissolving into a giggle,

'Take me!'

'It'll be our pleasure,' Winston replied.

Joyce closed her eyes wondering what the boys were planning. The first sensation was a feather-like touch on her hands and arms. Who was it? Were they using their fingers or lips or tongues or even their cocks? It seemed impossible to tell at first then she felt warm, moist breath on the soft skin on the inside of her upper arm and knew that that was mouth, while it was fingers caressing her forearms.

Then there was a light touch on her feet and her toes were enclosed one by one in a warm, wet mouth. Each toe was given attention and then the fingers and lips moved up her feet to her ankles, and then her calves, knees, thighs.

Now she was being touched down each side, the fingers circling up over her rib cage to her breasts. The contact with her nipples was expected but still she reacted with an indrawn breath and sigh. The skin of her whole body was tingling from the touch of six hands, thirty fingers, six lips and three tongues. She'd thought only her breasts and fanny were erogenous zones but every part of her was electrified and feeding sensations to her brain and pussy.

Both nipples were in the warm embrace of a mouth while down below the fingertips and tongue were on her inner thighs and drawing inexorably towards her quim.

Lips brushed against her smooth, hairless mound; the tongue dived into her crack drawing a cry from her while the other two mouths, assisted by fingers continued to tease her nipples and breasts.

Her thighs were pushed wide apart and strong hands slid under her buttocks and lifted her up. She opened her eyes to see Winston presenting his long, dark cock to her oozing fanny. Gently and slowly he entered her. That, along with the continued caresses of Johnny and Mick at her sides, sent ripples of pleasure bouncing around her body. She felt her vagina contract around the cock as he pushed in to its full length and she gave herself up completely to her orgasm. As Winston began to rock on his knees drawing his penis out a little then sliding in fully again she continued to feel the waves of pleasure wash through her. Now her desire took over.

'Harder,' she urged. Winston took her at her word and using the strength in his legs pumped her faster and deeper. She felt him come in a great gush of spunk, topping up her own climax. She expected Winston to collapse on her as he often did, but no, he withdrew, his detumefying penis slipping wetly from her hole. He slid back off the bed and his place was taken by Johnny. He was eager to fill her, his cock rock hard and his glans a vivid, urgent red. He crawled between her legs and slid his tool in to her gaping twat. She was ready, she was willing, she wanted it: she was on heat.

'Come on, Johnny, fill me up,' she encouraged. He shoved his cock into her until his large dangling sac slapped against her buttocks. Johnny was obviously eager to shoot his load, the preparations in the bathroom and the foreplay having brought him to a peak of readiness. Nevertheless the energy of his thrusts boosted Joyce to yet another high and she cried out loud when Johnny came, adding his semen to Winston's.

Johnny too pulled out with little pause and crawled around the bed to join Winston at Joyce's side caressing and teasing her breasts and arms. Now it was Mick kneeling between her legs, but instead of lining his prick up to enter her he bent his head to her fanny and lapped at the cream dripping from her cunt. He rubbed his face in it, licked and sucked at her, drawing his predecessor's ejaculate from her channel. Then he climbed up her and placed his mouth on hers. She felt the sticky residue, smelt the eggy odour and tasted it on his lips and tongue. It was like sucking the cocks of Winston, and Johnny at the same time as well as being kissed by Mick. She loved it.

Now he was ready to add his calling card. His penis slipped easily into her hot hole. She wrapped her legs around his thighs drawing him in until even his balls were squeezed between her labia. They rocked together and she felt his knob deep inside her twisting, rolling, thrusting.

Like the others, Mick had been waiting for some time to deposit his come in her vagina. As he spurted, Joyce felt yet more seismic trembling rip through her. Mick slipped out. Surely that was it. She'd had the three of them, one after the other. She was hot, sweaty and covered with their semen.

Winston held another glass of the fizzy wine close to her. She reached for it, grateful for the refreshment.

'Thanks, that was wonderful,' she said.

'Oh, that was just the start. The night is young,' Johnny commented.

Winston took the empty glass from her while Mick and Johnny rolled her on to her stomach. They proceeded to rub and massage her back and buttocks. It was excruciatingly delightful as they found and relieved little knots where her muscles had cramped during her orgasms. She gasped and groaned as they worked on her. Then she was lifted on to her knees and a tongue ran up the length of the crack between her buttocks. She wasn't sure which tongue it was but it was like a trickle of acid the way it fired off her nerves. It lingered around her arsehole, circling, pushing between the tight ring of muscle. She knew she was on the verge of coming again when the tongue left and a cock pressed against her fanny. Broad hands grasped her hips pulling her buttocks back, forcing the cock into her.

Having come once, the owner of the cock was now prepared for a longer build-up to his next orgasm. Joyce had little to do but give herself up to the tool ramming in and out of her cunt. Her whole sense of being shrank into the muscles of her vagina, contracting and relaxing around that reciprocating piston. That was about the moment when she ceased to be objective about her experience. No longer was she watching and feeling the hands, mouths and pricks and enjoying the sensation, now she *was* it. She gave up herself to the joy of being fucked, over and over again. Every nerve in her body firing, as one after the other Winston, Johnny and Mick filled her hole while all the time they continued to nibble and squeeze her tits, rub her clit, caress her bum, her thighs, her arms. Time after time she was filled with spunk and throughout each exuberant fuck she coasted on a tsunami of orgasmic ecstasy.

Eileen

She'd chosen the restaurant carefully. It was spacious with

tables widely spaced and separated by panels and pot plants. Each table was draped with a heavy linen cloth that reached almost to the thickly carpeted floor. The menu came highly recommended and the prices were high. She expected good service and she was determined to get it.

She had selected Mick as her dinner guest. He was very young, young enough to be her son, if she'd had children, but he brushed up well and it didn't look out of place a "mother" entertaining her handsome and athletic "son". He'd put on his interview suit and she had picked clothes suitable for the venue and the occasion. She had booked for the peak time of the evening and they had parked her car in the multi-storey car park nearby.

Eileen had asked for a table well away from the hustle and bustle of the entrance and the doors to the kitchen. Now having removed her cloak, she sat herself in the chair that gave her a view of much of the restaurant. Mick dutifully helped her move her chair into the table then sat himself opposite her. The waiter presented the menus and took their drinks orders.

Eileen looked around, noting where other diners were sitting and the movements of the waiters. She kicked off her court shoes under the table.

'You did do as I asked?' she said in a quiet voice, but loud enough for Mick to hear.

'What did you ask?' Mick looked confused.

'No knickers,' Eileen said, emphasising her pronunciation.

'Oh, yes. Yes of course.' his face turned pink.

'Good. Undo your belt and flies and push your trousers down.'

'What? People will see.'

'No they won't. Anyway you can put your napkin on your lap and pull the tablecloth over your knees.'

The wine waiter arrived and placed a pint of Watneys Red beside Mick and a Cinzano and soda by Eileen. He nodded his head and withdrew. Eileen lifted her glass and took a sip.

'Now, do it now,' she said.

Mick dropped his hands to his lap, shuffled and wriggled in his seat then pulled his chair closer to the table so that it pressed against his torso. He fiddled with the tablecloth by his side and took a large swig of his beer. While watching him and smiling wickedly at the thought of Mick sitting at the table with nothing on below his waist, Eileen reached below her knees and began to undo buttons. She was wearing a maxi dress in midnight blue velvet with tiny buttons from the high collar down to her ankles. She had left the bottom half dozen or so undone to facilitate walking and now she undid the rest up to her suspender belt. She pulled the edge of the tablecloth over her thighs and let the dress fall open.

Eileen raised her right leg and though the table was quite wide her foot reached Mick's knee. She slipped her nylon clad toes along the inside of his thigh causing him to splutter into his glass.

'What are you doing?' he asked.

'Just checking.' Her foot found his ball sac resting on the padded Dralon of the chair. She lifted her big toe and touched his cock, already erect. Her toes slid up his shaft and found that his knob was pressed against the underside of the table. 'Nice erection,' she said.

The waiter arrived with their starters. He placed the dishes in front of Eileen and Mick, smiled and withdrew.

'There. He didn't notice a thing,' Eileen said rubbing her toes up and down Mick's stiff prick.

Mick didn't reply. He tucked into his liver patè and melba toast, but his pink sweaty cheeks revealed his state of excitement. Eileen began on her escargot, winkling the tiny morsel of flesh from its hiding place, sucking off the tasty garlic butter then chewing it with relish. She took her time, enjoying each mollusc.

Mick soon finished all but the garnish of green leaves. He put his knife down on the plate and took another mouthful of beer.

'Right. Now you can get under the table,' Eileen said.

'What?'

'I want you to lick my cunt, right here, now.'

'You didn't mention any of this.'

'Why on earth did you think I invited you out for dinner,

with no knickers on if it wasn't to get you to do something like this.'

'Well ...'

'Come on. All you have to do is slide off your chair to your right and quickly crawl under the table. I'll tell you when the coast's clear.' Eileen looked around the restaurant. Although most of the tables were occupied, none of the guests were sitting so as to get a direct view of their table – as she had planned. The waiters were all busy serving the other tables and none was near to them.

'Now!' Eileen hissed and pulled her leg back

Mick pushed his chair back and slid on to the floor. He crawled under the tablecloth only once banging his head on the bottom of the table. Trying to look quite unconcerned at the disappearance of her dinner partner, Eileen continued to hook snails out of shells but opened her legs wide and slid her bottom to the edge of the chair. The first hot breath on her stocking-cased thigh made her flinch. Then warm, wet lips touched the skin above her stocking tops and a moist tongue ran up the soft flesh to her groin sending shivers up her spine. Eileen placed her cutlery on the plate and gripped the edge of the table to stop herself shaking. The tongue licked up and down her labia, first on her right then on her left. The lips and tongue searched within the folds of skin until they found the little bud of flesh and persuaded it out of its concealment. Eileen gasped as Mick sucked on her clitoris.

'Has madam finished?'

Eileen looked up astonished to find the waiter at her side.

'Oh, oh, yes, thank you,' she replied in a shaky voice. The waiter picked up her dish and side plate.

'And has sir, finished with his?' He nodded to the empty chair and the plate with its lonely lettuce leaf.

'Oh, yes, he has, thank you.'

The waiter added the plate to the pile on his wrist.

'Are you ready for your main course or do you wish to await the return of your, um, companion?'

'Oh, he'll be back in a moment. There was something he had to do. You can bring the next course. Thank you.' The waiter nodded and left. Eileen realised that she had been a little over enthusiastic with her thanks, but she could barely keep her voice level as Mick's tongue delved into her hole, rotating round the wall of her vagina and sending tremors throughout her body. Eileen felt her eyelids closing as her mind retreated to her groin, delighting in the sensations which almost but not quite took her to a climax.

She was brought back to the moment by the soft thump of a heavy china plate landing on the place-mat in front of her. She opened her eyes to see the waiter depositing Mick's plate in his place. He gave her a thin smile and walked away.

Eileen nudged Mick with her toe.

'You can come back now,' she whispered and glancing around added, 'no one's looking.'

She almost regretted saying it as Mick's mouth moved and cool air wafted over her wet fanny. The table rocked a little as Mick crawled out from underneath but he executed a swift manoeuvre into his seat with aplomb. Her juices glistened on his lips and chin.

'Thank you,' Eileen said, genuinely grateful. Mick gave her broad smile, obviously feeling more cocky after his secret exploit.

'No, thank *you*. That was fun. You taste lovely tonight.'

Eileen ate her lemon sole washed down with a glass of white wine, while Mick tucked into his steak occasionally supping at his beer. Their plates were soon empty and the waiter returned to take their dessert orders. They were alone again and the restaurant was really busy now.

'I'm looking forward to my crème brûlée,' Eileen said, 'but first I want a different sort of cream.' She placed her napkin on the table and after a quick look around the room pushed her chair back. She slid off to the left and deftly flicked her dress open while rocking forward on to her knees. She raised the tablecloth and crawled quickly under the table. The linen fell to the floor behind her and she was surprised how dark it was in the small enclosed space. Mick's bare, hairy knees were a vague paleness to either side. She edged forward and lowered her head to his groin. Her nose found his testicles pressed against the chair. She turned her head and grasped his cock between her lips, tugging it down and sliding along until she reached the swollen toadstool-like head. She opened her jaws wide and enveloped his knob, hearing a distant gasp from above the table. There wasn't much room to move without repeatedly banging her head against the table but she bobbed up and down on his cock sucking hard at the knob and rubbing her tongue over the little hole.

Eileen heard a voice, indistinctly above her and paused in her vigorous movement. She guessed that Mick and the waiter were conversing. She listened carefully and eventually heard footsteps moving away from the table. She redoubled her efforts, gulping Mick's cock down her throat, rubbing her teeth gently but firmly under the ridge of his glans. She felt the first gout of semen pulse up the shaft and burst into her mouth. It poured in, down her throat, spilling out through the corners of her mouth. For a moment it seemed it was never going to stop gushing out like a burst oil well. She recovered and swallowed, sucking every last drop of the rich, thick milk into her mouth. Finally when Mick's penis had begun to shrink she let it drop from her mouth. It slapped wetly against his chair. She felt him twisting around.

'It's OK,' she heard dimly.

Eileen shuffled back and emerged into what now seemed a brightly lit restaurant. She quickly stood and resumed her seat. She looked around. An older man on one of the nearer tables was looking at her with a quizzical expression. She avoided his eye and touched her napkin to her lips then focussed on the crème brûlée.

'Yum. That was good,' Eileen said.

'I'll say.' Mick nodded. 'I didn't think I would ever stop coming.'

They didn't bother with coffee, and while Mick groped for his trousers and wriggled into them again, Eileen paid the bill with a cheque. Having received a large cash tip the waiter cheerfully brought Eileen's cloak. She turned away from him so he could drape it over her shoulders and clutched her bag under the warm cloth. They walked back through the cold December evening to the car park. Their floor was dimly lit but a light bulb shone almost directly over the Ford Escort. There were still many places occupied by cars but there was space next to her car.

Eileen stood by the driver's side, then turned and faced Mick. She dropped the cloak off her shoulders onto the bonnet and having surreptitiously undone all the remaining buttons flung her dress wide revealing her naked body. Mick's eyes widened.

'I hope I have not misjudged your powers of recovery,' she said.

'Why?' he said, momentarily rendered an idiot.

'Because I want your cock in me now.' She reached for his elbows, pulled him towards her, dropped her hands to his waist and skilfully undid his belt and flies. She shoved his trousers to his ankles.

He grinned and looked down at his erect member.

'Satisfied?'

'Oh, yes.'

He placed his hands under her bottom and hoisted her on to the front wing of the car. Her cloak and dress cushioned her from the cold metal. He squeezed between her thighs, his prick questing for her hole. He found it and Eileen gasped as he pushed it home. She lifted her feet, her shoes dropping off and she wrapped her legs around his waist, her heels hard against his buttocks. She pulled him in so his balls slapped against the side of the car. Their hips jerked together driving him deep and producing a small cry from Eileen.

'Yes, do it. Give it to me,' she urged. They rocked violently so that the Escort's front suspension squeaked. Eileen threw her head back feeling the full ecstasy of the fuck. The bright headlights of a car shone in her face as it drove past. Did the driver see her ecstasy, she wondered. Still Mick pounded into her. There was the click-click of heels on concrete. Out of the corner of her eye, Eileen saw a man and woman approach, stare at them and move to the next car along. Eileen was oblivious to whether they stayed and watched or got into their car and drove off.

Finally and at long last she felt her orgasm building; a great tremor of excitement that began in her cunt spread up to her tits and burst through her head.

'Yes …' she screamed loudly as she came and felt Mick spurt into her.

'Really, Eileen. You do get up to some shocking things,' Joyce said, laughing merrily, 'and fancy poor, young Mick, having to do all that in a restaurant.' Mick's face blushed but his jerking cock belied his embarrassment.

'At least you didn't get caught this time,' Edith muttered, tugging on Willy's chain while his head rubbed against Susan's crotch.

'What will you get up to next?' Betty chortled, rocking Trevor on her knees, his upended buttocks glowing red after his most recent spanking.

'Oh, I've got a few ideas,' Eileen said, giving the three young men a wink, 'anyway; Susan's story was pretty out of the ordinary as well.'

'Yes,' Edith agreed. 'How on earth did you get all that food out of your fanny?'

'What?' Susan said dreamily from beside Edith on the sofa. Her mind was mainly on Willy's tongue delving into the creases between her labia. 'Oh, that. There was one of those French bee-det things in the bathroom. Soon washed it all out. It's quite a funny sensation feeling a fountain of water up your hole.'

'What was the rest of your weekend like?' Betty asked, caressing Trevor's small stiff prick that pressed against her thigh, 'Did your young man have any other weird ideas?'

'Not really, but we hardly stopped making love the whole time. We rarely left the apartment. I think he fucked me in every way I could think of in every bit of the place including the walk-in wardrobe when the maid came to make the bed. I can't wait till the next time.'

'And a nice bit of cash I expect,' Edith said.

'Oh yes, and that.'

‘But you’ve been busy too, Edith. You’ve taught Willy well,’ Joyce said, nodding at the young man. His answering nod made his cock and balls wobble between his legs.

‘He’s coming along. I might be able to release his wrists soon but he also needs training in how to use his cock to please a woman.’

‘He’s certainly a lot cleaner and whiter than when we first caught him,’ Eileen said.

‘Yes, I shaved all his body hair off this morning; don’t you think it makes him look much prettier and more innocent?’

They each agreed and admired Edith’s handiwork.

Joyce turned to look at Betty with the little man draped over her lap.

‘And you too, Betty. You appear to have found a pleasurable relationship.’

‘I’ll say.’ Betty joyfully slapped Trevor’s buttock. ‘Trevor’s a damn sight more obliging than my old man, good riddance to him, and he’s more appreciative too.’

‘And you enjoyed your special session, Joyce?’ Eileen asked. For a moment Joyce appeared coy.

‘Oh, yes, thank you. The boys were wonderful. They really exhausted me.’

‘How many times did they fuck you?’ Susan asked.

‘Oh golly, I don’t know,’ Joyce said anxiously trying to count up, ‘I lost count and then fell asleep, but they went on and on.’

‘The boys are good for at least five or six a night, aren’t you?’ Edith said drawing enthusiastic nods from Winston, Johnny and Mick.

‘That must be about twenty times then, Joyce,’ Betty said in an admiring voice, ‘no wonder you fell asleep. How did you feel afterwards?’

‘A little sore but very satisfied.’ The friends clapped and cheered. Joyce raised her hands to calm them.

‘Well, ladies, I think we’ve all done very well.’ Joyce looked round at each of her friends. ‘We’ve all experienced lots of joy in our sex. I think the Ladies’ College for Erotic Arts has been a great success.'

There was a chorus of "here, here" after which Eileen cried, 'What are we waiting for; let's get on with it.'